THE MOST
INTIMATE
PLACE

ALSO BY ROSEMARY FURBER

What You See Is What You Get

THE MOST INTIMATE PLACE

ROSEMARY FURBER

MAIA

Arcadia Books Ltd
15–16 Nassau Street
London W1W 7AB
www.arcadiabooks.co.uk

Published by The Maia Press
an imprint of Arcadia Books 2009

ISBN 978-1-904559-39-9

Typeset in Sabon
Printed and bound in Great Britain by Thanet Press
on paper from sustainable managed forests

Arcadia Books gratefully acknowledges the financial support of Arts Council England

Arcadia Books distributors are as follows:

in the UK and elsewhere in Europe: Turnaround Publishers Services
Unit 3, Olympia Trading Estate, Coburg Road, London N22 6TZ

in the US and Canada: Independent Publishers Group
814 N, Franklin Street, Chicago, IL 60610

in Australia: Tower Books
PO Box 213, Brookvale, NSW 2100

in New Zealand: Addenda
PO Box 78224, Grey Lynn, Auckland

In South Africa: Quartet Sales and Marketing
PO Box 1218, Northcliffe, Johannesburg 2115

Arcadia Books is the Sunday Times Small Publisher of the Year

Many thanks for encouragement and advice go to
Anjali Pratap, Paul Kennington, Mark Farley,
Martin Elliott, Jane and Maggie of The Maia Press
and, of course, my family

'When we want to read the deeds that are done for love, whither do we turn? To the murder columns.'
G. B. Shaw

I work down his shin with long, firm strokes. I ease the oil over the bridge of his foot and feel the fan ribs of bones under my thumbs. My fingers sweep around his ankle, and I am aware again of his bones under the skin.

I crack the neck of my alabaster jar, pour the oil into my palm and warm it. I spread my hands over his shin and hear him groan. It is a sound just for me.

I am smoothing the unguent around his toes now, my fingers sliding between them like fish in seaweed. He laughs out loud as I lift his foot high so that I can stroke his sole. His soles are lined and parched; they yield to the unguent under my fingers and soften. I take his Achilles heel between my thumb and first finger and pull rhythmically, and hear his intake of breath.

I am drenched in the aroma of smoke and of spikenard as I knead his joints. Bones again. His eyes are a sunburst of love. He says:

'May the Lord deal kindly with you, Mary, as you have dealt with your dead brother Lazarus. And you now deal with me.'

I long to smother him in adoration. I long to anoint him my Lord and King, and my rabbi forever.

He rests his hands on my head. Is he blessing me? He combs his fingers deeper into my hair and cradles my skull. My hair falls free from its pins over my face and shoulders. I must not let him see me cry. But I think he knows.

'You love me much, Mary,' he whispers.

I love you so much, Helen. I hear you speak to me from your book. I hear your voice in my dreams. You say my name: Patrick. Patrick. I wish I could wake and see you sleeping and defenceless beside me.

I long to spread you under me. It's simple. It's love. Since the day I met you I've been living more fully, even here in this prison cell, than I ever did before in my life. I can feel myself expanding to the edges of my body and soul.

What I adore about you most is that you never gave up. You were broken and you forced yourself to mend. You wanted to be a priest and you let no one stand in your way.

Nothing was going to stand in my way either. I loved you, Helen. I still do. I had to make sure you understood how much.

HMP GREYMOOR

Dr Julia Bailey, MA, LLM, PhD
Lancaster College
Cambridge

Dear Julia,

Don't come again. I can't stand it if you come again. You looked gorgeous. You always do but I remember especially – I remember this so clearly – that you looked more than usually wonderful walking away to the exit. Can you grasp how cruel that is? Did you dress like that on purpose? A dozen men you don't even know are boasting to me every morning about how many they've been giving you in the night. 'Hey, PatPrick, she got six last night, your bird, loved every minute of it.' In his dreams, of course, but that man was a screw.

What did you tell me? What did we say? I remember almost nothing except how you sat far back in your chair as if you might catch something from me, or the place. My ribs are still bruised with pressing into the table trying to squeeze close to you. You mentioned Mark. Twice. Is Mark fucking you while I'm in here? Is he? Is he?

This place is doing my head in, as they say in here. In your terms, I may be going mad. I'll try to do it discreetly. You don't understand, Julia. I don't see how you can. You say it must be awful for me in here and all that, but I wish you could know why I'm here, how it was never going to be otherwise, however things looked before. Maybe I should write it all down for you. If I did, I'd probably not send it. Maybe I will. Either way, please don't come again.

With all my love,
Patrick

Lancaster College
Cambridge

Dear Patrick,

Thank you for your letter, received yesterday. While I understand that you are likely to be feeling fragile at the moment, I have the following points:

1. The fact that you are on remand in prison charged with murder has nothing to do with me. Whatever you did or did not do, took place in an area of your life that you did not see fit to share with me. My visit was an act of friendship. You did say you loved me once.

2. I understand that I have become a victim of repeated multiple psychorape. Tell your friends, officers and inmates, that if they continue to violate me in their dreams I shall come down on them like a ton of legal bricks. Smedley v. Oxless 2009 (European Court of Human Rights) applies.

3. I am entitled to dress as I like. There is no prison rule against visitors wearing a strapless bodice and jodhpurs.

4. My relationship (if any, which is not admitted) with Mark is none of your business. It is months since you bothered to make any gesture of love, or even friendship, to me, so I had assumed that my life was my own. You treat me as though we've only just met. Who helped you give up smoking? Who put together your CVs? Who helped you to pee when you broke both your wrists in Val d'Isère?

5. You say you can't even remember what we talked about. I was just trying to keep you up to date with events in the outside world. I agree. There seems little point in my coming again.

6. Write your explanation to me if you wish. I do not promise to reply.

Yours ever, Julia

Did you dictate that to your secretary, Julia? 'I have the following points.' Did you have a good laugh about it together?

'You did say you loved me once.' How could you say that? I told you I loved you all the time, *and* I meant it! Or did I just say it in my head? Maybe I did. Anyway I need you in here with me, Julia. I need you here beside me. I need you to know the truth.

Let me take you back to Helen's room, to the last time I saw her, when I learned the real meaning of post-coital tristesse. Post-coital distress.

I sat there for hours looking at her, the dark red hair spread over the pillow, and her dress and the pillow red too, and my shirt, matching the red Christmas ribbons all over the place and I was thinking What a cock up. Of all the things – What a fucking cock-up. What am I going to do? I was angry. Not scared yet.

That's her phone over there, I thought, with my blood on it, next to the writing paper and a pyramid of books. Every joint in my body creaked as I got up and took her phone in my hand. It was cold but I could smell her smoky breath still on it. But who could I call?

I had the urge to hear someone compassionate, soothing and utterly on my side. As I stared at the keypad, the only number I could remember was my mother's.

'Mummy, it's Patrick.'

'Hello, darling. How are you?'

What could I say? I'm sorry. Very sorry. For myself mostly.

'All right,' I said. Pause. What could I say next? What could I say?

'I'm so glad you've called, darling,' her voice was posh and perky through the receiver, like a caricature, 'I've been trying to get hold of you. I left messages with your boss but he said he hadn't seen you. Have you decided about Christmas Day?'

'Ahm . . .'

'We've got Tim and Fiona and the girls coming. Seb's being indispensable in Brussels as usual, and I thought we could have quail this time instead of, you know, turkey's so dull, what do you think?'

'I'm not sure, Mummy. Look, I'm a bit tied up. I've got stuff to do here. I need . . . I need . . .'

'Well, it's up to you. Are you still a vegetarian, or has that worn off?'

'I haven't been vegetarian for four years.'

'Oh good. Well, let me know as soon as you can. Damn, there's somebody at the door . . .'

I need . . .

Mummy, I need . . .

'OK, darling? Still there?'

'Yeah. I'm still here.'

'Let me know soon, won't you, darling?'

I put the receiver down. I could taste blood. There was a ridge across my tongue as I licked my cut lip. It looks like blood, tastes like blood, must be a cock-up.

Was my tongue cut in half? That old taste slapped me right back to Tim and Seb and torture games, with me tied over my head in a sack and them rolling me round the garden over the gravel and the tree stumps, with me crying and crying through a sore mouth.

Suddenly I was so fucking angry I kicked a shiny little leather-topped table away from me. It rolled over and lay with two legs in the air, two on the floor and all the ash and fag-ends from the ashtray splayed on the rug beside the books. I looked over at her lying on the bed. At the elegant way her spine curved from the dress at her waist down to the divide of her beautiful arse. I decided to kiss her again. You won't bite me now, Helen, I thought. I'm going to kiss you, and you won't bite me again.

If only I'd never even heard her name. That was down to Cyril. I can hear his phone voice in my head now, the one that used to say 'Listen and learn, young man, from the newspaper king of thirteen south London postal districts, and wake up, you idle bastard!'

It was coming up to ten in the morning and I wasn't asleep actually. I was on my early watch contemplating that nurses' home just down the hill between my bedsit and the Thames. I could have watched the morning sky reflect in the glassy towers of the Isle of Dogs across the river. Instead my eyes were on that ugly concrete block with promising contents, just visible through the trees. Crows were fussing in the top branches that day and grey squirrels leapt about showing off. I could almost smell buds and new mown grass.

In the distance two police launches were cutting up the river, reminding me of Sword Rampant's latest video where their mighty axeman Gavin Whitehead steers his motorboat at a phallic angle with masterly flicks of his guitar while pretending to sing 'Older Than Winter'.

But I only noticed the river at all because the night shift wasn't up yet. Just another nine or ten minutes and some of the girls would stir from their warm scented beds and draw the curtains, wearing nothing but t-shirts. Short t-shirts.

Cyril's voice cut through me: 'Got a pen?' he asked.

'Yeah, hold on a minute.'

'I want you to go and see a Miss Helen Hubbard.'

'Helen Hubbard.'

'At the vicarage, St Paul's Road, Blackheath.'

'Gawd, Cyril, what's this, some holy bird?'

'Lady vicar, yep. She's got some new job in Chelsea that's famous apparently.' He gave a deep sniff. 'I've got her book here. I'll drop it through your door.'

'Fuck's sake, Cyril, why are you hitting me with this? I'm no godsquaddie, no way.'

'It's not a very long book.'

'Has it got a candle and a dove on the front?' I asked.

'What?'

'The book. It's got a candle and a dove on the front. Hasn't it?'

'Nope.'

'Cross made of barbed wire?'

'Nope. You might like this one. Look, it's what, a hundred pages. Can you manage that?'

I know you're not allergic to nuts, Julia, but I felt just like the time when we were still first years and that tosser Mark gave you some chocolate hazelnuts for your birthday and I ate the whole top layer to prove to him that you were my girlfriend, mine.

My throat swelled up, I couldn't swallow my own spit and my face began to boil.

My aversion to holy books can be dated precisely. It started on the 18th June 1995. That day my mother returned from Knightsbridge laden with bags and said that she had not been shopping, she'd been to church. From that day our house became Mecca to dozens of sad old girls with time on their hands and an over-developed sense of how lucky they were to have their husband's money. Every week my mother would play hostess at 'asperity' lunches for the harpies, all in cashmere and Chanel specs, who would keep to labelled water instead of gin and donate a fiver to charity each.

After the 18th June 1995 my father always described my mother as 'the Nun' because that's all he got out of her. He was right: she was never quite ours, never quite our mother ever again.

She wasn't his wife much longer either. Two years he stuck it, took a golfing sabbatical in Ireland and died in a bunker of a heart attack. He must have seen it coming because the day after his death, my mother received a postcard from him posted ten days before (a chilly picture of the eighteenth at Killarney) warning that in the event of his death, she was to mourn by sleeping only with black men throughout the first year.

She had other ideas of course. The bags she brought back that day didn't contain half of Harrods as usual, they were full of holy books, and gradually she was in our house less and less and the space she left behind filled up with books. *Meditations for the Busy Carer*, *Pilgrims in the Family*, *A Hard Coming We Had Of It*, *Mysticism in Action*, all that sort of stuff. *One's Personal Saviour*. No, I made that one up. And nearly every damned one of them had a candle and a dove on the front.

Cyril was still on the phone murmuring about his six hundred words when I noticed a blonde nurse draw her curtains in the room opposite. She was wearing pyjamas, pale blue, nice and tight round the upper thighs. But I was not pleased. She was the one who could usually be relied on to do a wide deep stretch in a short t-shirt . . .

'A hard coming . . . yeah.'

'What?'

'Sorry. I'm watching a girl get out of bed.'

'You dirty bugger. The lady vicar'll do you a bit of good. Have you got all that then?'

'What?'

'Wake up, for Christ's sake. By Friday week at the latest.'

The nurse moved round her little room making coffee. She had a truly great wide arse. Fat-bottomed girls, I love them. And slim-bottomed girls. And those in-between ones aren't too bad either, those ones with creamy little muffin tops peeking out of the tops of their jeans.

'Patrick!'

'Yeah, yeah.'

As he repeated the details and I took notes, I was struck by a brilliant idea. My pulse began to rocket just at the thought of it.

'Cyril, I'll do it. I'll be delighted. I'll even make it sound as though she's my personal saviour if you want, if you do something for me.'

'Try me.'

'Gavin Whitehead.'

'Never heard of him.'

'Never heard . . . You're showing your age, old man.'

'Fuck off.'

'He took over as the lead singer in Sword Rampant in 2006 when Pug died. You remember Pug, Cyril, the one with moustache hair down to the floor and platform boots he could park his pint in. A great life cruelly cut short. They're the only fucking group to drag British rock kicking and screaming anywhere near the twenty-first century.'

'Never heard of them.'

Never what? He needed a sample of the latest single:

'Ooooo – oooooooo – Wings that are o-older than winterrrrr.'

'I never heard such bollocks in my life,' Cyril droned, 'your point is?'

'My point is that the said Gavin Whitehead, the Sword's new singer, lives in Coleraine Road. In Greenwich. Our patch. Three streets from where I'm sitting now in fact. He really is God on two legs. I'll interview your vicar woman if you let me do Whitehead too.'

'Is he going to live long enough?'

'Gavin Whitehead is clean and serene. All green tea and baby rocket leaves. He'll outlive the economy. He's written a book too! Buy me his book, and I'll halve my fee.'

There was a pause during which the girl in the nurses' block stepped out of her pyjama bottoms and threw them across her room. She stood in the short blue top and nothing else, her fists resting on bare haunches talking to somebody I couldn't see.

I took Cyril's reply to be affirmative. It was two words.

'What fee?'

As soon as I put down the phone, tension squeezed my chest. I could almost smell my mother's prayer groups, their face powder and piety and their hands reaching out to bless me: 'God is calling you, Patrick, come and be alive in Jesus, come and be tight-arsed and superior like us.'

I stuck my fingers in my ears and was about to scream when I realised I had the antidote handy. Sword Rampant's first CD. Ten years ago it was the first album I ever bought and it still did the business. Ah yes . . . track one. No. Track two:

What is this I see before me?
Rugged crossroads, way to go.
Where's your spear, O trusty Satan?
Where's your arrows of desire?
My sword don't sleep, you better run now,
What you reap is what you –
So so hot in here, flames are all a-burning,
So much pain here, hearts are all a-yearning.

Or . . . *Rupture Bloody Rupture* might clear my head better with its rolling bass riff pumping to the chest-busting finale. Or, *In Thrust We Trust*, the one which starts with the cod church organ and culminates in a choir of schoolgirls being run over by a steamroller? So much choice. Where was I to start?

There was only one answer: slap the bass and volume up to max and hear the whole lot ten times through without stopping.

Then I might be in a fit state to phone the lady priest.

I didn't contact Helen immediately. I thought for once I'd look up religion a bit first. Once I started I couldn't stop. Church stuff didn't really take up too many of my waking thoughts. I knew the clergy were always at it but hadn't bothered much with the detail. Five minutes on the net and I could see that God was indeed all about love.

I suppose I should be grateful that my mum's religious madness took the Anglican form. Within seconds of searching 'Church' and 'sex' I was drowning in pictures of smug Cardinals and their haggard, valiant victims. Non-Catholics seemed to prefer sex with adults, like the Californian pastor sacked for inducing sexual frenzy among middle-aged women at his Creator-God Theme park (second-hand dinosaur ride for sale, one careful owner). A naked Galway nun had been sectioned under the Mental Health Act for saying that God doesn't exist and an Italian priest was on trial for alleging that Jesus did. And just in case I thought only the Christians were daft, two thousand people were converging on an Egyptian village to see the skin folds of a new born calf make out the words: 'There is no God but Allah'.

A quick search on Helen Hubbard produced nothing but a load of sites about cottages in Umbria. That couldn't be right. Then the screen offered something else: Rev. Helen Halberd. Over eight thousand sites began to march down my screen. Eight thousand. Some were snoreworthy articles in theological magazines with a circulation, I imagined, of almost ten people. Zipping past those sharpish, there were sites promoting a book and – hey, what have we here? – a clutch of sites in capital letters were shouting about how the author was a blasphemous handmaiden of the Anti-Christ who'd trashed the Virgin Mary. That couldn't be the one Cyril wanted me to see. Could it?

A related site was GodSense.com, topped by the face of a crinkly old lush. There was a deep cleft in his lower lip which made him look even more like the cat who's just shagged all the kittens and got clean away with it. The Reverend Neil Sarbridge. I remembered his name from that day's Evening Standard:

'Darling of Radio 4's Thought for the Day, Rev. Neil Sarbridge has been 'kicked upstairs' for not believing in the Almighty. In the wake of his disastrous GodSense shows at Wembley Arena, where he tried to impress a turnout of less than 300 with his revolutionary 'sham-free' theology, he has left his south London parish to become Dean of Lancaster College, Cambridge. "Even the church can't keep a good God down," he said, without clarifying whether he meant himself or some other deity.'

It wasn't just for my research that I spotted that. I remember cutting it out and writing in the margin 'Know this guy? All my love, Patrick. PS: See you soon?' I taped it into an old envelope and addressed it to Dr Julia Bailey, Lancaster College, Cambridge. Did you get it, Julia? You never said.

'Skiers survive three days on Mars.' I looked again. 'Skiers survive three days on Mars bars and melted snow.' Not a miracle after all.

Then I found something I've just about memorised, it was so fantastic. An interview with the Pope. Sales of his latest album must have been falling off or something, because there in the paper was Il Papa promoting for all he was worth, which is a euro or two more than the Anglican Church. Over a big photograph of the Holy Father looking like a piranha in drag ran the headline: 'Pope on the ropes. The spiritual leader of a billion Catholics talks forthrightly to Paul Kibitz.'

I'd first spotted Kibitz's work that time he claimed to have shagged Judi Dench, OJ Simpson and the Prime Minister of

Pakistan at the same weekend house party. Complete lies of course but so cleverly written that they all took it as a compliment and laughed off his apologies. He's been my hero ever since. What a master of the Insult Veiled. I used to wish, Julia, that some day Kibitz's name and mine would appear in the same major newspaper and then maybe you would be proud of me.

In the Pope interview Kibitz's name was in huge type of course, beside his usual mugshot of a bloodhound in formaldehyde. What'll he ask him, I wondered. The Pope's favourite colour? He'll not get much else surely. But that Kibitz is such a pro.

After the usual six paragraphs about how long it took to get a straight answer about whether he could see the Pope at all and how long he was kept waiting and how heroic Kibitz was to hold out against having his questions vetted, he played his first ace. When did the Pope lose his virginity?

'I think I shall borrow, if you don't mind, something a secular saint once said, someone you may be familiar with, of whose music I am fond, and disclose to you that I am, as you might say, like, a virgin.'

When I interview Whitehead, I thought, I'll carve a line of stubble from long sideboards down below the lobe up and over my upper lip, just a thin line, and I'll wear my beret, and I'll take no half-arsed answers like that.

Had the Pope ever been in love? The answer wound round the Alps, Pyrenees, the Urals and all until he said that he had been in Luvia in Finland, but never in love except with the one true God, in whose service is perfect freedom.

He has a good turn of phrase, that Pope, I thought. Service is perfect freedom. I liked that. Liked it a lot. Hadn't a clue what it meant but it rolled beautifully. I didn't half feel cheated later when it turned out he'd nicked it from somewhere.

After a few more volleys, the Pope began to respond like the perfect interview subject: he got tetchy. Kibitz was so subtle. By the time he asked, in all innocence, what was the Pope's favourite colour, it felt as if he was asking the old man if he was gay. Answer? Il Papa had all his 'collars' handmade by monks in Munich. Deuce.

PZ: 'And how does it feel to be infallible?'

Pope: 'I'm not gullible.'

PZ: 'I never said you were. I said . . .'

Pope: 'I may have led a sheltered life but I'm not gullible. How *dare* you!'

PZ: 'No, no, listen, I didn't say that, I said . . .'

Pope: 'Shaht ahp. *Shaht ahp!* You said what you said. You must never contradict me. How dare you, I am the Pope!'

This was Kibitz at work of course, so there was no guarantee that any of it happened at all. All the same, perfect journalism I thought then and I still think it. The perfect model for when I did the clean, serene rock god living so close to me that we could have the same postman. I'd treat my bills with more respect in future; they might have nestled close to Gavin Whitehead's.

I opened the curtain an inch. Sunlight blistered my eyes so I shut it again. I got back into bed and picked up my favourite book of all time: *Rock of Ages*, the amazing, unexpurgated rock and roll story of Sword Rampant by their roadie called Mugadossa, and Algernon Fox of *The Times*. It fell open at the story of Pug's first famous suicide attempt in the pond beside the Princess of Wales pub. Every time I sit outside that pub with a pint and watch the lights split the horizon between miles of grassy heath and a rosy evening sky, I remember that Pug wanted that to be his last view of the world. Or so he said in *Rock of Ages*. I smelt the pages. Glue and toilet paper. Appropriate really . . .

Seeing as how Pug was well filled to overflowing with substances of one sort or another, it was something of a mystery how he found his way into the Daimler at all. Then this old bat with a trolley bag rolled up to him, shouting: 'Young man, if you don't get out of that car this minute, I shall call the police. You riff-raff think you can just stroll up here from Deptford and steal cars belonging to respectable people . . .' Pug's electric window hummed open. He turned slowly, focused one eye on her and treated her to a unique rendition:

Who's this cross old bat before me?
Eye of newt and nose of dog,
Stand well clear, dear, Satan's Rising
Out of this here Blackheath bog.

She tried to yell over him, so Pug tried to close the window again but he kept getting his hair caught in it, and it was left to his trusty roadie, yours truly, to explain to the old girl as per usual that he was the greatest rock singer in the world and that it was his own car actually. I must have done a beautiful job. She apologised.

A minute later while I wasn't looking, Pug walloped the car straight into Drive, mounted the grass-covered hump along the edge of Princess of Wales Drive and headed all of fifteen feet towards the pond. Two wheels climbed the kerb and slumped at the low railing before the car stopped dead, the engine growling, Pug growling and the old woman laughing her drawers off. She must have told the Mail because next morning there it was in the paper: PUG DUG FROM SLUDGE, and how he'd never be as famous as Brian Jones in a month of Sunday papers. Little did they. . .

It was my mobile. Cyril. I put down the book.

'Patrick, you listening?'

Yep.

'I'm taking the little lady to the Maldives so we're going to put the paper away on Friday. I need the lady vicar piece by noon on Thursday.'

I laid my can of Special Brew reverently on the bed, propped up by a half-finished packet of chocolate biscuits. What day was today? Cyril said it all again.

'Yeah. No problem.'

'When did you see her?'

'Ahm . . .'

'Have you even phoned her yet?'

'Yeah, yeah.' I hadn't actually. Her number was somewhere . . .

'Good. Thursday's OK then?'

'Yeah.'

'Get her to talk about the two lesbian vicars trying to adopt a baby.'

'Right.'

'Patrick, are you awake?'

'Of course I am. I was busy on something else, that's all.'

'Well get off her and get on with some work. I'm off to lunch now.'

'Hang on, Cyril, when am I getting the money?'

'Money?' You'd think I'd asked him to share his vestal virgins.

'Thirty quid.'

'Sounds rather a lot.'

'For the Whitehead book. I'm not going near that lady vic until – '

'It's in the post, old boy.'

'In the post?'

Hnh. I'd experienced Cyril's 'in the post' before.

'Absolutely. And make it zing, old boy. The lady vicar piece, I mean.'

Make a lady vicar zing? She was bound to be fat and ancient in a beige anorak. But Cyril was as good as his word. Next morning I stood in my pants in the communal hall staring at Cyril's handwriting on the envelope, wondering how the hell I had sunk to this.

Her biog on the back was pure Mogadon: 'Having worked for 20 years as a London accountant, Helen Halberd (not Hubbard, Cyril had got it wrong) decided to be ordained as an Anglican priest. It cost her her lifestyle and her job. In this provocative bestseller her meditations on Bible characters combine with personal memoir to explain how the Bible has been misunderstood for centuries.'

Yawn. The contents list was even worse: Adoration, Lamentation, Desolation, Guilt. Vomit Bag had unaccountably been left out.

The best bit was the cover. No doves, crosses or candles, FIRE DOWN BELOW appeared in gold letters on a purple background above a naked bint with grapefruit tits and big legs. Bathsheba, apparently. No surname.

I took the book to bed, where my best thinking is done, and went back to scouring *Rock of Ages* for dirt on Gavin Whitehead. I knew he was the perfect expression of the Protestant work ethic: ten hours in the studio every day, one CD a year and straight home after every gig for lettuce juice and a tofu sandwich. And family prayers. The wife was into the God thing and in no time Gav was trotting along with her to church. That was his scene now. 'The new cool,' he called it. But no rock god is born like that. Surely there was heat and carnage earlier in his life.

I'd got beyond the first section of photographs and he hadn't even been mentioned yet. I flicked on through. . .

Whitehead was a novelty all right, a new whore bringing fresh skills to the brothel. You see, Gavin is what you might call a real musician. If he heard Kate Moss singing in the bath, he'd put his ear to the keyhole . . .

I woke up, and spilt my beer. In a panic I shook the precious books clear of the froth and cracked open the purple covers:

'*Desperation was overwhelming me. My life had become one of undiluted longing, of addiction without hope of satisfaction. I was burning up so much I could see only one solution: to extinguish myself.*

I used to drive across Blackheath every day with my fingers tapping the steering wheel as the traffic crawled along the A2. In various tempers we'd all make way for each other, or not, until we reached our destinations. The Heath can be exceptionally beautiful on some evenings when the wide dark sky is like a tent pegged down by the orange and red lights of the traffic.

That night rain was streaming down the windscreen. The wipers were swishing in a different rhythm from the Bach on the CD player and the tempo of the indicator clashed with both. I'd come off the A2 as usual and at least ten cars were between me and the mini-roundabout in front of the row of hotels. I'd been there so many times before. Suddenly I had had enough. I took it into my head to leave the road.

I closed my eyes, heaved the steering wheel through one hundred and eighty degrees and stamped on the accelerator. The engine thundered and I remember being aware of an insane excitement and a lot of rumbling and bumping along grass before the impact into the side of the church. The car was a write-off. The church sustained several thousands of pounds' worth of structural damage. I was in hospital for three months.'

Good old Pug. My hero.

But Bach? Pug liked Bach? I turned the book over and choked. I had been reading the words of Helen Halberd. Undiluted addiction? Insane excitement? Thousands of pounds of structural damage? Maybe this old bird was worth a look after all.

It was raining that first night I went to see her too.

Now, as the politicians always say, I want to make one thing absolutely clear: it was never my idea to see Helen Halberd in the first place. I was only doing a job.

My note of Helen's directions got steeped pretty soon in the downpour, so I did several circuits of the Blackheath one-way system before I wiped my visor in the slanting rain and saw the sign for St Paul's Road. I stopped outside a gabled house that could have fitted several versions of my place in its servants' quarters, parked the Honda under a tree and trudged to the front door.

There was no response to the doorbell, so I grabbed a black knocker the size of a tennis ball and was giving it a hearty seeing-to when the door swung open and I nearly fell into her arms.

She was taller than me, what my mother calls big-boned, with a lot of untidy red hair. She was wearing a black cardigan buttoned up to a white polo-neck which I took to be a dog collar at first, and black jeans. Not bad looking for an old bird. I made a note: 'If singing in bath, not put ear to keyhole.' We swapped apologies and she led me down the dark brown hall through a stained glass door to what might once have been a drawing room with paintings in proper frames and an ornate fireplace at each end. Now it was a bedsit full of books and junk shop furniture. She apologised for the mess – the place was just temporary until she started her new job.

My coffee came in a mug with a church on it. How did I ever come to this? I would murder Cyril when I saw him. I unfurled my wire-topped reporter's notebook, dead professional, turned on my dictating machine and bounded in, pleased with myself, with the first ace on my list:

'Why's the Church in such a mess?'

She curled up on the sofa and tucked her bare feet under a cushion. She blew on her coffee and I noticed brown lipstick. Had she heard my question? I was about to ask again louder when she told the coffee that it was important not to confuse God's work with the work of the church. She sat back as if that was it. Finito. I put on my winsome face and leaned forward to lure her into some crashing disclosure: 'You said you got a new job coming up.'

Another pause as she reached under the cushion for a packet of cigarettes and lit one. No sign of her offering me one.

'Something classy,' I said, 'in Chelsea?'

She gave a half-smile. She still hadn't looked at me.

'You're . . . censorious,' she said, 'as if you don't expect me to smoke. Is the little intimation of hellfire worrying you?'

'No, no, you do what you like . . .' I didn't ask her for a cigarette. I have my standards. They're low but I have them. 'I've given up actually.'

'So have I,' she exhaled luxuriously, 'Several times.' She allowed herself a playful smile, then: 'Have you ever been to church, Patrick?' Her eyes were on me like power drills.

I was about to go Excuse me missus, I do the questions here, when in a musty place at the back of my head my mother squinted at her red leather Bible at the very end of her outstretched arm. 'As the sparks fly up the chimney,' she whinged, 'I am born to woe'. Maybe that's why my mother took to religion so happily, so that she could indulge her taste for gloom.

'My mother does,' I said, holding her gaze. 'Not me.'

'Very wise,' Helen said, letting our eyelock drop. 'And the church you don't go to, is that the Church of England?'

'We're not here to talk about me, fun though that is,' I said. I was only a little bit flustered as I searched my list for my next ace: 'Do you believe in God, vicar?'

'You can call me Helen if you like.' She leaned forward and tilted her solemn face to me: 'Do you, Patrick? Believe in God?'

Before I knew what I was doing, I was going on about believing in something greater than ourselves but I wasn't sure what.

'God, that sounds trite. Sorry. And sorry I said God in front of you, I mean, oh bollocks, that's so trite too. Oh fuck . . .'

'No problem,' she giggled, 'don't worry what you say with me. It's fine.' Her delicious downward smile faded and she was all business again: 'For me the only real question about, what shall I call it . . . about belief is this . . . Is it very complicated or is it very simple? I used to think it was very complicated, so I read a lot. Then I decided it was both so I talked a lot, I preached. Now I know it's very simple. So I just get on with my work.'

I'd been watching her tongue move as she spoke. She broke a moment's silence: 'Shall I say that again slowly while you write it down?'

Bloody cheek.

'No thanks. It'll be on the machine.' And far too boring to use. What next? Time was getting on. There were pubs out there in need of my custom. I looked down at my reporter's notebook where my list of lethal questions would have been if I'd got round to writing them down. Beside my latest stick man doodle of Gavin rock-god Whitehead, done while I'd been kept on hold for almost an hour, was a note of my chat that day with his agent's temporary assistant PA:

WHITEHEAD on tour – where? (I forgot to ask), back next month, call again then.

I knew exactly what I was going to ask Whitehead when I got to interview him, and what I'd wear, and what I'd get him to autograph for me.

Her phone went. I watched her arse sway like a swingboat at a fair as she crossed the room to answer it. She must have known I was looking because she pulled her jersey down as she spoke.

'Eh yes,' she went, 'he's here now, no, no, he hasn't asked.'

As she spoke, she reached to a bookcase and tilted one of the books out with her middle finger. The entire bookcase wobbled in time with her arse as she pushed the book back. Almost arousing actually. What was the question I'd not asked?

Back on the sofa, she checked her watch and was straight back to business, maundering on about working in the City for years. I didn't listen much. Get anybody to talk about themselves for an hour – it's not difficult, ask any therapist – and you can usually cobble something together. I was content to watch the way her little finger played along the seam of her polo neck at her throat.

She caught my eye and laughed again.

'This is all in my book, you know. You haven't read it, have you?'

She was definitely new to this game, I decided. Didn't know the protocol, that I would pretend to have read it, and even make some fatuous compliment, and then she'd proceed in the knowledge that I hadn't really and gave me the gist.

'Can you just remind me?'

'My book,' she laughed, 'my book is a tawdry piece of pornographic blasphemy composed by a whore of the Anti-Christ.' She was looking at me as she blew smoke at the ceiling. 'But I'm sure you knew that really.'

Blasphemy, yes. Porn too! Where?

'Porn?' I asked, as delicately as I could. I swear you'd have thought I was more interested in the latest weather report for Alaska.

'Porn. The Old Testament's full of it actually. Have a look at the Song of Songs.'

I scribbled fast: Song of songs.

She wasn't laughing any more. 'And all I was trying to do in my book is show that the gospels weren't written to be taken literally.'

'You wrote porn in your holy book?' I couldn't get it out of my head.

'I didn't think I had, Patrick,' she pursed her lips, 'but some people saw it that way. You could always read it and decide for yourself.'

'Can't wait. And you got the new job in Chelsea because you wrote porn?'

She was speaking in a 'good with children' voice now:

'Not exactly. Do you know anything about Omega Wave?'

'Is it like a Mexican Wave?'

She tapped her lower lip with her thumb. It was a gesture I

would see again in dreams, but it lasted only a moment before she flicked her hand through all that red hair of hers and was serious again.

'No, Patrick, Omega Wave is a blend of . . . it's when the Holy Spirit, as they call it, fills you and you fall flat on the floor in the grip of a supposedly religious experience. It started in a warehouse near an airport in the Seychelles. People were so full of "the Lord" they couldn't drive their cars straight and when they got stopped, all they had to do was touch the traffic cop on the shoulder and he'd fall over too. Everybody was saved. Just by touch. And nobody took much notice really until St Martha's Chelsea brought it to this country.' She blew a sigh.

'We wrote them off as a lot of public school mummies' boys ditching their inhibitions. If we mocked them long enough it would go away. But Omegitis has damn nearly split the Anglican church. World-wide. Here, in the States, Africa, everywhere.'

'Doesn't everything.' I asked, 'What was the sex angle?'

She leaned forward. I could smell her scent of roses through the smoke.

'Some people were knocked flat for days, Patrick,' she said. 'Like that topless model who advertised the healthy vegetable waters and turned out to be a 40-a-day smoker – Chesty Mornings. She fell forward of course.'

Good one, I thought, I'll use that as if I thought of it myself. While I was writing it down, she murmured on: 'The Church of England does tie itself in knots about sex.' At that word I looked up. She was staring back at me and my guts flipped.

'But deep down,' she was formal again, 'it's all about money. The church was skint long before this recession. Bring on a sexy, new charismatic movement that hooks in all these high-earning professionals wanting to be seen as good guys. Of course the Omegists said these were all "new Christians". They wouldn't have been giving to church at all if the Omegists hadn't nailed them. Well, that was true, but in some barely definable way we all looked silly, and shabby, and the home team ended up with less and less.'

She sat forward, so close to me she sprayed her cigarette ash on my trousers.

'There were huddles and conflabs until all the bishops lost what was left of their hair,' she said, 'and then suddenly last New Year's Eve it seemed to resolve itself. St Marty's curate was an – '

'St Marty's?'

'Sorry, St Martha, Chelsea. Their curate was an amateur Kaballist, I think. He had worked out that by squaring the number of capital Ps in his favourite version of Revelation or something, the end of the millennium was actually the thirty-first of December last year. So while the police were all busy protecting drunks from themselves in Trafalgar Square, the entire congregation danced from St Marty's down to the Albert Bridge and threw themselves in the Thames.'

'The Chelsea Lemmings.'

'Good boy. You *have* done some homework.'

I preened like a teacher's pet.

'The curate – '

'The Kaballist?' I interrupted, to prove I was listening.

'Yes,' she exhaled smoke as if I'd just said something of the highest sophistication. 'Yes, he took a bump on the head in the crush or something and – how do we put it? – he met his Maker?'

'Tragic,' I beamed.

'Indeed.' She wasn't smiling. 'And the bishops have got together to plug the gap with someone of an entirely different slant.'

'Who is . . .?'

'Me.' She sat back with her arms wide: 'People criticise the Anglican church for being too broad'

'Believing any old shit?'

She licked her teeth: 'You could put it that way, but that's what I love about it actually. The breadth of belief. The tolerance.' She brushed ash from the tip of her knee three times. 'In this church here in Blackheath there's a man who loathes the whole concept of homosexual love, for his own reasons, and there's another man who's been happy with his same-sex partner for thirty-two years.

Every Sunday they're at the same altar together serving the Eucharist, the best of friends. That's the Anglican church to me.'

'Anything goes?' I blurted.

'We work together whatever our differences. The bishops are clever. That's why they're asking me to move to St Marty's, even though it's in a different diocese. It's unusual for the dioceses to co-operate like this . . . but St Marty's needs diluting.' She squeezed the butt of her cigarette to annihilation. 'And so, apparently, do I.'

'Ha!' I sat back. 'A chess fork.'

'I don't play chess.'

'Sounds like the bishops do.'

She gave another downward smile and shook herself another cigarette from the packet.

'What's your strategy?' I asked.

Lighting up, she narrowed her eyes at me through the smoke: 'My bishop said I should pray.'

'I'd get a kill dog.'

'Now, Patrick,' she looked at her watch, all flirting gone, 'much as I'd like to continue . . .'

'One more question please . . . wouldn't you rather be a Catholic? Know where you are? On sin and that?'

She laughed like a builder from deep in her guts. I was shocked, and a little bit thrilled.

'If I were a Roman Catholic, I'd still be making tea at the back of the church,' she said. 'Please don't misunderstand, I have the utmost respect for the Roman church, I just prefer to be among people who don't have it all sewn up.'

'It's all daft if you ask me.'

'Maybe it is all daft,' she laughed, 'The mumbo jumbo? The funny kit?' She tapped her lower lip with her thumb again.

The doorbell rang.

Helen rose and smoothed her palms down her thighs: 'I'm sorry,' she said, 'but . . . you know.'

I followed her back into the main hallway, now lit by a single dangling bulb. Helen opened the front door to an anxious little woman twisting her fists in her anorak pockets. There was a stilted moment while I moved all my stuff into one hand to shake Helen's hand with the other. The little woman was so eager to get inside that she shoved between us and nearly knocked me bodily on to the porch. What idiot ever said women were the weaker sex? I tottered down the vicarage steps like Fred Astaire in the moonlight, desperate to keep my balance.

The rain had stopped but the air was still clammy. Had I aced her, I wondered. Had I actually managed to do a Paul Kibitz and ask the Rev. Halberd something she couldn't answer without looking stupid? I couldn't believe my own genius.

As I rocked the bike off its stand, I realised I hadn't put my back-pack on properly. So I balanced the bike against my knee and swung the bag so that it would loop behind me and land in a single graceful motion in the centre of my back. I missed. The bike slid away in the mud and juddered to horizontal on the grass at my feet. That's when I realised that the two women were still standing in the porch under a Georgian fanlight seeing me off. Or making sure I went, one of the two. I heard that trucker's laugh of Helen's again, and the little woman joining in, and wondered what that question was that I hadn't asked.

Three days later, in spite of Cyril blasting me on the phone twice an hour about his deadline, I was still at my desk building pyramids of empty biscuit packets and beer cans with nothing on my screen except:

INTIMATIONS OF HELLFIRE
by Patrick Price-Johnson

You were distracting me. Yes, you, Julia, my dearest, the love of what I dared to call my life. Not in person unfortunately. That was precisely the problem. You'd sent me a text to call you urgently, then you'd gone unavailable. I left messages on your mobile, direct line and at the law faculty, and you ignored them all. Eventually I called the porter's lodge where they took my name as if they were blessed if they'd ever heard of the lovely Julia Bailey, doctor of law and youngest ever occupant of the Snorebag Chair of Land Law Studies, having any male friends outside Cambridge. I heard nothing more. All night I wrestled with the A checklist – pregnant, STD, dear John – and knew that of those it could only be the last, what with you being such a scrupulous advocate of body-bag sex. Body-bag life really. Come on, you know it's true. You even wipe your chess pieces after I've touched them.

Would I have minded if you wanted to ditch me for somebody else? Could I have managed without sherry parties in the Master's garden where I listened quietly as eager freshers congratulated you on the impenetrability of your bloody book on Leasehold bloody Reform? Could I have survived without waiting for the invitation once in four or five weeks to come and share your beige bed in your beige Cambridge rooms, having got kind of used to a jolly, and for me rewarding, day-by-day bunk-sharing experience when we were undergrads together? You used to swing into my room and drop your coat by the door, your jeans by the desk and your underwear on my head, remember?

I lay in the bath for about three hours that day contemplating that drawer where you keep your bras, each one with its matching pair of pants folded inside the cups, and wondered what you were getting up to without me. You knew what I did; I had the empty cans and biscuit packets to prove it. I would sit in my bedsit staring at Canary Wharf and the nurses when I should have been writing for Cyril, and I'd wonder about you for hours. You thought I was assailing the greasy pole of broadsheet journalism but for years I was interviewing Brown Owls and charity walkers and longing for you.

Would I hurt if you ditched me?

Bloody right I would. Occasionally it had crossed my mind to try another woman just to see how it went. I even got as far as chatting to one or two in the pub. But they always laughed too much or not enough, they were too stupid or not stupid enough. Mostly they didn't know how to buy a fucking round.

When it came down to it, nobody measured up to you, Julia. It was as simple as that. You were my woman, the one I wanted (in about two decades) to be the mother of my children, the one who would keep me in fags and footie tickets until I made it big. As soon as I got a column with my mugshot on it, we'd move out to some classy little stud farm around Cranleigh (next to Eric Clapton) or Haslemere (close to Slash) or Cookham (near everybody else) where you could devote yourself to me and our good-looking offspring and maybe write books about cookery or minimalist gardening. You'd be the perfect nouvelle feministe, you know you would.

What about the B list, I thought as I topped up my bath with more hot water. Did you want to be escorted to some college fixture? Had I forgotten your birthday? The anniversary of some first or other of ours (first kiss, first party as a couple, first shag, first holiday together, first time you left me)? The B list was anybody's guess. I always suspected you made them up.

A powerful strategy was called for. I phoned for two tickets for Norwich at home to Crystal Palace in two weeks' time and sent you that rather dated postcard with muscle-bound pectorals cradling a baby on one side and details of the match on the other. If anything was going to get your attention, that should do it. It was so bloody typical of you to come on all needy and then disappear. Have you any idea how disruptive it was to my work? Every time I sat down to write, another worry about you would assail me.

Was it the anniversary of the first time I got you into conversation? I bet you don't remember it. I was helping with the barrels for the Norwich fan club AGM in our first term, anything to get close to some beer, and you waited with your clipboard until we'd got them all on to the table before you pointed out that you'd ordered Shepherd Neame, not Bishop's Sweaty Gusset or whatever it was. The guys and I downed three pints each without drawing breath to prove the Gusset was just as good. I asked, who's the bossy bird? and swallowed my gum when they said you were the vice-president.

I want you to know something, Julia. Confession time here. Purely in the hope that it will annoy you so much you'll come and see me again. Thump me if you like, but please come. I fell in love with you that day, so hangover heels in love I didn't dare tell you this but I'm daring now. I support Charlton. Good old Charlton Arthritic. Like my dad. I always have and I always will. Not Norwich at all. Sorry, my love, but now you know. That's how much I've always loved you. Enough to deny my own team.

I'd have dropped everything to rush to your side but I had to get the vicar piece out of the way first.

INTIMATIONS OF HELLFIRE, I read again. I thought, Fuck me, what can I put? The afternoon nurses would be out soon, though the spring branches were thickening up so I couldn't see as clearly as in deep winter. But if I was ever going to make a living at this I'd have to get stuck in. I decided to go back to first principles and listen to the recording. I even went as far as to close my curtains to cut out all distraction.

Sitting alone in my warm room lit only by the glow of the laptop screen, listening to the recorded sounds of the traffic outside, and my own sniffing, and Helen's words seeping into me through earphones, I had an extraordinary sensation of muddle clearing. It was almost as if I had wandered by mistake into a dark, glistening cathedral in a foreign country and was inhaling unfamiliar smells while holy murmuring far away washed over me. By a mysterious process something indefinable turned wordlessly in me and I seemed to become focused, finely tuned, for the first time in my life. Why this happened I don't know – and God knows, it was all too short-lived – but time after time in all sorts of contexts Helen Halberd would succeed where my church primary school and my mother and even the combined efforts of the Cambridge English faculty had failed. She made me aware of my soul.

Paradox upon paradox, she said on the recording, and I muttered it after her. Paradox squared and cubed. Muddle made clear by mists of incense. A young man stretched on an instrument of torture combining beauty and ugliness, torture and love, misery and bliss, desperation and hope.   A young man praying the classic prayer at the moment of his death: Take me, God, wipe it all away and love me, hold me forever in the safety of your love. Even that young man, who was God himself, did not know as he died if his prayer would be answered.

That's what I should have written. Her words, straight on to the page. I didn't understand them of course. Hadn't a fucking clue. If only I had, simply quoted her words. Or even slapped down a chunk of her beautiful book. Oh Julia, if only I had.

The crowds were getting absurd. They were clamouring, tearing at his clothes as if he were a mighty man of wealth, pushing him and pleading: please don't go without helping us, Jesus, we love you, we need you. Someone screamed and as the crowd surged, Jesus began to topple. Before I could help it, we were forced together with his belly and thighs against me. He grabbed for my arm. In the middle of the tumult he spoke my name softly, 'Mary'.

'Help me Jesus, I can't – ' I reached for him, his sleeve, anything to keep me steady.

'Be still, Mary. Trust me.' The crowd swayed again and he held my shoulders.

'Why have I found grace in your eyes, Jesus?'

'You are loved, Mary. Does it frighten you?' he whispered. 'This storm will pass. Don't tremble, hold me, hold me, this . . . I . . .' Suddenly – and I don't know if anyone could see – his mouth was on my mouth, hard.

The crowd stilled, the world stilled.

We both laughed. It was a laugh full of sex.

'I cannot breathe without your eyes upon me, Mary.'

I was walking on waves, eternally kissed. My limbs tingled as if hummingbirds held me suspended a heart's beat above myself and I learned for the first time that the world is made of torment.

The crowd swirled again. I was gulping, buried in waves of strangers, their malodorous cloth, their roaring. Their hands came at me, pulling my arms, my shoulders, my breasts. My nostrils closed against their stench. Darkness closed over me and I sank.

'Jesus!' I cried, and nothing came from my mouth. 'Jesus!'

His face rose to the crowd over us and he roared:

'Let this woman breathe!'

The heads above us parted. Blue sky flowed in, then air. He knelt and cupped my face and three times he breathed on me – 'breathe, Mary' – from that barrel chest of his.

I obeyed, the storm in my heart calmed and I felt life flow back to me. He dragged me upright and there among the crowds he took both my hands and held them high as if in victory.

The crowd cheered as though I'd been brought back from the dead. Indeed I felt as if I had and would have sworn that was the case if anybody asked.

Then he spoiled it. As he always would. He dropped my hands and was gone again. Back to his men.

Back to his men.

That storm-tossed kiss gave me hope that I had come under wings I could trust. I yearned to wrap myself around him, touch him, taste him, hold him deep inside me. I long for him still.

Hope.
It's crueller than a butcher's skinning knife.

I had my email to Cyril ready: For the South London Chronicle (NB: for EASTER, Cyril, you asked me to remind you, EASTER), approx. 600 words. All that was holding me up was the attachment.

The best bit of any interview is always at the end, when your interview subject is relaxed and they think you've finished and they're safe. Naturally that's where I started my piece about Helen:

INTIMATIONS OF HELLFIRE

by Patrick Price-Johnson

'Everything we do in church is daft,' purred Rev. Helen Halberd through her own cigarette smoke, 'from the mumbo jumbo to the funny kit.' But lack of faith in the Almighty has done nothing to hold back her career. On Easter Sunday Ms Halberd takes up a new job at St Martha's parish church in Chelsea, famous for the 'Chelsea Lemmings' who were so full of the Holy Spirit last New Year's Eve that they danced through London to the Thames Embankment. Their vicar, the Rev. Aloysius Richkind, led them straight into the river where – God moves in mysterious ways – he drowned. 'It was tragic,' Ms Halberd smiled.

Ms Halberd, a 46-year-old former accountant, sees her sex as an advantage. Like journalism all the best jobs in the church go to women these days and I wanted to ask her why at her age she'd not taken the new glamorous 'nouvelle feministe' option of children and domestic accomplishments.

Yawn. I plugged in the headphones again, scanning the recording for something to tickle the lacklustre south-east London palate. Lean pickings, I thought then.

Now I know parts of what she said by heart. As I sit here in this cell, it's as if her soft, smoky voice is flowing around me like a blessing:

'*I wrote that book . . . I don't know why, I yes, I do, I wanted to work out why I became a priest. My vocation, if you like. I don't know if it's right to say I was "called" by God, I'm always suspicious of people who go on like that. It feels arrogant to me. And I don't know if God has ever spoken to me really, not in the way those people mean. I . . . how do I say this? I became a priest because of love. Somebody said that priests are priests because they're useless at anything else but that wasn't true of me. I was a City accountant. A good one too. I had a pretty predictable briefcase life. Happy to leave a "relationship" and the babies thing until later.*'

She lit up at this point. I remember her snapping a match between finger and thumb to extinguish it and her wry smile as she exhaled:

'*I never used to sleep much. I remember that. Up at six, quick run round the park, then a shower and off to my desk. I gave conscience money to a national charity every month and enjoyed spending the rest. I had this huge television with all the channels. Five remotes. I don't remember ever sitting down to watch it.*

'*Work does make you feel alive. It feels like life. But it's not life. Money's useful of course, don't get me wrong, we all need money. But work for itself is arid. It's love that keeps the blood warm in the veins.*

'*Then I met . . . a person. It was Good Friday, not long after I came out of hospital after my accident. A bank holiday so I was working at home and I took a quick walk across Blackheath to get the numbers out of my head. There was this crowd of people singing by Whitfield Mount. It's a rough bit of the Heath near the tea hut, lots of gorse bushes, and it was such a gorgeous, breezy day. Surreal really with the lorries thundering behind us along the A2. And I found myself being taken for a meal afterwards at the house of somebody I'd never met before. Before I knew what was happening to me, I was sitting beside this priest.'*

Who was the priest? I should have asked Helen at the time, there in her room. I could have done with a third party quote, to make me look thorough and investigative. It was not too late to phone her and ask . . .

'Hi. Ah. Sorry, yes, ah, what time is it?'

Her voice was sleepy soft. She couldn't still be in bed, could she? I informed her that it was one-thirty. Lunchtime.

'Sorry, yes, I am half . . . we had, ah, we were doing a candlelit vigil last night, I didn't get to sleep until six.'

Yes, that was definitely my idea of a hot night out too, I nearly said, but the kindness in her voice was melting me. I could almost smell her warm skin, the scent of her bed.

I introduced myself, asked who the priest was who'd changed her life and was wondering if my phone battery had died when she said: 'What did you make of that bit of Matthew's Gospel?'

That threw me.

'I left a note in your crash helmet. Have you found it?'

'No.' Patiently she said:

'Why don't you go and look now?'

I found my helmet and upended it. Tucked inside the padding was a folded piece of A5. Come to think of it, I had felt something a bit scratchy. (My head's not my most sensitive organ.) It read: 'If you can explain Matthew 27, verse 53 to me, I won't insist on copy approval. Helen Halberd.'

Had Cyril promised her copy approval? Shit.

I looked again at her words. Dramatic tails dangled from each Y and P.

When I moved into my bedsit, my mother was so thrilled to get me out of her house, she sent me a package marked 'Bible enclosed: treat with care'. It was delivered duly battered and covered in boot marks. I ripped it open and sure enough inside was an Original Revised Amended Edited Updated Cross-referenced Modified edition in easy language for happy Christians who were born yesterday. Or the likes of me.

I'd chucked it under the bed with my archive of Kerrangs but its moment had come. The pages kept flopping over themselves. Psalms, Leviticus, wrong way, forward, there was Luke. Where was Matthew? Matthew Mark Luke and John, I whispered, Matthew must be back a bit. Aha, Matthew 15 . . . 22 . . . Matthew 27. I had to lick my thumb to get the page I wanted . . . Yes!

> '53 After Jesus came back from the dead, saints came alive
> out of their graves too, just like him, and walked around
> Jerusalem showing themselves to lots of people.'

Dead saints roaming around Jerusalem like extras in *Night of the Living Dead*? What the fuck? I went back to the phone.

'Ms Halberd, are you there?' She was yawning.

'You can call me Helen. Yeah?'

'I found it.'

'And?'

'I've no idea.'

'Did you know that bit was in the Bible, Patrick?'

'No.'

'Matthew's the only gospel that has it.'

'I called actually,' I said, 'I just wanted . . .'

Oh God, how could I ask her? I could hear you in my head, Julia, saying Just Do It, Patrick. So I did: 'Who's the priest you met on Good Friday in your book?'

No answer. I felt the back of my neck prickle.

'Why do you want to know?'

'Well, I'm supposed to get comparative quotes where I can. You know, so and so says you're such and such'

'Not all clergy are happy to share themselves with the press.'

Was she flirting? Even so, I needed an answer:

'I know but . . .'

'I think I need to see what you've written so far, Patrick. Please don't take it personally but – '

'You'll be quite safe with the *Chronicle*,' I said, 'we're south-east London's finest – '

'Quite, but I think I do need to look it over. Can you email me?

Please? Then if there are issues we can talk again.'

Shit bugger and fuck, I thought, now what have I let myself in for?

A penny dropped inside what passes for my brain. Gavin White-head lives in Blackheath and he's a regular church-goer. Could the church he goes to be Helen's?

'One last thing.'

'Patrick, I'm really tired.'

'Yeah but . . . do you know Gavin Whitehead at all?'

'Who?'

'Sings with Sword Rampant, I just wonder if his kids are at your church school. I know the Sword have lost their edge since he joined but he looks fantastic, great hair, great act and, well, he's our local hero, man, I'd give anything to meet him.'

She was sniggering again. 'The rock star? Yes, I have met him. It's not easy, you have to fight your way through every mother from Deptford to Plumstead but he seems nice. He doesn't throw his religion at you.'

'What? How he's got two Bentleys, three Rolls and keeps the Bugatti for Sundays?'

'I'll ignore that.' I could feel her smile. I won't tell you where. 'He doesn't come to my church, no. He goes to St Marty's actually. The Omegists' church.'

'Is that what they call it? St Marty's-Actually?'

'Now, now.' She was definitely chuckling, 'I did ask him once why he goes all that way to Chelsea just to go to church.'

'Nothing to do with all the horizontal totty of course?'

'Patrick! You should go and see for yourself. You might like it.'

'What?'

'Go to St Marty's. He'll be nice to you there. You never know, he might even convert you.'

Whww. No way that was going to happen. They say there's one born again every minute but it wasn't about to be me. Not until the day they had a happy hour on communion wine and an all-female choir in bondage gear.

'You could do me a favour,' she said slowly as if she was about to entrust me with the mission of my life. 'Ask him for me what *he* makes of that bit in Matthew. Ask him if he's ever heard of midrash. It's important, Patrick.' A tremor in her voice sent hooks into my heart. 'My future could depend on it.'

I could never have become a Christian, let alone a priest, if I thought the gospels were to be taken literally. I have far too much common sense for that and am still dazed by otherwise rational people who don't. I was so lucky! From the start I was taught about midrash.

The gospels are Jewish books written by Jews in a literary form they called midrash. That cannot be said often enough or clearly enough. We are not dealing with news reports. Nor are we talking about some quaint oral tradition here: midrash is a theological and literary system of the highest complexity and beauty. Its purpose is to interpret and develop Scripture (a process called exegesis) and it has two main forms: Halakah (interpretation of the law, the holy Torah) and Haggadah (which covers almost everything else).

This process of midrashim is many centuries old. It began when the temple of Jerusalem was destroyed in 70CE and it was at its height in the great Mishraic-Talmudic period between 100 and 500 CE, overlapping with the time when the four gospels were written.

Which brings me to the exciting part: all four of the canonical gospels – Matthew, Mark, Luke and John – use haggadic midrash to express experience of God through the life and death of Jesus of Nazareth. It's the same technique used in the Hebrew Bible to try and understand Jewish history as a continual revelation of God's love and justice.

This offers us a paradox. According to the gospels Jesus was tested and eventually tried by the hated Pharisees, yet his story is related to the world in the Ancient Jewish midrashic *form. And Gentiles have managed to misunderstand it for nearly two thousand years.*

How does haggadic midrash work? An example: God helped Moses to part the Red Sea and save the Israelites. Moses died, and when Joshua inherited his mantle, the Israelites needed to be shown that their new prophet was in the same tradition and just as worthy. So Joshua was reported to have parted the river Jordan. Elijah was described parting the Jordan in his turn. Likewise Elisha. When the time came to place Jesus within this pattern, Jesus was described as striding into the Jordan to receive baptism from St John the Baptist. There it's not the river waters that part but the heavens themselves, allowing God Himself to validate his 'beloved son'. The pattern was honoured and broken at the same time: Jesus was in the tradition of the great prophets but as far as his followers are concerned, he was in an entirely different league.

When Moses met God on the mountain, his face shone so brightly that it had to be covered. A first century Jew hearing that Jesus was 'transfigured' in the presence of God so that his face shone with an unearthly radiance (Mark 9, Matt 17, Luke 9) would have a sense of Jesus not only within the Moses tradition but at the zenith of it. Midrash.

I hope that experts will pardon my amateur attempt to explain this. I expect to be criticised for an overly narrow and technical approach, but I enjoy trying to understand the gospels in this way. I find it a daily search for richness, and adore that we need not reconcile apparent contradictions or insult our God-given intellects to appreciate the sacred.

For midrash is not a source of dogma. Quite the opposite. It is a process of seeing each new holy experience within its tradition, thereby expressing the timelessness of God while developing our understanding. It is a magnificent way to express the glorious complexity of our relationship with God. Human life glows happily within this technique, and the lack of simple answers in the spiritual realm becomes not a torment but a treasure.

Perhaps I can be forgiven a literary parallel which might appeal to our Western minds. If I tell you a love story in which a man envelops his beloved in his overcoat, you might think of Bridget Jones and know that the story will probably have a happy ending. If my love story features a young Princess in a wedding dress kissing her Prince on a balcony, you might anticipate a story of turbulence and tragedy. By referring to the great stories of the past, the new story is placed within the tradition. This augments the new story and the old one, and makes them all timeless.

Let me push this a little farther.

The story of Herod trying to kill the Jewish babies to erase the newborn Jesus would link in the first century Jewish mind with the Pharaoh trying to kill off the Jewish babies in Egypt while Moses survives hidden in his basket. Herod may or may not have been aware of baby Jesus' existence. I don't honestly imagine that he was. But the incident is related in the gospel to place Jesus within the tradition of Moses.

Likewise, Jesus' Palm Sunday procession is an echo of a reference in Zechariah where the king indicates his humility by entering Jerusalem on the back of a donkey. If Jesus came to Jerusalem on a donkey, he would have been conscious of the Zechariah story and Jews watching him would have known of it too. It's quite possible that Jesus didn't ride on a donkey at all. It is enough that the story tells it so. Likewise it's possible that there was no star to indicate where he was born. How can a star indicate a particular address? No, the Star in the East is a deliberate echo of the births of Abraham, Isaac and Moses.

There is no shortage of further examples. The gospels weave them intricately into almost every line. In midrash, prophecy is not about fortune-telling. It's about pattern, the pattern of our relationship with God. These are devices designed to impart a sense of Jesus as God within the Jewish history of a sense of God. They are emphatically not lies. Quite the reverse. But they are not necessarily true in the post-Enlightenment, Western sense either.

They could be literally true of course. Except where they contradict each other, and more of that later. As my evangelical friends point out, God can surely do the impossible, is that not what being God means? These friends also say that deconstructing the gospels too thoroughly leaves nothing to believe in at all. It leaves no room for 'faith'. But for me, stripping away ridiculous literal interpretations – which were imported in error and should never have been there in the first place – liberates me to meet God in a new and deeper way.

This debate is not new. It has been developing among academics for many decades. My purpose in this book is to bring the debate to you, the non-professional reader.

I propose to do this by example. I am going to retell some of the Bible's greatest love stories. Each one is told from the woman's point of view and is refracted through those going before. As I write, I shall explore my own theology and vocation. This book is an adventure for me. I trust God will guide me safely through it.

One person's adventure can be another's snooze on the beach and after a quick flick through Helen's book, I still hadn't found what I would describe as porn. I'd ask her for details – chapter and verse – when she came back to me about my article.

Meanwhile I had a much greater hazard to negotiate: a trip, my beloved Julia, to see you. You still hadn't told me why you'd texted me so urgently. Presumably whatever you needed, you got from some other poor sap. But my tickets to Norwich and Palace had come through, which rendered me fantastically sensitive and caring as far as you were concerned. About bloody time, I thought, and packed for the weekend.

I still hadn't sent Cyril a single word, and I still hadn't identified Helen's significant priest, but I was feeling luckier than Ronnie Wood on day release with his latest waitress. I was walking around the Norwich ground with you, my darling Julia, and I was young. Your black hair fell like water down to your bum skimmed by a tight navy skirt and long dark tights. I longed to juggle your tits in my hands but I know what you'd have said. It would have gone on for several convoluted sentences, hours even, but it could be summarised in one word: Plonker.

Arriving for the start of a Norwich City game with you was always one of the most exhilarating experiences of my life. Driving past the coaches with the windscreen wipers swinging and through the streams of lads on foot all with their collars up and hats down against the lashing rain, bellowing and singing and pushing each other, and me feeling more and more pumped up from inside as you drove us straight through to the season ticket holders' car park by the stands. Then the slump would begin with you picking through the puddles whinge by whinge in case your latest boots got ruined. The alcohol-free lager, the elbowing through layers of small boys to get to the games machines, the smell of steaming anoraks, the feel of melted Mars bar in the mouth blending with a smuggled swigette of scotch (while you sipped fruit tea from your flask), schoolboys squeaking as a goal looked likely and then that most quintessential of football sounds, AWWW, that AWWW of thousands of male voices when nothing has happened after all. My own shout felt like a clawed beast just in front of my face aching to do untold damage in the world but then it's the usual, a scoreless draw and a trip round the supporters' shop.

I'd put a hand on your thigh as I shared with you my thoughts on how unleaded the whole football thing had become since the days when my father used to take me when I was little. We took our lives in our hands, yeah, but what heroes we were coming home. You crossed your legs, and my hand fell like an empty glove between us. 'Now what?', my hands were up in the air as if you'd pointed a gun at me, 'Can't I touch you any more?'

'You're so . . . masculinist,' you whined and adjusted your narrow hair band (no totty mane-tossing for Julia) and I got the old story, as if I'd never heard it before, about how you were entitled to dress as you liked without it being taken as a sexual invitation by me or anyone else. Even in those boots? I thought, but felt too bullied to speak. Wondering at the sheen of overhead lights reflecting on the hair of this glorious woman beside me – who had been known to claim to be in love with me – I felt at least entitled to hope.

After the match, in the fan shop, God only knows why but you went straight to the children's section.

'Aren't these sweet?' you were saying, pulling out a sherbet yellow baby suit with NCFC written across its chest in green. I went to find you a thong with 'I've scored at Carrow Road' across it, knowing full well I hadn't, nobody had, and that as to later on I would need extra time.

The cash desk woman held the thong up to the light, leered at me and said 'Big enough for you, sweetheart?'

I was about to give her a lecture on sexual harassment but found I was blushing too much. I nodded over at you still moving baby clothes along a rail, with a 'What about her then?' The woman winked: 'Yeah, they'll look great on her.' Even better in a pile on the floor of course. The woman went on:

'She's so slim, I hate her.' Then she called right across the shop to you: 'He's not the one you was in with last time, is he, love?'

Ha ha, I said, Ha bloody ha.

On the way back to the car I put the knickers in their paper bag into your coat pocket and whispered in your ear,

'I've got pints of it for you, darling.'

You mustered a thin smile and waggled your finger in your ear. You still hadn't said why you texted me. Needless to say I hadn't asked. I was too terrified of the answer.

In the car you started moaning about your work. Some City git, a solicitor, had come up to talk to your lot about employment prospects for newly qualified lawyers. Fair to middling seemed to be the verdict, and you'd taken it badly when he said that what you were teaching them would be as much use as the Pope's balls. Since when did that hold back university lecturers, I said, and got another look.

'They're all so earnest,' you were saying, 'so bloody tidy. You know what I mean?'

'I've never liked solicitors much either, I have to say.'

'No, the undergrads. They all look so old, so sensible. They wear ties and pin-striped jackets and polish their sensible shoes.'

'And that's just the women.'

'Yeah.' Christ, I'd got you to laugh.

'We weren't like that, were we? Where's their imagination, Patrick, their fire?'

'You mean they should put crisp 'n' dry on their hair and wear silly corsets like our lot?'

'And that was just the men.' You cracked a joke! Like old times. Things (not a million miles away from my fly) were looking up.

As you eased your little car out through the stragglers and the sun carved a slice through the clouds, you finally asked what I had been doing lately.

I slipped the Sword's latest into the CD Player.

'I still haven't got through to Gavin Whitehead but I'm not taking it personally, yet,' I said.

'Keep trying.'

Will do, I thought, but what if we turn out to have major religious differences, like I think he's God and he's not? I sang along with the Great Man,

There's a way back to you and it glitters like gold
When my heart dries and cracks into splinters.

Without you, babe, I'm cold, petals wither and fold
Like wings that are older than winter.

'Oo-oo-ooo, oo-ooo-ooooooo,' we sang, 'wings that are older than winter.'

Hear the call to be free, where there's spring in the trees
And the mushrooms are dancing for Jesus.

This is where you started giggling.

Throw the sins off your back, hang a cross in your shack,
For you know, every day's a new dawning.

You were laughing so much, snot was shooting into your hand but I knew better than to mention it.

'Oo-oo-ooo, oo-ooo-ooooooo,' I yodelled, 'every day's a new yawning.'

You blew your nose a few times, and managed to say, 'What does that song remind me of? It's definitely like something.'

Nonsense, I said, the Sword's music might be a bit samey since Pug died, brain dead really, but it's nothing if not original.

The truth is, I often think back to the old days when I saw the Sword in sweaty pubs. They had such energy then. I watch them now, the classic stadium rock act, and we're all headbanging ourselves silly to the old stuff with our phones held high as if it's actually going to bring Pug back. We're trying to conjure up his resurrection.

'She knows him, you know,' I said.

'Who?'

'The lady vicar. She knows Sword Rampant's singer, Whitehead. She said I should go to his church. He'd have to be nice to me there.'

I told you how my bike fell over and Helen laughed and how she was going to St Marty's-Actually and in no time I was holding forth as though Christianity was something I'd just invented.

You stopped me dead. You knew all about Helen Halberd already, the Chelsea Lemmings, the new team at St Marty's, the lot.

'How come you're so well informed?' I asked.

'Neil was after that job.'

'Who's Neil?'

'Our new college dean. You know . . . Neil Sarbridge.' Something about the way you braced your arms against the steering wheel as you said his name unnerved me.

'When?' I said, trying to get you to meet my eye. Not sensible as we were approaching a double roundabout.

'Patrick, are we playing marrieds or something?'

'I just want to know.'

You pulled up, checked your face in your rear view mirror and ran your tongue over your lower lip: 'We had lunch.'

We were silent for the whole drive back to Cambridge. The Backs were doing their picture postcard bit with willows and pale Venetian light and I shut my eyes to hold their beauty in my mind until we turned right after Silver Street and approached the familiar lumpish brickwork of Lancaster College. One of the undergraduates had written a message on his window at least a foot high, upper case, in shoe whitener. TITS AND BUMS.

'That's Leo's room,' you said. 'He's joined my post-nouvelle feminisme group. To wind me up.'

I said nothing. Safest.

In your rooms with your coat off, you looked small and neat, like a doll. Watching you move around your sitting room opening and pouring bottles of Belgian beer, I was reminded again of the day we both graduated. We'd had to queue in Senate House Passage for hours, in 90 degrees in our gowns and fur capes, and you kept standing on tiptoe to see over everybody else. Almost every time I see you on your tiptoes I think of that day, how proud I felt of your first (and my third), of how I had never loved you so much. I haven't been given much chance to love you since.

'So where did you have this lunch?'

'The Pickerel.'

'Who else was there?' For the first time since we left Norwich, you looked at me.

'A whole pub full of people, Patrick.'

'I see.'

'No, you don't see.' You mopped under my glass. 'I had to meet him.' You sat down and twisted your legs around each other like rope. That was when I first became aware of a nasty vibration between us, by the name of Sarbridge.

'You wouldn't believe the trouble he's causing,' you were saying, 'nearly all the girls in the college have got it now. Religion. Candlelit vigils all night, Bible meetings all day.'

'Sounds like you could do with a candelit vigilante?'

'Patrick, they crawl round the quads all night moaning that they're saved, then fall asleep in their supervisions. And it's all his fault – '

'God's?'

'No. The Dean. That's why I took him to lunch.'

'You *took* him? *You* took *him*?'

'You should write him up, you know, there's some scandal about him, I bet it's why he's here. Not safe out in the real church, so they hide him here with a fresh crop of undergrads every year thinking he can't do much real harm.'

'What's he like?'

'Not much to look at. Red face. Funny lip. He's clever. Something fake about him though, I can't quite . . .'

Your diffidence was almost convincing.

'Just another middle-aged shagger priest, by the sound of it,' I said, 'can we talk about something else, love?'

'I'm sure that's why he's been put in this backwater. You dig him out. Write him up for a big paper. Ask that woman Halberd. She should know. He's from Blackheath. Like her.'

'Julia. Look, these holies bore me stiff. I was just doing a one-off for Cyril.'

'I'm just trying to help you make a bit of proper dosh for once.'

I stood up. The Belgian beers were blending nicely with my blood and there was something about the pink rising in your cheeks, the light in your eyes. You were excited, Julia. You were very excited. And you were with me.

I crossed the half way line between us.

'It's just . . . he's poison, Patrick. I know he is.'

I reached forward and laid my palm against your cheek. Miraculously you didn't brush me away. I was within striking distance, yes, and with one of those quirky moves against the run of play that makes it such a funny old game Price-Johnson was in the area, it looked as if the whole pitch was just there to do his bidding, all it would take was some neat dribbling, a bit of footwork, keep the hands steady and . . . Was he going to hit the post? . . . no, it was looking good. Looking good.

You said afterwards you would have had more fun flossing your teeth while listening to Gregorian chants but you really seemed to like it at the time. For me the result was clear.

One nil. And an away game at that.

I must have said so, or similar, out loud.

You shredded me with a look and said: 'Just get the dirt on him, Patrick. Get it soon.'

Dearest Julia,

My mother sent it. A clip from the *Telegraph*'s engagements column. For god's sake Julia, the *Telegraph*? You and the tosser Mark? Whose idea of rock is his fossil collection? I'm guessing he kept on his bicycle helmet to propose? You couldn't have said yes in full sight of those ears. No, Julia, no, you can not do this!

A curse on everybody called Mark. May every one of them die painfully, alone, with their dicks caught up the red hot exhaust of a juddery old Harley. But why confine yourself to a few lines of small print? Take out a whole page ad, why don't you? Go ahead. Marry him. Don't fucking mind fucking me. But please wait. Not for ever, or even until I come out, I know I can't expect you to want a jailbird. Just hear my story first. Please try and understand. It's important.

All my love,

P

I didn't send that one either. I'm too miserable to do anything much. I've been lying curled up on my bed, turned away from the light, trying not to imagine you and the tosser Mark together. You said once he was 'a safe pair of hands'. I don't like to think about his hands. Where they might be on your body. Sometimes I can't help it, I do see his hands on you in my mind, and it makes me feel as if my guts are full of maggots. Soon my whole body will be full of maggots all wriggling under the skin, and in my head as well. I have to do something to stop them and all I can think to do is cry.

But I'm not going to cry. It's not good for your health around here. So this morning I decided to get up and do something. I could do with a new challenge. Something that will bring me comfort and at the same time annoy quite a few other people. So – I'm trying to make them get me a copy of Helen's book.

The library here has miles of shelves but by the time this new model prison opened they'd run out of money to fill them, so there's nothing much there except thrillers with the last page or two torn out. The chaplain's no use either, ridiculous old buffer with breath like a dog's fart, but there is a screw who brings me the odd thing. He's not the one who was fantasising about you, by the way. (They seem to have shut up about that, more or less. Congratulations. You're obviously far more frightening than the Crown Prosecution Service.)

No, Julia, you're too old for this bookish one, being over the age of twelve. He's brought me a sinisterly stained copy of *Sacrifice to Beelzebub*, full of capital letters and exclamation marks, but he can't get hold of Helen's book. Which is out of print.

I can feel her book, feel it and smell it, but I haven't got our copy any more. The libel lawyer kept it. Do you remember, Julia, how we lay in your bed, that weekend of the football match with the curtains closed right through to Monday morning? It was one of the most satisfying weekends of my life and I'm trying to remember every second, and conjure you back. You nipped out for DVDs and pizzas on Sunday but apart from that it was just like being under-graduates again after a freshers' party with FUCK OFF YOU FUCKERS WE'RE BUSY FUCKING stuck outside the door.

Helen left me a voicemail while we were busy actually, saying that we really should discuss what I'd written and could I call and arrange a meeting. You had made a start on Helen's book with a red pen: 'She says she hardly knows him?'

You were such a marvellous sight propped up against three white pillows wearing nothing but your glasses.

'She bloody well does,' you said, 'look at this acknowledgement. After two pages of publishers, grief counsellor, therapists and so on, she mentions NS.' You'd marked it with four vertical red lines: 'Finally, how can I express my appreciation to NS for his inspiration and encouragement? He led me through the fire. That he did not get burnt too is testimony to God's gentle care.'

'Pass the vomit bag.'

'NS,' you said, remember? 'Neil Sarbridge.'

'Could be Nobby Shawcross.'

'Who's he?'

'Drummer for Steel Virgin.'

'I don't think so. Who's this priest she's on about the whole time?'

'Judas Priest she's on about?'

'Oh wake up, Patrick, you are infuriating sometimes.'

'What? You said Judas Priest and I'm in trouble! What?'

'You can be perfectly clever when you want to but it's such hard work dragging it out of you.'

I hate it when you go on about how useless I am. That's why I'm writing all this. I want you to see it the way I saw it for once. How it was for me. Oh Julia, how I wish you were here now to disagree. I want you so much. The real Julia, not the one in my head.

Anyway, suddenly you performed an act of genius. Not a sexual one, sadly. Almost as important as that.

'How can you not see,' you said, 'this book isn't a "faith safari" at all. It's all about sex.'

You'd found the elusive porn, I thought: 'Show me!'

'Not in so many words but . . . Look, look at this about Ruth here. Halberd says it's "*A simple tale of two people falling for the good in each other.*" Rubbish. It's a simple tale of how to catch a man.'

'Pff, disgusting. I love the way you hate all that Bridget Jones stuff.' Well trained, me. But had you found the porn?

'Listen,' you said, 'Ruth's mother-in-law tells Ruth to wait until the guy's drunk, then go and lie down beside him in the night.'

'She does?'

'Yeah.'

'Where? Where is she? Bring her here!'

I made a grab for the book. You held it high above our heads and read aloud:

'*And it came to pass at midnight.*'

I love it when you put your arms over your head. Your armpit was irresistibly close. I couldn't help it, I had to kiss it full on before I ran my tongue down the swell of your breast.

'Patrick! I am sick to death of it!'

I pulled away horrified: 'Of my tongue?'

'No, I mean – '

I latched on to your nipple and gave it a soft tug. It sprang to attention, as solid as a liquorice torpedo from the school shop.

You pushed me away: 'No, it's all this obedience stuff, you know, why's it always the women who have to take the orders?'

I did as I was told and surfaced: 'Didn't you say a woman told her to do it?'

'It's unnatural. Every chapter's the same, another woman trapped, taking orders, well I think we've moved on a bit since those days and it's typical of the church to try and keep women locked into the outdated mores of a defunct culture, this far, *this far*' – your thumb and forefinger showed a distance about the same length as my now dwindled penis – 'frankly from the Taliban!'

'Can I have permission to kiss your navel, Julia?'

You straightened your specs and perched the book on your belly but I could tell from the smile that I had your attention.

'*It came to pass,*' you read, '*at midnight that he was afraid.*'

'What was he afraid of?'

'Doesn't say.' Then, '*He moaned like a baby in a bad dream.*'

I did a bit of moaning myself.

'*and sat up with his eyes wide to find, behold, I lay at his feet. "You are kind and virtuous, Ruth."*'

'Terrific,' I sat and crossed my arms, 'I've never heard anything more erotic.'

'Patrick, listen! *"I will forebear to touch you. Lie with me here until morning and be my comfort." Never in my life had I felt more naked than when he covered me with his skirt.*'

'Covered her with his skirt?' I folded my arms. 'Like he's Axl Rose or something?'

'Who?'

'Guns 'n' Roses.' I made a rock fist.

'I don't think so,' you went on primly, you are so fucking sexy when you're prim, 'Halberd explains the skirt thing. There's a bit in Ezekiel apparently where God says to Israel, *"Thy time was the time of love and I spread my skirt over thee and covered thy nakedness."'*

'So Ruth was naked?'

You leafed back a page or two.

'Not literally, no. But the skirt means he's protecting her. It's sweet really.'

So you're against obedience but you're all for being protected? I pulled the sheet over us both and was trying to 'protect' you when you slithered away and dumped me on the floor. You leaned over the edge of the bed showing some deliciously squeezed cleavage.

'That's the whole point, Patrick. The skirt thing is *not* about sex. Why can't you be a gentleman like this Boaz character?'

'How can I be a gent when we're naked together?'

On you went about how the skirt business could remind a modern reader of Bridget Jones being wrapped up in Mark Darcy's overcoat. Which doesn't mean sex either but a happy ending blah blah.

'That's what Halberd says. Isn't that fascinating?'

I was kneeling by the bed.

'Not as fascinating as the fact that one of your nipples folds in on itself and the other one doesn't,' I said. I was in the perfect position to see if the tip of my tongue would fit into the pinkish-brown half-centimetre horizontal groove of the closer one. Again I got the shove.

'Patrick! You just don't get it, do you?'

'What?'

Your hands were flailing tantalisingly close to my body. You grabbed the book in both hands: 'Don't you see,' you purred, 'what this book's about? The obedience thing's a smokescreen, it's not about that, it's not even about God really. She's using intertextuality to write about love.'

Intertextuality. Ah yes, that stuff. The word buzzed into my head like a cartoon bee and flew out again. My academic years were behind me and were going to stay that way. You spanked Helen's book deliciously.

'Halberd was in love with somebody,' you said, 'but she's a priest so she can't say it straight out. So she's written this book. It's a love letter.'

'What makes you think that?'

'I mean, look at the detail. She reaches for Boaz, look: "*My finger rose to my lips, then moved across the greatest chasm in the world to the cleft of his lower lip . . .*"'

I reached for your lower lip and stroked it lightly.

'When are you seeing her again?' you asked.

'I haven't phoned her back yet.'

'Make it soon. Look at these pictures. Here she is at Neil Sarbridge's meeting. His GodSense thing at Wembley. That's him there, look. They're together.'

I stretched up for a look in the central pages of the book.

And there they were, hand in hand on a laser-lit Wembley stage with her grinning at him fit to burst and him clocking the camera in an open-necked polo shirt with his grey beard blending down into chest hair, middle-sized, middle-aged and full of himself. With a deep cleft in his lower lip.

'You've got to bust him, Patrick.'

'I can't. It's not my – '

'It's complete hell as long as he's in the college, he's got to go!'

'I'm only being paid to write about her. I'm not Miss bloody Marple.'

You flounced off to the bathroom and slammed the door. What next? I thought, what fucking next? I got myself a medicinal beer and waited in the middle of the bed for about twenty minutes. What was I supposed to do? Put my own work on hold while I rid you of this turbulent arsehole? It was a bit much . . .

You walked back in and stood, still naked, under the chandelier so that I could take in every detail. You could have removed my beer from my fist and replaced it with lemonade, I was that knocked out. I looked from your neatly trimmed pubic triangle, very nice, up your lovely little belly and deep navel to the two perfect pendulousnesses to . . . Lipstick. Blusher. Stuff on your eyelashes. Very nice. And there was a bruise beside your left eye the size of a wineglass, redness of a swollen lip below your left nostril and a dark splodge criss-crossed with blue and red on your chin. I hadn't heard any noises of you knocking yourself about. You looked like something out of *Night of the Living Dead*. Or indeed St Matthew's gospel.

'It's make-up. Feel.' You lifted my hand and put it on the place where your lip was red. It came off on my fingertip.

'What?'

'But they won't know that when we're at High Table in two hours' time. I'm going to say you did it to me, and they'll believe me, unless you dig out the scandal on the Dean!'

It was such a hot day that we laid down our sheaves and took off our scarves to let our throats have a taste of the sun's good rays. The light reminded me of my mother blowing down her blouse to cool herself as she laid out my wedding feast under the trees. So far away. I looked across at Naomi, my mother-in-law, twice my weight and all of it sorrow. What could I do to shake her out of her misery?

'This reminds me of my wedding day,' I said, 'the last day I knew any happiness in this world.' I was imitating her scowl and the way she rocked as she spoke. The other gleaners chuckled and someone said:

'Yeah, bloody marriage, I went into mine with my eyes shut.'

'Your father closed one,' called another, 'and your brother closed the other!' The first one giggled:

'It's just as well! If I'd seen the groom first, I'd have run a mile!'

Laughter gripped us. Naomi's back was quivering as she shook out her hair but I couldn't tell if she was laughing or crying.

'My big day, I was that innocent,' I said, 'I asked my mother what fornication meant. She took my veil in her fingers and she said, "Ruth . . . fornication like this, your father's got us the very best wine!"'

Men across the field turned to see what the noise was about. Even Naomi snorted and fanned herself with a handful of stalks.

'Oh you're a naughty girl, Ruth,' she wheezed, 'making me laugh like this and our men all dead, oh you're making me sweat in this heat!'

Next thing I knew, she was loosening the straps of her dress and sitting naked to the waist in the furrows. I watched the sweat roll down the arc of her back and remembered a very different day, a day of storms. The day we laid out our dead husbands together.

I'd been about to wipe the creases of my husband's palms when I turned his hands over and looked at the backs. Scars covered the knuckles like lace. Most of them had answering scars on my head and body. I'd heard my blood in my ears, and dropped the dead hands unwashed. Naomi had been watching me move around his body and rested her hands on my shoulders:

'Ruth, my dear one, after the funeral, you must go.'

'And leave you alone in a dead village?'

'You disobeying me, girl?' she growled. I nodded.

'Go, silly girl, why do you wait?' she said, 'You must go and leave me here to die.' That night she slept under the winter moon and begged the Lord to take her.

Next morning she came to me with a new plan: she would go home to her own people in Bethlehem in Judah, and take me with her. I cupped her wrinkled face in my palms.

'Whither thou goest, I will go,' I said, 'Thy people shall be my people and thy God will be my God.'

'May the Lord deal kindly with you,' she patted my hand, 'as ye have dealt with the dead and with me.'

Many nights we shivered together, and cried and prayed. A thousand times she was dangerously ill with grief, but somehow we found the strength to go on. Now here she was rocking with laughter in the harvest fields, dangerously well again.

The men couldn't have that. Two of them stamped over to us, their faces as dark as justice. They yelled at Naomi to cover up, she was an insult to God, an abomination. I thought she looked beautiful, smiling at the sunshine on her breasts, but I had to protect her. I was unwinding my shawl from my waist to cover her when the men hushed. A third man was walking towards us like a bull in the sunlight, a head taller than any of the others. His skirt swung like the barley. Someone bellowed: 'That old woman's a disgrace!'

Naomi pushed my shawl away and sat quietly.

'Naomi?' The big man stood over her.

She looked up. His eyes were a sunburst of gentleness as he mimed pulling straps up over his own shoulders. This silent command was enough. Naomi pulled her dress back up.

'Boaz! My kinsman Boaz!' she shouted. The syllables of his name made her mouth pucker and smile. 'I remember you when you were the height of that gate,' she said, rising to hug him, 'with eyes as bright as fish and twice as serious. Look at you now, a mighty man of wealth!'

He glanced at me, and Naomi started singing my praises. There'd never been such a daughter-in-law, she said, I was a famine widow, very good through all our travails, very honest, very clean. Boaz and I heard none of it. He pulled some barley ears from their stalk and let them trickle from his fingers. They were strong, fat fingers with knuckles were as soft as a scholar's. Not a scar to be seen. I heard the bend and flow of barley heads in the wind and my heart repeated silently Boaz, Boaz, with a pucker and a smile.

He helped me to my feet.

'Follow my reapers,' he said, 'I have told my men to drop more barley for you so that you and the old woman can eat.'

Obedience had never been sweeter. He lifted my chin: 'Wilt thou come hither and eat of my bread?'

I did not dare look up for fear of the heat in his eyes.

'At meal time,' he went on, 'wilt thou dip thy morsel in my vinegar?'

Naomi chortled: 'You used to be such a modest boy, cousin. Sounds to me as though you've learned a thing or two! I'll bet your "vinegar" is the finest wine for miles!'

The women's laughter rippled around me. Boaz raised his fingers to my cheek but dropped them before we touched.

That night Naomi was as excited as a child in a puddle.

'They'll be feasting on the winnowing floor,' she said, 'Go and wash thyself and put on thy best raiment. Don't make thyself known to Boaz until after he has drunk his fill and his heart is merry. Then go in there and uncover his feet and lay thee down.'

'All that thou sayest unto me I must do,' I said, and my heart tingled.

The men were rowdy on the winnowing floor. Their talk turned to singing and the singing was close to fighting when suddenly all *was quiet and Boaz's voice rose above the rest, a fine tenor of deepest sadness. The applause faded and Boaz swung away from the table to lie down alone.*

I came softly close to him, as Naomi had bidden me. As I uncovered his feet and lay down, he murmured soft vowels to himself but he slept on. And it came to pass at midnight that he was afraid. He moaned like a baby in a bad dream and sat up to find, behold, I lay at his feet. I trembled like a horse in lightning as my finger moved across the greatest chasm in the world to rest upon the cleft of his lower lip.

'All that thou sayest unto me I will do,' I said, then folded my hands under my chin. I waited for the abrupt removal of my garments and my dignity. In the next moment I fell in love.

'You are kind and virtuous, Ruth,' he said. 'I will forbear to touch you. Lie here with me until morning and be my comfort.'

Never in my life had I felt more naked than while he covered me with his skirt. I lay wide awake until morning.

Next morning while you were in the shower, I thought I'd do a bit of clearing up. So I cleared up that half-bottle of red that was looking lonesome on the table, the last half-inch of a bottle of scotch, some chocolate cake, an overripe banana and half a packet pizza lying cold on the draining board. I washed down the lot with a cool Trappist beer.

You came out of the shower swathed in that dressing gown the colour of battle dress. If I could do one thing to improve the human condition, I'd burn that dressing gown. But it had your beautiful body in it and soon your beautiful body might be out of it again and in my arms, so the dressing gown had a reprieve. You put on the kettle.

'I've been thinking, Patrick.' Gawd. Now what? I'd already agreed, while kissing those fake bruises off your face last night, to pursue your Dean Sarbridge to the ends of the earth.

'You know that Whither thou goest thing?' you said.

Time to distract you by nuzzling your neck.

'Slither thou hither, you're making me shiver,' I said and pulled aside the collar of the dressing gown. It felt like corrugated card-board.

'Stop it, Patrick, be serious.'

'I couldn't be more serious,' I said, 'My love is a river I want to deliver.' I pressed myself against your bottom.

'For God's sake, Patrick.'

You bumped me away, which only made me want you more.

'Do you ever think of anything else?'

Not often, it has to be said. Why do women never understand this?

'That Whither thou goest thing,' you said, 'I've heard that before and I always thought it was for lovers. But it's not. It's what Ruth says to her mother-in-law. I'm sure I've heard it at a wedding . . .'

The W word. Wedding. Avoid, avoid.

I took your hand and started kissing your finger tips. You reached for a blue cloth and wiped the worktop where I'd been leaning.

'We've got five minutes,' I whispered. 'Whither thou goest, I will come . . .and I promise not to come until you've come first.'

'I've got to go to work, Patrick!'

'Oh go on, Julia, it won't take long, I promise.'

You pushed me away and drowned two teabags in boiling water.

'Milk thistle for me,' you sang. It was probably to cure some obscure female thing. I had no wish to know what.

'Mexican Wild Yam OK for you? It's calming.'

You passed me a concoction the colour of camel's piss. I looked forward to my second breakfast, the full fry-up and a pint of builder's tea on the way home.

'It's obviously about him,' you said.

'Who?'

'You know,' you looked up. 'It says he was red-faced?'

'Grey beard.'

'And that funny lip, Patrick, it's – '

'Sarbridge.'

I put down my mug and laid my hands on your shoulders: 'My clever whatever, come, be mine forever.'

'But what's she saying about him?' you asked. 'It's got to be more than just "falling in love with the goodness in each other."'

'He moaned like a baby,' I said, 'pretty clear to me.'

'Yeah but Ruth's all kind and virtuous – '

'Bollocks,' I said, 'she dipped his morsel in her wossname. And she's excited, it definitely said Naomi was excited.'

'Naomi's the mother-in-law, idiot.' You slid away from me again.

'What about the feet?' I asked, 'she uncovered his feet. That's got to be code for something.'

'Exactly. And we have to find out what. I'm sure Halberd's telling us that she and her priest had an affair but she's subtle.'

You turned and parked your bum against the oven: 'Which is why, my darling cutting-edge investigative journalist, you are going to have to get me some more facts. Then we'll crack the code and get Sarbridge out of college, where he does nothing but distract the female undergraduates en masse. And *you* can write it all up for something a bit more august than Cyril's rag, OK?'

I covered your face with kisses and was working my way down to your throat when I felt your hand on the back of my neck. I heard a clump as your mug was set down out of the way. I felt your other hand on my chest, working down.

I loved this midrash game. We were getting somewhere at last.

I dreamt this morning I was in a newer, bigger prison in which I had a suite of rooms on four floors. 'In my Father's house are many mansions,' my mother said as she showed me into my new sitting room with a bar in the corner, a six-foot television screen and computerised billiards. Sitting on one of my three personal lavatories, I was wondering whether to wake up when Robbie Williams came in and squatted on another bog at the far end of the room. 'My mum used to like you,' I said and asked if he planned to be long. He said About four years. Shit, I said. I don't need your permission, he said, looking pleased with himself. No, damn and fuck, I said, I'm in the finest prison suite known to mankind and I've got to share a bathroom with Robbie Williams. As long as he doesn't sing. 'Worse than that,' he said, 'your victim's here to see you.' And she was. Helen walked over to me in her red dress and stroked her thumb across my lower lip as if she was about to kiss me deeply, as I sat there on the bog, my eyes closed. For the first time in months I would feel the delight, the bliss of her mouth. I waited and waited until my bum was cold. I opened my eyes. Nobody was there after all, not even Robbie.

Waking up in my real cell here wasn't so bad. At least I've got it to myself. The rest of the wing found out what I'm in for and nobody wants to join me. Paradox, I thought. To get the best out of prison these days, make sure you commit something big. Aggravated rape, or murder of course, and you'll get a nice cream room to yourself with its own toilet. It's not huge, you can pee into the toilet bowl straight from your bunk if you want to, but they do leave you on your own twenty-three hours a day. A little light burglary and you have to share your cell and toilet with some tattooed hard case and get harassed about cleaning duties and gardening the whole time.

Paradoxes. That a woman of 46 provoked more erotic passion in me than Julia Bailey, the class of 2002's babest of all possible babes. That in trying to get closer to her than I am to myself I have wound up here in what should be hell but is sometimes almost close to peace.

Paradoxes, Helen. I wanted to get so close to you, I would have ripped open your rib cage with my own fingers so that I could crawl inside and lie there in your body among your wet, beating heart and soft lungs for comfort.

I came down hard after that exquisite weekend in your rooms, Julia. I'd phoned Helen after my second breakfast and arranged to call on her that evening but in Deptford Creek I ran out of petrol. I caught the bus, feeling like a right dick with my helmet on my arm, then I had to jog another half mile or so back to the bedsit for my dictating machine. A neighbour had left a bicycle outside, unlocked, so I borrowed that and arrived late at the vicarage with my back splattered with mud. The tosser had no back mudguard.

Helen took my jacket. Before I could stop her, she put it on the floor and was kneeling over it with her red hair forward hiding her face and her black skirt taut over her arse. I was transfixed by her bare feet and the movement of her arse over them, close to my own in towelling socks, as she solemnly worked a white teacloth into the padded seams over the shoulders of my jacket, making long, smooth strokes down the cracked leather. I thought that my mother wouldn't do that much for me.

She hung it on the back of the oatmeal chair near the window, made us coffee and then walked to her desk. I sat as good as gold with my fingertips pressed together.

'I've got to take a cremation service tomorrow morning,' she said, 'I thought some of this might do but I'm not so sure now. Often it's local people who've never been to church before. The trouble is they come to church to find God and what they get is people.'

She prized a paperback from one of her rickety bookcases – had she built them herself? – and slung it at me. On the cover was a sick-looking dude with a plate behind his head.

'What do you think of that?' she asked.

The words fogged in front of me.

'Canticle of the Furnace?'

'Yes.' She took the book back and read: '"*The arrows fired from his bow of love have struck me. These strokes have been made by a loving lance.*" Why's there so much masochism in Christian theology? "*The sword is long and wide and it has pierced me through and through . . .*"'

She cocked an eyebrow: 'He's talking about how he fought Jesus and lost. And ever since Christ "*loved him with a true love*".'

She kissed her thumbnail absent-mindedly: '"*Love has set me in a furnace, a furnace of love.*" Beautiful. But I can hardly use it at the cremation service of a little girl keen on rabbits, can I? Even if it is by St Francis.'

She squeezed the book back on to the shelf and looked at me with her fingertips together all business-like: 'Your article.'

She produced three sheets of my carefully chosen, double-spaced words, now covered in spindly, red edits.

'There.' She handed it over. 'You can forget my alterations and write what you want if you can explain that bit of Matthew's Gospel to me as we agreed.'

I wasn't going to be caught out in the ignoramus enclosure of the zoo. I went on the offensive.

'I want to know the truth about Neil Sarbridge. You do know him, don't you? There are pictures of him in your book.'

She uncrossed her legs and stuffed both hands into the loop of black, pleated skirt between her thighs: 'The clerical world is pretty small, Patrick. It's hard not to know most people a bit.' She eased her neck luxuriously. 'He used to be at St Felix's just across the Heath. But I wouldn't say I know him at all well. He's at Cambridge now, I believe. How was Cambridge?'

Had I told her I was going to see you? Must have done. I muttered about the Backs and the football match and you, and then

. . . Why I don't know, maybe it was something about the quiet of the room, the wideness of her eyes listening. Before I knew what I was doing I was telling her about you, Julia, about how much I still loved being with you after seven years, my whole adult life, even though I got on your nerves sometimes, quite a lot actually, but I found myself saying that some day, you know, not that we'd talked about it or anything . . . and Helen was listening so gently and I was rambling on, saying that even that weekend just gone I'd thought it was the last thing in the world I wanted – avoid, avoid – but there you go, before I was thinking straight or at all, it was out there in the air with a new life all of its own.

I told her I wanted to marry you, Julia, but I didn't know how to ask.

Helen raised her eyebrows the slightest flicker. Then I remembered why I was there. Neil Sarbridge. When did they last see each other?

She stood up, slowly brushed down the pleats of her skirt and went to the window to light a cigarette. As she looked out across the Heath, a slice of sunlight caught her, lit her hair to amber translucency and edged her left breast with a line like the blade of a new knife.

'When a man is in love, he often does want to possess his woman.' Her voice sounded slightly swallowed, as if she was addressing a bank manager who was being unreasonably reasonable: 'Legally as well as physically. Something like a quarter of men want to marry a woman after just one date, did you know that? They call it romance but it's actually about ownership. Man owning woman. Three hundred years after the Ten Commandments, King Solomon was the proud owner of more than three hundred wives. And twice as many concubines. Women he owned but who didn't have the status of marriage.'

'Yeah. Like sex slaves, right?'

She laughed and came and sat on the chair that had my jacket over it. She offered me one of her cigarettes. Heroically, I refused.

'I don't know why I'm laughing,' she sat back, 'it's not funny. It's just you . . . make me look at things anew.'

She made a half-pout when she said that last word, smiled, then half-pouted again. Was it supposed to be a compliment? I was too mesmerised by her lips to think.

'Anyway, my point is that the commandment against adultery is closer to the one about coveting livestock than violating a marriage bed.'

Bed. Neither of us dared look at it. Double, in the corner under a rust-red Indian coverlet and six or seven tasselled cushions.

She combed her hair with her fingers, pausing at the crown to hold a tight knot for a few seconds: 'Ask your friend Julia if she wants to be owned.' As she let go, she sighed as if releasing pain: 'Some women do.'

She paused and looked down my body, leaving a tingle which rose from the soles of my feet to my open mouth. I was about to bridge the chasm between us and take her hand when she spoke again.

'Can I ask you something,' she said, 'about my book?'

She was formal now, as if the answer was bound to be Jesus.

'It'll help me know if I, you know, got my point across successfully. Or at all. Don't worry, you can't get the answer wrong. Can you just tell me what you think my book is about?'

'Jesus?' I ventured.

She laughed: 'Could you be a little more specific?'

I left school years ago, I thought, I didn't need this. Holding her knee, she leaned back into my jacket. Maybe tomorrow I'd be able to smell her off it, her smoky smell.

'My book's theme is obedience,' she said.

I looked down and clasped my hands together as if I was about to pray. Where did *that* come from?

'Esther's story is about whether women can be forced to obey. Of course they can't. Nobody can. God understands that, even if human beings don't.' She sat forward.

'Esther was chosen from thousands of girls to be the king's new wife,' she said.

Suddenly I remembered. You had read me bits from that chapter, Julia! You were spotting echoes from the Ruth story, phrases from

Ruth's story that had changed slightly.

'Go, go, silly girl, why do you wait?' was in Ruth's story. And look, you said, in Esther it became 'Come, come, silly girl.' Ruth had cupped Naomi's wrinkled face in her palms; Uncle Mordecai had cupped Esther's face in his wrinkled palms. Esther's uncle 'stooped to lift some crumbs from our table and sighed as they fell from his fingers.' That echoed Boaz handling the barley ears in his field. There were so many allusions like that, overlaps. What did they mean?

'You tell it as if Esther and Ruth's stories are like drawn from the same,' I said, 'you know, the same phrases, the same but different. Like, you know . . . intertextuality?'

'Well, well,' she said, 'I am impressed.'

Her voice flowed into me and seemed to pool in my groin. Her cigarettes lay on the sofa beside me. She nodded at them, and at me. I took one. As she leant forward to light it for me, I could see an inch or two of crepey cleavage framed in her white blouse. I found myself imagining how it would feel to touch.

'You could put something to that effect in your final paragraph there.' She pointed at my draft article. 'I could write it for you now if it would help.'

My brain was gyrating in the glare of its first nicotine hit for two months: 'Why not?'

It would do no harm. Cyril would probably cut it for being pretentious.

I handed her back my three sheets of immortal genius and watched her put on little spectacles. Suddenly I could see you, Julia, jabbing your finger at Helen's chapter about Esther, then clambering over me and out of the bed, pushing all our pens and pages everywhere.

'Where's my Bible?' you said – *you* had a Bible, Julia? – and looked exceptionally delicious bent naked to search your lowest bookshelves.

'Yes!'

You pulled out a confirmation Bible and unzipped its white leather cover. You scanned the list of contents as if it was Halsbury's

Laws of England and found the Book of Esther in seconds.

'Halberd uses one translation. But here in this Bible it says something else.' You smacked her book. You smacked your Bible. 'World of difference.'

What difference, Julia?

'Come on, Patrick, keep up – ' you were excited now – 'look what Halberd's written in the last line of her chapter on Esther. It undoes everything she's written about Ruth being all virtuous and chaste. Everything.'

I still couldn't see the significance but I put it to Helen all the same. I did actually say to Helen: 'In the authorised Bible'

'The approved version,' she said.

'Approved version it says that Esther touched the *top* of the king's sceptre.' She breathed smoke at the ceiling: 'Isn't that a marvellous image of her domination of him,' she said, 'in both public and private domains?'

'So why did you say . . . what you've got in your book is . . . Why, wh–, why did you change it to what you said in your book?'

Helen's face had such brightness in spite of the lack of make-up. A teasing smile lit up the corners of her eyes. It dawned on me that I was having the most erotic conversation of my life as she said: 'Mischief?'

I was dishing up when my uncle Mordecai came in. He thumped his stick on the ground and bent over cackling. He laughs a lot, my uncle, so I got on with stirring the soup. He'd tell me the joke in his own time. I put the tureen in the middle of the table and set about finding the bowls.

'You can't put that there, Esther,' he grinned. 'The King says so.'

'And why does the King care where I put my soup tureen?'

Uncle Mordecai perched his big heels on the table and said: 'Because he has issued a declaration . . .so that every man may find rest at home with his women. Every man is to bear rule in his own house. The King says so. And I want that soup tureen here.'

He gave a wicked smile and pointed at the spot by his feet.

'I pray that you may find happiness, uncle,' I said and parked my fists on my hips. 'And safety.' I turned the arc of my back to him and checked on my rolls in the oven. Done. Out they came and –

'He means it,' said Uncle Mordecai. 'All wives in particular have to give to their husbands honour, apparently, both great and small.'

He picked his teeth, still grinning.

'Come, come, silly girl, why do you wait?'

'I'm not waiting, uncle. I'm working. What do you want of me?'

He rocked back in his chair: 'As if the King's say-so is going to change the nature of women one jot, har har.' He sprang up and came to me. He cupped my face in his wrinkled palms and said: 'You rule me, young lady, and have done ever since you walked in here at the age of four.'

It was true. My uncle had taken me in after my parents died of fever and it had long been a joke between us that I was obedient to him as long as he asked of me whatever I wanted.

'Women are the boss,' he chuckled, 'always will be, and that's how we love it. Where do you want me to sit, Esther?'

I pulled out his chair for him, said 'Here, please,' and when he'd sat down, I kissed his bald head.

He explained that a proclamation had indeed been posted beside the well. The King had been giving one of his seven-day feasts, so the rumour went, and was showing off all his splendour. He had commanded his Queen Vashti to come and join the merry-making so that he could show her off too. She would not come.

'How dare she have a mind of her own?' Uncle Mordecai quipped, 'there'll be blood in the streets for this.'

A few days later I was dishing up stew when my uncle came in from his walk and slumped in his chair.

'The King's at it again,' he said downcast.

I added more salt to my pot: 'What is it this time?'

'He's banished Queen Vashti.'

'Good for him,' I said.

'He seeks a fair young virgin to replace her. They're rounding up virgins, Esther.' Uncle pinched the top of his nose: 'They'll be here soon, for you.'

'They won't want me, Uncle. We're Jews.'

'True. You might be safe.'

We shivered that night in our narrow beds and cried a little too, and prayed for men and women everywhere more than for ourselves, and soon found the strength to sleep.

In the night my uncle had a dream of linens and gold and lapis and furs and many kindnesses, and in the midst he saw me in a jewelled diadem.

'I've had a think,' he said in the morning.

He stopped to lift some crumbs from our table and sighed as they fell from his fingers: 'To be Queen may not be the worst fate to befall a young girl.'

My mouth fell open.

'Go, go, silly girl,' he said, 'why do you wait?'

So I washed and anointed myself and dressed in fresh cotton, and when the King's Guards came I was ready. My Uncle Mordecai followed our caravan to the city: 'Whither thou goest, I goest,' he said, 'for I need to keep an eye on you.'

I was kept for twelve months in the house of women, for purification. Each day ten maidens would be taken to the king. Whatever they required in the way of raiment or jewels would be brought to them and their paraphernalia became ever more outlandish. One had sixteen trunks of silk and another forty barrels of rose oil.

When my turn came I took nothing but the cotton slip I had come in.

Two chamberlains led me to the court. I will never forget my first sight of that place. There were white and green and blue hangings fastened with cords of fine linen and silver rings and pillars of marble. Couches of gold and silver lay upon floors paved with marble, red and blue, white and black.

When the King appeared my courage drained away and I tried to hide out of sight, but I could see him looking over in my direction. He sat in his throne as strong as a bull in the sunlight, and bade his servant hand me a golden vessel full of royal wine. As the liquor reached my lips, I raised my eyes to the King over the lip of the vessel. He smiled.

'You're safe, child.' I saw gentleness in his eyes. 'What is your name?'

'Esther,' I replied. My heart was bursting as I bowed before him. So many new colours and tastes and scents, and the king himself, oiled and handsome, was master of it all.

'How could your queen fail to come to you?' I heard myself say.

'Are you an obedient child, Esther?'

'Always, my Lord.'

The King sprang from his throne. My eyes winced in the light reflected from its gold. The ornaments on his dress clanged as he bent and took the vessel from my hand. With the other, he clasped my hand.

'You're trembling, child. Are you afraid?'

'Yes, my Lord.'

'Well, there's no need. Do you like horses?'

'I don't know, my Lord. We have a mule.'

'Well, come with me and see my beasts.'

Gently he led me to his stables and introduced me to his favourites. He watched me stroke and nuzzle them. He raised his slim fingers and stroked my cheek. He nodded.

Suddenly he strode out into the yard where his many chamberlains were waiting.

'I have found her!' he called. 'This is the one!'

The men all smiled and applauded as I came from the stable into the sharp sunlight. I'd heard the King's words but could not believe.

'This is the one,' he called again and sank on one knee in front of me.

'Esther, I command you to become my queen.'

His smile was a burst of tenderness.

'Then, my Lord, I will not protest. I choose . . .to obey,' I said. And we both laughed.

That sense of being singled out, being drawn from a huge crowd, I will never forget. To see him walk towards me would always excite me, make me smile, and remind me of that glorious day.

I was duly crowned. As he came softly close to me to set the royal diadem upon my head, he whispered that he loved me above all women. And it came to pass at midnight that he lay beside me, put his finger to my lips, 'Ssssh', and led me through the fire of first lovemaking with care as sweet as God's own love. I still smile in my heart to think of it. He knew his mind but heard my wishes too and said I was his finest counsellor. And so, I was obedient to his every wish, as long as he asked of me whatever I wanted.

My uncle had followed me to the city and was making full use of his new status as the Queen's Uncle. One of the King's favourites, Haman, resented him however and insisted that my uncle bow to him. Uncle Mordecai refused, so Haman, always short of temper, announced a threat to kill all Jews in the city in a single day.

My uncle cast off his clothes, put on sackcloth and ashes and cried a loud and bitter cry. The slaughter started, and he begged me to help.

'What can I do?' I protested, 'I am an obedient wife, as I was an obedient niece.'

'Exactly,' Uncle Mordecai spat, 'you can work him like a bobbin. Go! Save your people! Quick! He won't harm you.'

I assented with a heart of lead because I knew that my husband loved Haman with a love higher and deeper than his love for any woman. He could choose to swat me like a gnat.

'I will go unto the King as you command.' I said, 'If I perish, I perish.'

I put on my royal apparel and stood in the inner court of the King's house. I recalled the day I saw those white, green and blue hangings for the first time and my King may have been reminded of the same. He sat upon his royal throne and watched me approach, my head lowered in obedience and adoration.

'Esther,' he said, 'Esther. You seek to bring me counsel?'

I paused close to his feet. The King held out his golden sceptre, the symbol of his power over kingdom and palace and all that dwell therein.

'Esther,' he said again, in the soft murmur he used only when we were alone. I lowered my eyes further and drew near. I touched the top of his sceptre, and ran my finger around the tip.

After that second interview with Helen, I zoned in on the nearest pub for a pint to calm my heart rate. Had she meant to be so exciting? Or was she like that with everybody? She knew I had a girlfriend, so she couldn't really be coming on to me, could she? The further I walked from her place, the less likely it had to be. By the time I came in from the Heath, my hopes of ever getting close to her felt as small and dank as the bar. In fact, as I sat and watched the froth on my beer settle, I realised that Helen Halberd had once again deflected me brilliantly from the point. Which you noticed of course, the minute I called you. A roar from the snooker table forced me to turn up the volume on my mobile.

'Mischief?' you yelled again.

'She said it was the publisher's fault,' I replied.

'Do you mean it was a mis*print*?'

'No, she didn't say that. She said the publisher wanted the book to wind up the extremists.'

'Not difficult.'

'Where the sales figures are apparently.' You said something but the snooker guys drowned it. I turned to the wall and yelled at my phone: 'Then all the internet petitions started and she got called the Whore of the Anti-Christ.'

'What? Patrick? Hello?' The pulse in my ears drowned you out as I became aware that the entire snooker crew was watching me.

'Yeah?' I said, an octave too high.

The snooker guys mimicked me: 'Yeah??'

The pub went quiet.

'There's a theology group in college here doing dissertations on Halberd's view of obedience, you know, Patrick. Are you suggesting they should be studying mischief?'

'Their problem, love, not mine, I'm just telling you what Helen said. And there's no need to shout.'

'No Need To Shout!!!' The snooker guys were closing in on me.

'Who have you got with you, Patrick?'

'Nobody, love.'

'You're in a pub, aren't you?'

I downed my pint and hurried outside.

'No, I'm not. I'm in the car park. Can you hear me better now?'

'You didn't ask her the right questions at all,' you said, 'you didn't ask her if they had an affair.'

'Who?' I said. No echo, thank God. My predators were still inside.

'Sarbridge, you idiot! And Halberd! Look, have you got a pen?'

'I'm standing in a pub car park, Joo.'

'Get one!'

I was feeling in my pockets when the snooker crew tumbled out of the pub door.

'Shit.' I said it under my breath but they heard.

'Shitttt!' They all went and pointed at me holding their noses.

'You're going to see her again, Patrick, and this is what you're going to say. Patrick? . . . Are you listening? . . . Patrick?'

I should have run away. Instead I slouched round to the front of the pub with my collar up, hunched small.

'Patrick, listen!' you went. 'We've already been over both stories.'

'About the arc of the back?'

'First it's Naomi's back turned to Ruth, then Esther turns her back on her Uncle Mordecai. Halberd is using these old texts to tell us something. But those are family relationships, they give us no clues about the affair.'

A yelp of pain made me look back to the pub exit in time to see a small terrier shoot recklessly into the road as if someone had just kicked its nuts. Indistinct male jeering confirmed that the pub snooker crew were still in the car park, for now.

'What about the shivering together at night?' I whispered, trying to keep the fear out of my breathing.

'Yeah, but in one case it's Ruth with the mother-in-law, and in the other case it's Esther and her uncle. Family relationships. And Esther and her uncle are in separate beds. It doesn't start cooking until we meet Boaz and Esther's King. Now, in *those* bits – '

I could hear you flapping pages to and fro. Did I dare ask whether you had on that Norwich City thong I bought you?

'Yes,' you said, 'listen to this, Halberd says that both men are like bulls in the sunlight. Boaz and Esther's king. I've a suspicion that's code for sex.'

'But you said the Ruth and Boaz thing was pure and virtuous.'

'They get married.'

'I can't believe Helen would be anything but virtuous, Julia. She's too nice.'

An ambulance screamed past, scattering geese off the pond.

'Julia? Hello? You still there?'

'Does that mean you've tried it on with her, Patrick?'

'No!'

'How come you know her so well all of a sudden?'

'I don't! I don't know, I just . . . you know . . .'

'Don't underestimate the clergy, Patrick, they're at it the whole time. Look at any newspaper, any day of the week.'

So true.

'Write this down.'

'I can't, I'm walking to the station.'

'Remember it then: Boaz lifts his hand to touch Ruth but he decides not to. But with Esther and the King – '

I looked behind me and saw the biggest of the snooker crew, a real behemoth, loping after me.

'Sorry, Joo, gotta run – '

'Stay where you are, Patrick!'

I kept walking.

'The king raised his slim fingers – '

'Weren't the fingers fat?' I asked.

'Well done – that's Boaz. The king raised his slim fingers and stroked Esther's cheek.'

'Not what I'd call a shag fest.' I was half-running down the hill now, divided between the fear of offending you by hanging up and the near-mortal thrashing I'd get if I didn't.

The snooker behemoth was about twenty feet behind me. I swear saliva was dropping from his long lower lip.

'No, but you remember Ruth came softly close to Boaz and lay beside him untouched all night? Well, the king came softly close to Esther-'

The snooker behemoth nearly caught me when suddenly he bent double, sucking air into his chest. I took a sharp right into some posh road and walked smartly.

'And it came to pass at midnight,' you said. 'Next thing you know he's – '

'Shagging her tits off,' I panted.

'Halberd puts it more sensitively. She says he led her through the fire of first love-making.'

'Same gist.'

'I don't think they shag people's tits off in the Bible, Patrick.'

'You want to look at the Song of Songs, Julia. They do little else.'

'How do you know that?'

'Helen told me.'

A police car blared up and slid to a two-wheeled stop just behind me where four police guys bounded out and had the behemoth from the snooker table on the ground in seconds.

'When did she tell you, Patrick?'

'Ages ago.'

'You never said?'

'You never asked.'

I heard you do one of your prissy sighs. So I said: 'I didn't know it was obligatory.'

'What?'

'Tell you every time I talk to another woman. This couldn't be the real thing, is it, Julia? It's not, you know . . . jealousy?'

I grinned and lit a fag. Fresh air always made me want to smoke, and so did the merest confirmation that you cared about me after all.

You did one of your deflating laughs.

'Put that cigarette out, Patrick! You promised.'

I held the phone at arm's length and blew smoke at it, still grinning. The phone squeaked: 'And don't *ever* call me Joo.'

I put the phone back to my ear and could hear you thumping at your book, punishing the pages.

Maybe it was the nicotine that did it. Or it might have been the sight of that bastard from the pub being shoved into the back of the police car. Best place for him. He flicked me a two-fingered salute as they went past, which I just managed to catch in silhouette. I knew he was really wishing me well. By way of a similar gesture, I wished him a comfortable night in the cells. We understood each other.

Little did I know that we'd meet again at Her Majesty's Pleasure, with nobody to protect me.

You were flapping pages so angrily, you could have been trying to rip the book apart. Whatever the reason, a suggestion arrived in my brain that could have been battering at the windows of my sensibility for hours and suddenly soared clear through the window. I exhaled luxuriously at the street light, lost for a second or two in my own brilliance.

'Joo-ulia, there's a bit in the introduction, no, in the acknowledgements section. You haven't ripped that out yet, have you?'

Flappety flap.

'Remember that nauseating list of people she thanks? One of them's called NS?'

'You thought he was some rock star?'

'That was a joke, Nobby Shawcross. Yeah, read me that line.'

'She says, *How can I express my appreciation to NS for his inspiration and encouragement.*'

'Go on.'

'*He led me through the fire. That he did not get –* '

And there it was, as clear as a pimple on a stripper's bum.

'He led her through the fire, Joo. He Led Her Through The Fire.'

'You mean I'm right?'

'I mean you're right, my love. Helen Halberd's book *is* all about sex. She did shag Sarbridge, she must have done!'

We'd cracked it! I was going to make it big! With Sarbridge

lording it around Cambridge and her about to be all controversial in Chelsea, I was bound to get a proper commission at last. Maybe from the *Express* or *Mail*. Maybe even the *Telegraph*.

It was time I had a good look at Sarbridge on the net too. I needed all six glorious minutes of Metallica's *Creeping Death* at top volume to settle my stomach afterwards.

He had pages in all the free net encyclopaedias, all suspiciously identical from the details of his school prizes in Devon (isn't that like telling people in the pub your GCSE results?) to a 'wacky', fake shot of him playing tennis with Sir Cliff. His radio talks were attached along with yards of holy tomes he'd contributed to, all with bland enough titles. Even an 'Open Letter to Rev. Sarbridge' purporting to be from some vein-busting old fart was tepid compared with the online punishment Helen had endured.

What turned my stomach was his website, GodSense.org. There were more pictures than text: him with his shirt off gardening, laughing with children in wheelchairs, handing coffee mugs to toothless drunks, that sort of thing. And there was the photograph from the book of him and Helen running hand in hand from the wings on to the Wembley stage. The caption read: 'Let's all just love each other, for God's sake. Whatever the question, big or small, stupid or clever, painful or sweet, the answer is always Love.'

In her preface Helen quoted from 1 Corinthians 13. I have it here in my mother's Original Revised Amended Edited Updated Cross-referenced Modified edition (she's sent me another bloody one here to the prison) and you'll be pleased to know, Julia, its language is pretty careful about women. I don't remember which version Helen used either. Something humane, I expect. Anyway here it is, just verses 4 to 7:

'Love is gentle, long-suffering, serene. Love does not boast or feel proud. It is not envious, arrogant or rude, but keeps its

temper, forgets slights and is always quick to forgive. Love turns away from evil and loves honesty, it values trust and truth. Love gives succour. It protects. Love lives forever in hope and never gives up. Ever.'

Love gives succour. It protects.

Did I ever tell you that when I was seven, I had to read a huge chunk of Corinthians at my Aunt Susie's wedding? The adults thought it was sweet because my voice hadn't broken yet like Tim's and Seb's. Mummy stood me on the kitchen table and made me practise it every night for four weeks – charity vaunteth itself not, charity is not puffed up, all that – and afterwards, every night, Tim and Seb would each take one of my arms and swing me to crash my balls against the newel post in the hall before I went upstairs to bed. They said they wanted to see me puffed up like a toad.

But reading the same piece in Helen's book, sadness hit me in waves. I wept for her, and for St Paul too who wrote those lovely words and must have known the same desperate love without being loved in return. He knew the waiting and waiting for a sign of some sort, and when the loved one *is* there, when the loved one is breathing the same room's air or is under the same sky, that pure, giggly, fool-making delight, restrained of course, held in at all costs in case the moment the crucial words are said, the beloved vanishes.

St Paul knew all that, poor man, he must have done, and I've wept for him. And now too, once in a while, I weep for myself.

I was going to write for a proper newspaper at last. Several, you reckoned, if I got it right. While I worked out how I was going to spend the copious fees, you sent me Helen's book covered in your post-its and red scribbles, Julia, along with ten pages of instructions on how I was to corner Helen again. You reckoned that I'd waltz into any newspaper office in the country if only I got her to admit the affair outright. So . . . come Thursday evening I was on her doorstep yet again, ready to quiz her about her affair. I was ready to watch the smoke curl from her mouth too, and the way she'd tuck her legs beneath her and stroke the outer curve of her thighs.

'I can only spare you ten minutes,' Helen said as she led me to her room. She was looking rather Goth in a long black skirt, black top and clerical collar. 'I have a PCC meeting at eight.'

She reached for a decanter.

'Which is the best excuse for a stiffener I know. Scotch?'

'Thanks. Just a large one.' It was what my father always said at about noon as he poured his first gin.

Helen smiled and poured two large measures into plain tumblers. We toasted each other.

'PCC?'

'Parish Church Council,' she downed her drink. 'Now Patrick, I thought we'd covered everything.'

From the depths of her warm sofa I breathed in the delicious scents of her room, part furniture polish, part fried bacon, large part smokes and scotch. I was aware of an inane smile on my face and drank fast. The scotch careered through my chest, knocking on doors and swinging them wide. I sniffed again. I wasn't going to cry, was I? Christ no, I was here to do battle.

I'd forgotten your notes of course, Julia. And the book. What was the gist?

'I've gone through your book with a fine-tooth comb.'

She smiled and tapped open her cigarettes: 'What did you make of Bathsheba?'

Nothing yet of course, we hadn't got that far, but I was not to be deflected.

'It's Esther I want to ask you about.'

'Congratulations. You've got to page 40. Have a cigarette. Scotch without smoking is so dry somehow.'

I managed to hold my fag still while she lit it. She sat back and blew a queue of smoke rings.

'My misspent youth,' she grinned, ' every priest should have one. And that can be on the record if you like.'

This could all be diversionary. Any minute she'd leap up and show me out, and I'd have missed my chance. It was time to go in hard:

'Esther gets led through the fire of, you know . . .'

She was poker-faced, locking eyes with me.

'Sex, Patrick,' she said.

Sex, Patrick? I felt a sharp catch in the gut followed by throbbing heat as my prick yawned and stretched. I moved my bag into my lap.

'Eh yeah I . . . in your acknowledgements – '

Suddenly she was up fussing on the desk for an ashtray. A pile of ancient hardbacks hit the floor. With her fag clamped between her lips, she dropped to all fours to gather them up. I joined her on the floor and jostled some books in my arms until they tipped over the floor. Suddenly she sat back on her heels hugging the books and said: 'My God, my God, why have you forsaken me?'

A bit dramatic, I thought, until she smiled.

'Do you think Jesus really said that?'

'What?'

'Those words. They're supposed to be the last words Jesus said before he died.'

I said yes, I thought it was quite realistic really, come to think of it, the sort of thing a bloke might just say in those circumstances. I leant over to stack her books on the desk.

She clambered to her feet and for a millisecond I had a sense of her involuntarily leaning closer to me before she raked her hair.

'Did you know,' she asked, 'that it's a direct quote from Psalm 22? Probably written about a thousand years before Jesus was born. So if you said it today, it would be as if you were quoting something like Chaucer. Or Shakespeare – To be or not to be – as you stood on the scaffold.'

She reached for a Bible, leafed through for Psalm 22 and placed a finger on the first verse as if it might escape. Before I knew what I was doing (do I ever?) I took hold of the Bible too. We stood side by side as if we were choristers sharing one hymn book. In spite of the cool of its pages under the whorls of my thumb, I began to tremble.

'Verse 1,' she said, 'there, look.'

My God, My God, why hast thou forsaken me?

She ran her finger down the page toward my pulsating thumb, to some more stuff about piercing his hands and feet and casting lots for his gear and so on, and then we were into The Lord Is My Shepherd. I loosened my grip and dug my hand into my pocket to stop it shaking.

'Midrash, Patrick.' She closed the Bible gently and sat down again. The sweet bonds around us for those few moments dissolved.

'Does that mean Jesus actually said it?' she went on, 'or is it midrash? Or prophecy? Or all three? Take nothing at face value, that's all I'm saying. What you see on the page, maybe it did happen, maybe it didn't. Do you remember when I explained to you about the zombies at the end of Matthew's gospel?'

'Night of the Living Dead, yeah.'

She smiled: 'I love your use of language. And were the zombies actually there after the crucifixion, do you think?'

'It says loads of people, you know, saw them everywhere.'

'Yet there's not a single historical record. Not one, Patrick.'

'So resurrected corpses weren't running round Jerusalem?' I genuinely wanted to know. I also wanted the conversation to go on forever.

'Of course not. But clued-up Jews reading Matthew's Gospel then would have recognised a hint of something in the Book of Daniel about the end of the world and the coming of the happy-ever-after.' She rose to her feet, tugging down her blouse. 'Now I'm afraid I really must – '

I was too busy tingling from contact with her Bible and a glancing kiss she left on my cheek on her doorstep to care about my investigations. I don't know whether it was the scotch or what, but on my bike on the way home I had a near miss with a white van. I reckoned I could do with some food to help me gather my wits and found my way somehow to the Swan.

I had spent the first half of my teens desperate to be old enough to get into this pub, mainly because Sunday lunchtimes featured pork pies and the sort of strippers who went round the bar in their underwear begging for change in a pint mug before they got on with their acts. Or so I'd been told by reliable sixth formers whose parents thought they were in the local evangelical church at the time. Two days before my sixteenth birthday they cleaned the place up. Not entirely. They kept the marshy carpet, the blind barman and the chronically filthy glasses. They just got rid of the strippers. No justice in the world.

I sank back into mulberry velour and rested my cranium against the 'wood' panelling.

I didn't dare phone you, Julia. Six sausages and three pints later, I came out under a silky black sky and just managed to cock a leg over the seat of my moped at the third attempt when I spotted a motorcycle cop sitting under a tree. He was engrossed in his phone, texting his mistress or something, but I couldn't risk it. I wrestled my leg back off the moped and began to push.

As soon as I was back home, I hit the laptop. Not, unusually, for porn. I wanted to Google Helen. I just wanted a quick look at her face before I went to sleep. There she was in a po-faced religious weekly beside a snotty review of her book. I magnified her nose first, then I zoomed in on her mouth. Top lip. Lower lip. The mouse slid under my hand like an award-winning dancer. Lovely. I flopped on my bed and let the room vibrate gently.

Through smoke you come to me across a courtyard of gold and of angels. 'Come, Patrick,' you whisper, 'you are chosen. Cast off your sackcloth, and do me honour. Come into my power and all will be well.' Smoke trails over my face. I try to catch it, hold it, gentle, long-suffering, I long to come, I tell her, I long to have and to hold you forever.' But she's gone, Helen is gone, her breath of frankincense and myrrh, and I reach, I can't hold, come back to me, Helen, don't leave me, I beg . . . and cry a loud and bitter cry.

I woke sweating. I pushed the duvet off my face and drank in air, dark air lit only by the green display of my alarm clock. I swung my boots off the bed and sat up, too fast, then slammed back among the pillows, closing my eyes against the waltz of the room. My face was wet. It couldn't be tears, don't be daft.

Those pub sausages must have been dodgier than I thought.

In this meditation I have allowed myself to follow the modern feminist tradition of speculating about the pregnancy of MARY OF NAZARETH. All sorts of theories have been promulgated: was she raped by a Roman? By Joseph? By the donkey?

I don't think it matters. Mary's obedience led her to horror, but from there to love where she did not expect to find it. I admire Joseph's tenderness for the sad girl in his care. May we all find our Joseph.

I'm still trembling. Nobody told me it would hurt so much. When I asked my mother what it would be like when the baby came, she gave me one of her east wind smiles and said:

'Hurts getting them in there, hurts getting them out.' Then she kissed me and wept.

I watch the arc of her back as she cleans up the baby. I don't want to see it. I hope she goes back home soon and takes it with her. It came too soon, the baby. It's small and might not live. God willing, it won't.

I'm to get in this bath. I'm still bleeding down my legs and shivering.

Like the night my father came to me.

On that day three seasons ago, he was in the stable yanking the girth too tight on our mule when he heard me creeping past.

'Mary,' he barked, 'in here.'

I went in, keeping clear of the mule's hooves. He could lash out when my father was about.

'The deal's done,' he said. 'I've got you a husband.'

He pulled the girth even tighter.

'Two mules and three fields, he's getting. You better be worth it.'

'Who is he, Father?'

'Joseph of David.'

'The old one?'

'Nothing wrong with old wine, girl. Like I said, the deal's done.'

He punched the mule on the side of the mouth to force its mouth open for the bit.

'What do you know about marriage, Mary? Your mother told you?'

'What, Father?'

He stuck his tongue far out. It shone and jumped like a terra-cotta fish. He snapped the stirrup down and mounted the mule, which shot out of the stable rocking him back in the saddle. Yanking the reins, he yelled: 'Wash yourself, girl, and dress in fresh cotton. You're going to find out, tonight!'

My mouth fell open.

'Go on, silly girl, what are you waiting for?'

That night I was lying on my bed with the curtain drawn round me. There was ale on his breath as he came unto me and sat on my mattress.

'You are highly favoured, you know, Mary. You are blessed. Many a girl your age would be glad to have Joseph as a husband.'

'Thank you, Father.'

'So it's time to show your father how grateful you are.'

My heart was bursting with fear when he leaned over and rubbed his stubble against my cheek. I could smell the sweat caked into his shirt.

'Don't be afraid, Mary,' he said, 'you're an obedient child, aren't you? And there's something you need to know before you meet Joseph.'

He licked my mouth and pushed his tongue between my lips. His weight was on me now and his hand reached under my bedcovers, low. I protested but he would not listen. He grunted, putting his big palm over my mouth to cover my mewing for help.

'My power shall overshadow you, girl. I shall show you the secrets of the world. And Joseph will be right glad that he has a girl that knows and will not be afraid in the house of her new husband.'

I was whimpering, shuddering. His brute fingers were doing unspeakable things under my covers.

'Stop trembling, Mary. What are you afraid of?'

His other hand yanked hard on my hair.

'Silly girl, why are you crying? This is our secret.'

I couldn't breathe. Pain shot through my body, south to north. He twisted my hair tighter in his fist.

'Be it upon me according to thy word,' I cried. I closed my eyes and wept.

I weep still to think of it. I shivered that night alone, and bled and cried, and prayed for the strength to live on.

He's at home now with my three sisters.

When Joseph discovered that I was to bear a child, I tried to hide out of sight. But he found me, and cupped my face in his callused palms.

'The sin is not yours,' he said gently, 'but it is time to return to your kin.' I thought of long afternoons playing with my sisters, and soon everything was arranged.

The night before I was to go home, Joseph found me sobbing on my bed.

'I'm lost,' I said, the tears juddering my body, 'my mother hates me, and my father . . . my father . . .'

The tears ripped out of me: 'If I perish, I perish.'

Joseph kissed my forehead and wept with me. He said nothing but I think he knew, for he let me stay with him.

'Why have I found grace with you?' I asked him.

'You're so young for such misery,' he said, crouching beside me. So, it came to pass that he and his kin cared for me until my time came, and my mother chose to arrive.

His kindness astonishes me. Last week I had a cough so he brought me a pink posy. He shows me books and we sit together reading. I love his aroma of smoke and cedar shavings. He could swat me like a gnat if he wished but he has never touched me except to lay his hand on mine to still my fear.

*I hear Joseph coming. I lower my head in obedience and respect.
He pauses close to my feet.*

He has a bundle in his arms. He presses my shoulder softly.

'Mary?'

He holds out the bundle.

'Please, Mary.'

I turn away.

'He's beautiful, Mary.'

I'm weeping into my hands.

'Will you hold him? Just once?'

I have been brought up to obey.

*'All that thou sayest unto me I will do,' I say, but the minute the
words pass my lips, I think of sweat and stubble and blood down
my legs, and dread weights press upon my heart.*

*'Please, Mary,' Joseph says in the soft murmur he uses only when
we are alone. 'For me?'*

How could I not, for Joseph?

That chapter bewildered me. It hung in my mind for days. The
horror of it, the desperation, it felt so true. Did it mean that Helen
was raped? I hated to think that. I longed to feel her tears ebbing
away on my shoulder as I soothed her hair under my fingers and her
breathing eased and she found safety at last with me.

But first I had to photograph a Brownies' Easter tea party and
interview a couple in Charlton who'd been married for seventy
years. You might have thought I only had Helen Halberd to pursue
but Cyril was always waiting for several other scrag ends of balls-
aching boringness. Life in prison is charmingly streamlined in
comparison.

The Brownies were straightforward – the pretty ones and a
dogged Brown Owl grouped around a five-foot fluffy rabbit with 40
vapid words of print – but the oldsters were endless trouble. Each
one joshed the other with deadly mockery, as you'd expect, and they
disagreed with each other on point after point. After an hour there
wasn't a single fact they agreed on. Not their dates of birth or the
number of children they had. Not where they met, or even the date

they married. And every time I tried to photograph them, she spat her teeth out into her apron pocket and they both clenched down the corners of their mouths.

I was too busy to answer your voicemails too. I was actually terrified to tell you that I'd seen Helen and got nowhere again. By the time those pub sausages had run their course, I'd decided to use them as my excuse and tell you I'd not gone near the Rev. Halberd because of food poisoning. A sympathy ploy that cut no ice with you at all.

Cyril wasn't happy either. He was so not happy, he chopped half of my piece about Helen Halberd. 'Not only late,' he grimaced, 'it's dull, dull, dull,' and I watched him blank out swathes of my deathless prose on his screen and tap them away to Hades. Not that it was the best piece I'd ever written or anything but the interview had been his idea and usually he hardly cut my stuff at all.

'That's where you start,' he said pointing at my first mention of the Chelsea Lemmings. 'What have I always taught you?'

'Keep to the sex and violence?'

'And the mad bastards. The genius is to overlap all three. So do we need that boring stuff about her life before? No. Do we want her worthy plans for the future? No. Who'd she have the affair with?'

'We haven't-'

'Who's we?'

'Me and Julia.'

'Ah.' Cyril's eyes rested on a distant parking meter in Woolwich High Street. 'How is the lovely Julia keeping these days?'

'Great, thanks.'

'If she's involved, there's a chance you'll get your facts right.'

'We're going through the vicar's book-'

'I'm not paying you to read, Patrick, I'm paying you to write.'

Not paying me much either way, I nearly said.

'It's full of clues, to her affair. But we haven't got her to admit it yet.'

'Who?'

'Helen Halberd.'

Cyril's eyes turned to me showing vacant.

'The priest in the piece, Cyril.'

'Right. What clues?'

Was I going to take Cyril through the complexities of midrash before he'd started on his lunchtime half gallon of ale? I tapped my teeth: 'Her book's full of these love stories'

'Terrific. Get pictures. Plenty of pictures.'

'They're Bible stories, Cyril.'

His forehead knotted, making him look more obtuse than usual: 'Sod Bible stories, who reads that shit these days?'

'I thought – '

'Did I ask you to think? Bring me the lady vicar dirt, that sounds tops. By the end of tomorrow. Right, I've got work to do.'

Cyril pulled a slim black briefcase from under his chair and toddled off to spend the afternoon getting quietly off his face with his Masonic chums.

Which left me next morning (the Friday) weary but on the track of sex, violence and, if at all possible, mad bastards. Helen's church website had said there was a school service that day, which should be short, and I couldn't think of a quicker way to get my answers.

I stopped the bike by the Swan and walked over. Cars were pulling up at the church and parking one after the other as tightly as bricks newly laid on a wall. Children in green uniforms skipped out of each one and ran loose all over the Heath before their dowdy mummies gathered them up to cross the road and led them hand-in-hand into church. A couple of them could have been the spawn of a local rock god but nobody stood out from the crowd.

As I crossed the road, I rested my eyes on a line of hotels and pastel Georgian houses stretching away towards Charlton and the Shooter's Hill water tower. A batch of thunderclouds lowered there as if Thor and his chariot might burst forth like a Sword Rampant album cover. Helen's church, in the foreground, shone up to the heavens like mother-of-pearl, clean and good in a heathen world.

My moment of near numinism was shattered when I pushed the

church door open. A pale woman with tight grey hair opened her mouth and screamed. I was going 'Madam, I come in peace, I just want to see the priest,' when Helen came out herself in a full length black cassock with tiny buttons all down the front. Under it I noticed black patent, pointed, high-heeled boots.

Helen vouched for me, explaining to the vicar's wife, for it was she, that I was not a day-release murderer but a journalist. But the mistake was understandable, it was so hard to tell the difference sometimes.

I could have kissed her. In fact I should have kissed her, opportunities being so few, but with teachers bossing the children into sitting quietly in the pews and the parents gossiping in huddles, this was not the best time. Besides, I had another purpose. Zeal was rising through me. I wasn't just doing this to expose Sarbridge any more, and get him out of your college. I was on a crusade. For sex, for violence and, I really mean this, Julia, for truth.

The notion that Helen might have been raped was still nagging me and I wanted to do my best to make sure something like that could never happen to her again. I'd been awake much of the night imagining it actually, and had the eyebags to prove it.

The vicar's wife bustled away muttering to herself. Cursing me probably. She wouldn't have been the first.

'It's mutual!' I called up the aisle.

Helen folded her arms, emphasising the curve of her breasts in her cassock.

'Are you sure you're a journalist?' she asked.

'Ye-eah.' I smiled. She did not smile back.

'I've never known a journalist chase as thoroughly as this.'

I dragged her book from my pocket, its many Post-its fluttering.

'This isn't just about . . . your journey to God, is it? It's a midrash mishmash about you and Neil Sarbridge?'

The inner corner of her right eye twitched.

'We've covered this, Patrick.'

'No, wait, please – ' Tears were starting in my eyes at the thought of her pain, 'were you raped, Helen? And Sarbridge helped you?'

She spoke through clenched teeth: 'This is not the time or the place, Patrick.'

'Did *Sarbridge* rape you?' I was ready to emasculate him with rusty razor wire. She sighed.

'Midrash does not mean that things happened literally, Patrick. I have not been raped, OK?'

'So why did you write that?' She raked her hair:

'I was trying to say something about how I'd felt raped by my previous moral values, but it was out of them that a new impulse grew in me and I needed to be taught to obey it. Now please . . .'

'But you did have an affair and that's why he's had to go away to Cambridge. That's true, isn't it? Otherwise the book's only half true, and isn't half true the same as a lie?'

She looked as if I'd hit her.

'I keep telling you, Patrick, the purpose of midrash is to teach. Now I've got to take this service. Please go. Or stay . . . if you must.' She swept away to the altar. I followed.

'But I don't get it,' I said, 'is this book of yours about Sarbridge or not?'

She kept walking.

'You're hiding an affair,' I called after her, louder than I'd intended.

She paused and turned. She'd avoided my eye so far. Now she did look at me. A hard look. Like a punch. Her equivalent of saying Outside, pal, and bring your friends if you've got any: 'I'll thank you to keep your voice down.'

She looked so brave and defenceless and beautiful. I longed to tell her how elated I was just to be there with her under the same roof. My mother had been telling me for years that if you don't believe in stars whizzing round pointing at stables and virgins getting pulled by angels and dead men walking, we're damned, tossed out of the party, plain and simple. Helen was saying there was another way of looking at it, of being able to believe in Jesus without feeling like a complete idiot, and I was dying to tell her that if that way was real, I was definitely interested.

But I didn't. I said none of it. She'd disappeared into a side-room beyond the altar. I had no choice but to make the long walk to the back of the church and watch her work.

I never deserved to be with Helen in that sanctified place. I certainly never deserved to go up to her altar rail. But while she was explaining to the children about Daniel in the lion's den, tying it up somehow with Jesus in his tomb, I sat with my hands clenched between my knees, unable to take my eyes off her. If I relaxed for a second, I might weep. Chairs creaked on each side of me as people leaned away, fearful of my intensity. Then Helen's voice blessed the bread and wine and she was inviting us up to join in.

I knelt on maroon velvet at the altar rail and held my crossed palms high, as my mother had taught me when I was confirmed. I bowed my head and heard Helen say, 'The body of Christ,' as she laid a small cube of bread in my hands, white in front of the black of her cassock. My vision began to flutter at the edges. I looked up. She was looking back at me, level and serious, as if the entire performance was for me alone. Our eyes held, and in those precious seconds my life changed for ever.

But I was a long way from being able to admit that. Not to you, Julia. Not to Helen. Least of all to myself.

I was desperate to speak with her again. At the church door as people were leaving, I hovered at the edge of several conversations, all banal, until one of the mothers asked: 'Where's your proper robes for church? You're not properly dressed. If I went into work without my proper uniform on I'd get the sack.'

Helen watched her own toe move a pebble for a moment before she replied:

'I don't bother with the surplice and robes in front of the children. I found church a bit intimidating at that age and . . .'

The mother cut in: 'And you say there's no stone and no cave, what does that mean, you don't you believe in the Resurrection at all?'

'Never ask a liberal priest that one,' Helen grinned, 'please, it's more than our job's worth.' In seconds she'd gone again, almost running back to that side-room without a thought for me. One minute I'd been high on waves of joy and anticipation, the next shipwrecked. Alone.

Which is probably why the minute I got back to my bedsit, I sat down at my laptop and rattled out a thousand words of sheer damage.

I shake my hands into the bucket and watch the drops ripple away. I'm alone out here at the back of the house with the sun's heat on the back of my neck and trembling in my breasts. There should be a voice in my head shouting at me to stop. Save myself. All I hear is his whisper, hot and moist, saying this is too good to miss.

They came into the house like an ocean, waves of them laughing and talking, so many it was hard to remember all the names and the pile of cloaks was like a mountain. My sister Martha hissed at me: 'What are you gaping at? Go, go, silly girl! We're in the kitchen, you and I, until the guests are all fed.'

I wanted to obey but Jesus wasn't having that. One minute we were sitting in the kitchen with a dry heel of bread each. The next they were all edging up the benches to make room and taking a bit of stew from this one and some rice from that until Martha and I had as much as anyone.

I'd heard about Jesus of course. John the Baptist had been such a beauty but there was always something arid about John. No sap. No humour. Handsome as a bull in the sunlight but somehow not whole.

Jesus was not like that. He was such a great guest for a start. I caught Martha smiling when he wiped up his gravy with big chunks of bread and caught the drips down his chin. He made her laugh, the way he held up his plate like a little boy for seconds. Martha never laughs. He liked his wine too. He belched. Laughed till he was bent double and we were all coughing with mirth. And when he was quiet, oh when he was quiet . . .

I love his hands. They're fat and red like a butcher's, hands that know how to work, and every time he talks they fly like doves.

'Martha!' he called as she disappeared into the kitchen yet again, 'Martha! Will you come and look at this table!'

He reached after her, those hands of his fluttering, 'Come back,' he yelled, 'you're not going to see it staring into the sink!'

'What's wrong with the table?' she said, her fists on her hips in the doorway and the breadknife still in her hand. Jesus sat back and linked his hands behind his head: 'It's a marvel, Martha, that's what it is. And you've done it. You and Mary. Come here and just look at the beauty of this table.'

It was the table my grandfather made for his own wedding but you could hardly see the wood for Martha's big bowls of rice and chicken. The olives and tomatoes were mine, I had grown them from seed. There were my terracotta bowls of oils I'd gathered and flavoured myself. I sniffed my fingernails, yes, the garlic crushed by my blade was still there.

'Don't you feel the privilege of it, Martha?' Jesus asked.

Martha gave him one of her east wind smiles.

'A dogsbody's privilege?' she snapped.

The laughter stopped dead. Martha broke the silence by starting to apologise but Jesus was up and around her like a wind. She was embarrassed to be held by him – nobody touches Martha – but she did not struggle and her eyes were laughing.

'That's it exactly, Martha.' He was squeezing and rocking her. She teased that if he kept up this nonsense, she would have to cut herself free. Before anyone could stop him, Jesus whipped the bread-knife out of her hand and held it against her throat.

Martha's eyes flicked. In the silence I could hear her suck breath in and hold it. Jesus spoke in her ear, loud enough for us all: 'You are a knife, Martha.'

He swivelled her so that we could all see the blade.

'We all are,' he said aloud, 'some of us are knives that stab . . .'

Lazarus was on his feet now. He's a gentle boy, my brother, but honoured guest or not, this was past a joke. Jesus saw his begging eyes and lowered the knife: 'This woman,' he gripped her tighter, 'Martha here, she's a knife that feeds.'

Jesus released her, rolled the knife to show that it was the blunt side he'd held against her neck and held his hands high. The disciples cheered as if they'd known it was just theatre all along, and bent to their food again.

But Jesus hadn't finished. He smacked the table for quiet again and this time his smile was all tenderness:

'We came to this place empty and you have filled us. What greater honour can there be? You know, when I'm dead and gone' – one or two or the disciples faked yawns at this point as if he was always going on about this – 'I want you all to keep doing this. I want you to remember this night!'

'Don't worry,' Martha murmured, beckoning me to follow her back to the kitchen, 'I won't forget it in a hurry.'

Jesus wouldn't let her go. He folded a glass of wine into her hand and sat her in pride of place where he had been. She set to chopping the bread and sharing it out, laughing and flirting with the men, refilling their glasses. Cutting her own throat with her finger.

Which meant that nobody noticed when he came and sat beside me. I smile in my heart to think of it. The fresh linen of his shirt mingled with something darker, sweat, as he held out his glass.

'Can I have a drink please, Mary?' His eyes were a sunburst of mischief as if he'd asked the naughtiest question in the world. I knew he'd be off soon to sit by someone else so I didn't obey immediately.

'They say you're a Great High Priest, Jesus,' I said, 'is it true?'

'I love questions, Mary.' He leaned closer and whispered, 'What do you want me to be?'

'Isn't it the priest's job to share out the wine?' I asked and held my own glass up.

'You want to keep me thirsty, do you? I could die of thirst right here beside you and then what would you do?' He pursed his lips, 'Would you give me the kiss of life?'

Smiles were binding the two of us like ship's rope.

'I've never understood why you preachers are so reluctant to die?' I said, pouring wine for us both. 'Isn't paradise your prize? Your privilege?'

'Where's the hurry?' he purred. 'Mind you, with a beautiful woman like you beside me maybe I am in paradise already.'

Nobody had ever called me beautiful before. Suddenly I was imagining shoulders and flesh and weight all together, for a matter of seconds, then they were gone like a thunderclap leaving nothing but air behind. He took my hands in his.

'Look at the beauty of these hands,' he said.

I looked down at the rough skin, the broken nails and peeling knuckles.

'As long as you care for others, Mary, the Lord will deal kindly with you.'

I frowned. I was uncomfortable being talked about like this.

'But you're capable of more,' he said. 'And you know it.'

I blustered and said I was perfectly . . .

'Look at me, Mary.'

Obedient, I looked up into his hazel eyes.

'You could follow me, Mary. You could be my comfort.' His breath waterfalled down my face as he spoke. I reached for a bread roll, one I'd baked myself that morning. I had to do something to avoid what he was asking. I felt him watch me as I sank my thumbs into the roll's soft centre and pulled the halves open like ravenous teeth.

'They're going to do that to me, you know, Mary.'

'What?'

'Break my body. Like that bread.'

He took one half and dipped it into his wine: 'Open your mouth, Mary.'

I'd tasted wine before, of course. But this morsel from his fingers exploded around my tongue like wine from the first untainted fruits of Eden. Something unfurled in me and opened in the wind.

I'm too ashamed to remember what I finally wrote about Helen. But the shame did not set in immediately.

I had no luck with the *Express*, nor the *Mail* or *Telegraph* either. *The Times* ignored me, didn't even return my calls. I was about to give up when I tried *The Truth*. You won't know it, it's a new paper for old lefties. Just the sort to be tempted into a bit of clergy bashing.

The hardest part was persuading the Features girl that I'd actually written anything before. I emailed her my latest Brownies piece and lo, I had my chance.

Why? To impress you, Julia. But also I wanted to discover what it might be like to sit inside the head of my hero Paul Kibitz, the Vanquisher of Popes and actresses, the Master of the Insult Veiled, and know how it felt to be a proper journalist for once.

That's what I was like in the daylight anyway. As soon as I lay horizontal at night, something else overcame me.

It was Helen. I longed to be inside her, just once. I'd lie twisting and yearning in bed, muttering her name. I wanted to hold her, to comfort her. Her book was so full of pain, what I'd read of it, and I wanted to cradle her, be easy with her, to sit by her and kiss her fingers and smoothe her hair. I loved the sly way she looked at me sometimes when she thought I didn't know. She watched me as if she was studying some exotic insect who might fly away at any moment. Then she'd throw back her head and laugh that trucker's laugh of hers.

Did she laugh during sex? I had to find out.

Anyway – I remember sitting in The Cat and the Canary with you, Julia, overlooking the ornamental docks on the Isle of Dogs, close to the printers so that we could be right there the minute the article came out. I bought ten copies of the first issue and read you my precious words a dozen times, and my byline two dozen, and swore that I'd carry a copy next to my heart for as long as I lived.

They weren't my precious words actually. My first and last paragraphs were cut and the stuff in between rearranged so that it was almost unrecognisable. I had written the thing with care, believe me. The crucial words sex, affair and adultery had been scrupulously avoided. It was one of those pieces where it is left to the reader to see the smoke for the trees. And what does the headline say? VICARS CAUGHT IN ADULTERY. My name was misspelt too – they left the h out of my surname to make it fit the line.

Who cares? I'd made it. I was in a national paper at last.

A couple of days later, it hit the mat. A threat from her lawyers.

The Number One Governor came to see me last night. The prison's biggest of big, fat cheesy cheeses. As my absentee legal advisor, Julia, tell me: if you were me, I mean oh God, Julia, help me please, I need somewhere warm and soft to cry, like between your breasts, and I need your finest legal help. What do you make of this?

At about half eight I was just moving a knight to g6 to skewer the Number One Guv on the p-mail when I looked up and found him smarming around my cell.

P-mail is Greymoor's intranet by the way. There's no internet access in here. (That's why my Spod-the-Inhaler blog has gone silent.) If you disclose on your admission form that you play chess, you qualify for a laptop in your cell but you have to play the old sod on p-mail once a week. In prison you'll try anything.

He had two glasses in one hand and a bottle in the other which he swung on to my desk. It looked like a rather fine vintage port.

'You were at Rugby, weren't you, Price-Johnson?' he smirked.

'No. Streatham College, sir.'

'Not many of us educated chaps in here,' he went.

'More than you'd think, sir.'

'I've just had a rather magnificent dinner with Rugby's most famous old boy, the Rt Hon. Nigel Futhelby-Futhell. We had roast ostrich, oast rostrich, and green beans. Washed down by this stuff. No, not this stuff, some Bulgarian Cab Sauv. Not *the* best, nearly best's good enough for an old Rugbian. Har har. And now he's gone. Gone. Before we got to this stuff. So I wondered if it might just interest you.'

He was speaking as if I was the deaf lady treasurer at his golf club. He starfished himself in my armchair and sighed. Almost immediately he woke with a snort, adjusted the two glasses on my desk and, with excruciating care, filled one of them to the brim. Then he crouched on his knees to slurp.

'So you're an old Stringham, eh?'

'Yes, sir.'

'Know Jamie Malpass-Jones?'

Slurp.

'I'm afraid not.'

'Hugo Parry-Evans?'

'No.'

Slurp.

'Jeremy Smythe-Stockwell?'

'No.'

'Sure you were at Rugby?'

'No. Streatham, sir.'

'Why didn't you say? Have a glass of this, old boy.' Little by little I savoured the aroma, the burning descent of my first alcohol in three months. Within seconds I was pissed.

He's very dapper, our Number One Governor. His suits are immaculately cut and his cotton-lawn shirts are ironed until they shine. I know this because I do the ironing. Yes, believe it or not, Julia, they have forced me into domestic service. He spent the next minute or so tweaking his collar in my mirror, smoothing his few grey strands back over his bald patch and adjusting his cuffs. He didn't seem to notice a wine stain like a map of India just left of his tie.

'Have you had dinner?'

'Oh yes. Dinner, sir. Confit of duck with braised fennel. Roast peaches in amaretti to follow.'

He wouldn't see a joke coming if it was as big as the moon covered in naked tits.

'Good, good.'

'And porridge.'

'Porridge?'

'April fool.'

'Ha ha. Very good. Did you enjoy it?'

'Delicious, thank you.'

'Good, good.' He picked a bit of fluff off his lapel.

'You will let me know if you have any complaints, won't you? Wouldn't want you to be . . . unhappy at all.' The chumminess in those last three words took me straight back to school, my first day, in a new blazer three sizes too big, when I was about to enter the big boys' urinals for the first time. Without any direction from me, my buttocks clenched.

He came to peer over my shoulder at my laptop. It's a clunky Tandy, years old but adequate for my purposes. As sincere as a MacDonalds *maitre d'*, he asked again if everything was all right. Then he came out with it: 'What exactly is it you're writing all the time?'

So that was it. Journalist in jug rattles Number One Guv. He thought I was writing about him.

'Just a few thoughts,' I muttered. 'About my misdeeds.'

He perched a buttock next to my keyboard. 'This colour of blue suits you.' He pointed at my prison sweatshirt. 'It brings out your eyes.'

Was that a threat?

He went on: 'I hear the lads want you to be President of the Chess Club.'

It was news to me. Not happy news. This place was like being back at school; my best bet was not to be noticed.

'I'm not surprised,' he went on, 'I loved the way you forced me into back rank mate in 17 moves yesterday.' His face was horribly close. 'Who taught you to play with such ruthless beauty?'

'My mother.'

'Ah, Mother.' He gave a wan smile at the ceiling, then swung close to my face again: 'I could help you, you know.'

I was edging away as far as I could without falling off my stool.

'My old friend Jezza Highhand – Lord Highhand – is head of FILCH,' he said, 'I bumped into him at a livery company dinner last week. Drink up your port.'

'Is FILCH the new chess organisation?'

'Absolutely. We could enter you for a few jousts, you know. Might even get you a rating. I want to teach you the Parkhurst

Opening.' He rested his chin on my shoulder. 'And the Ford Open opening. And, I'm a little old-fashioned, I still adore the Queen's Gambit . . .'

'And the Stringham high?' I offered.

'Ha yes, we could have such fun.'

He sprang away, sat heavily on my desk and managed to cross his legs. His upper leg bobbing with excitement, he reached right across me for my little Kasparov computer set and arranged the pieces between us.

'All I want is a little close match play, one on one, get my meaning. Mano a mano. You can start.'

I was beginning to understand. There could be material gains for me in defeat by the boss. I wasn't too proud for that. I even offered to take a handicap and surrendered my two bishops. He grabbed them, stuffed them suddenly up my nostrils, and kissed me.

I won't bore you with the physical details except to say that my nose is still bleeding a bit, and that as kisses go it was nasty, bristly and short. I pushed him away.

'Come, come, Price-Johnson.'

'Not with you, sir.' I didn't really say that but wish I had. What I did say, in a sort of whimper, was 'I'm not gay.'

'You surprise me. After all, what's a little close-contact sport to an old Rugbian like you?'

'Old Stringham, sir,'

'Really? Are you sure?'

'Oh yes, sir.'

'Well, what's a little close-contact sport to an old Stringham?'

There was a pause a man could drop to his death through. Then in one continuous motion he rose, strode to the door, turned back and wavered beside my desk again, swigged back the last of my port, gathered up the bottle and both glasses (damn him) and said: 'Ha ha. April fool. Got you, Price-Johnson, didn't I, ha ha ha ha ha.' And left.

So, Julia. What do I do? He could lose his job for assaulting a remand prisoner, especially if it gets spread over five pages of a

Sunday tabloid. I dare say I'm not his first. On the other hand . . . On the other hand I am never doing a newspaper exposé of anything ever again. I've learned the hard way. If I let him win a few times, do you think he'll get bored and leave me alone?

That was a fortnight ago. I haven't been able to write since. My hand's too sore. You're right, Julia. Men are horrible. We're filthy, appalling sadists of the first order. Men distilled by month after month of their own company, well, it's not nice.

The evening after the Number One Guv's visit I got ambushed in the library. I was tucked in a corner out of sight, deep in the *Guardian*, when the room went dark. I looked up to find the strip light obscured by two massive sets of heads and shoulders. One was the behemoth I'd met in the pub car park all those months ago. He turns out to be an armed robber called Kitten who comes back inside every time he needs a haircut. The other was his friend Peeler. Peeler's not in the police by the way. He's called that because every time he rapes and murders some little clubber, he's in the habit of peeling the skin off her tits with his flick knife. Lovely boy.

My hand hurts but nothing's broken, nothing visible. Nothing I haven't coped with before. My mistake was to get noticed. I'd even been thinking that six months of being left to my own devices was pretty cool.

You know me, when I'm hurt I go flippant.

They'd heard that the Number One Guv had developed the habit (hardly a habit, I bleated, it was just the once) of sharing his alcohol with me. Well, that's such a sweet thought, PatPrick, they said as one of them took hold of my arms behind my back. They'd brought me some drink too. A bit like white burgundy, they said, yellowish in a plastic cup with an acrid bouquet.

I said something daft like Isn't the Uglies Convention down the corridor. Ha ha, they went and throttled me. Then Kitten held my nose and when I opened my mouth to breathe, he tipped it in. If I paused Kitten spread my hand on the desk and offered to bash it with his fist. I let that happen just the once. Bastards. Can you get HIV from being force-fed human piss? What about subhuman piss?

It was Helen who said that the mouth is our most intimate place. Isn't that so true? Why prostitutes shag but don't kiss? I keep hearing that Marlowe line in my head, I remember from school: 'Sweet Helen, make me immortal with a kiss. Your lips suck forth my soul.' Every time Kitten's fist reappears in my mind, in that half light just before and after sleep, I try to exorcise it with memories of Helen at her altar rail in her long black cassock and those pointed, patent boots, as she places the bread on my tongue and says in that sweet, dark voice of hers 'the Body of Christ'. The Body of Christ. The Body of Christ.

My hand's up like an inflated rubber glove, a purple one. I'd give almost anything to lose myself in alcohol. The most cruel thing that bastard Governor did that night was remind me. Those three or four sips.

I'm sorry to burden you with this, Julia. I won't do it again.

Her lawyers' letter was pretty frightening. 'We, Fukk, Yew and Pissoff (or some such), are instructed by the Rev. Helen Halberd in the matter of Halberd v. Johnson-Price etc.' Our names were linked there in print, in the worst possible way. There was a draft apology for *The Truth* to publish, with my name correctly spelt both times, followed by a request for £5,000 damages to be paid to a charity of the Rev. Halberd's choice.

There was nothing from Helen herself, no card or sweet note to soften the blow. So cold, all of it, so clinical. I longed to hold her and soothe away my offence.

Instead I put it all back in its A4 envelope and hid it under the sofa.

A couple of days later a second letter came. Neil Sarbridge this time. He wanted to see me. He would be in Blackheath the following

Monday and would call on me at 11.30 a.m. unless he heard to the contrary.

Of the two letters, the second intimidated me more.

That Monday morning I was so nervous I couldn't work, walk or sit down. I had just decided to make a run for it when there he was, at 11.28 a.m., at the front gate.

I stared at him from the doorway. Shorter than I expected. Well fed but hardly what you'd call built. I could take him, no trouble.

Or so I thought then. Sitting here today, my ribs are aching, my fingers are slow – these last few pages have taken me two days – and if I waggle the bridge of my nose, it still crunches. I'm not taking on anybody for a while, I can assure you of that.

At least I don't dress like Sarbridge though. I have my dignity. Why is there still no legislation against old hippies making total sartorial sapheads of themselves? Sarbridge was wearing . . . well, you know his look. Wide trousers about four inches too short, red handkerchief knotted under his chin (the beard had gone) and a faded, navy fisherman's smock. A fisherman's smock. Had he ever caught as much as a stickleback in his life or was it supposed to be heavily symbolic? I could see no dog collar. No briefcase or A4 envelope in his hand either, so he hadn't come to deliver another invitation to court.

'Your gate doesn't shut,' he called out from the bottom of the path. 'You got a drop of oil and I'll fix it for you?'

I couldn't think of a reason not to, so I brought out a can of oil. After a few minutes of lifting and swinging the gate, he gave it up as a bad job. Wiping the oil off his hands on his red neckerchief, he introduced himself as Neil Sarbridge.

My room felt unusually small and cluttered as we sat there with mugs on our knees. He spread his legs wide, worked his mouth like a boxer trying to remember his own name and stirred his tea. Where was the famous charisma, I thought? Or was that privilege only for the ladies?

Music was thumping in the distance, probably in the nurses' home, the cosy nurses' home full of warm nurses in their warm nurses' clothing and even warmer nurses' underwear. I'd have given anything to be there instead of here with Sarbridge.

But I did have a plan: no apologies, no flannel, but I'd let him start. He sat back into the sofa with confidence I could never have mustered in those clothes. Confidence drawn from the fact that he was probably here to tell me he was going to sue me until my so-called career dropped off. He plunged forward, dangling his knuckles between his knees, and announced to the floor that he had read my article. Somebody had put a copy of *The Truth* in his pigeonhole, undergraduates probably. Their idea of a joke. He glanced up. I wasn't going to treat him to a reaction.

'What I want to say is,' he cleared his throat as if he was nervous, 'I like parts of what you wrote. It actually mentions our theology. Your explanation's not quite right but at least it's not misleading. That's pretty unusual, you know. For a journalist.'

I thanked him, chuffed. The last thing I'd expected from him was magnanimity. *The Truth* had indeed kept in one of Helen's paragraphs, for intellectual gloss. He laid his thumb against his mouth, then: 'You conflated a Unitarian approach with an overly Platonic interpretation of St John though, were you aware of that?'

He'd aced me, the po-faced bastard. He knew he could pull a stunt like that to blind me and I wouldn't have a fucking clue what interpretation of St John was in that article, if there was one at all. And I'm probably not quoting him correctly anyway, but that was the gist. The merest twitch of the lips disclosed his total satisfaction with himself. He wasn't going to leave it at that either. How could I have taken at face value, he went on, that Jesus and Mary of Bethany were lovers? Where did I get that, madbollocks.com?

Well, I had had help on this actually, hadn't I? One of the finest in the business, I wanted to say, in the comely shape of Helen Halberd. I'm not sure why I didn't say her name straight out. Maybe I wanted to watch him wriggle a bit longer in suspense . . .

'Who was your collaborator?' he said, and studied the floor-boards as if bracing himself for the answer. 'Was it the Reverend Halberd?'

'She did collaborate with me, yeah.' Though she knew nothing then about being featured in *The Truth*.

'Did you two work . . . very closely on it?'

'Yep.'

He glared.

'She . . . Helen . . .' Her name filled my mouth. My tongue felt too big to speak. But I couldn't let the bastard intimidate me like this.

'Helen likes the idea of Jesus being this big, rangy, sexy guy,' I said. Sarbridge rocked slightly, closed in on himself, as if the slightest annoyance could push him to violence.

'Who's dead keen on wine and food and women and – '

My voice died away. His tongue slid over the divide in his lower lip, then: 'Is she well?'

'Who?' I asked lightly.

'Ms Halberd. How's she keeping?'

'Yeah. She's great.'

He sucked air in through his teeth: 'She's what?'

'She's great.'

He was up, pacing and punching the air: 'I ask you *how* she is and phw, your generation has no idea what an adverb is any more, do you, do you, you call yourself a writer, nobody teach you, you say *well* for how you are, great or good for *what*, Helen is good, a very good person, a *great* person, those are adjectives, when I ask *how* she is, an adverb would be nice so is she well, or is she ill, is she well ill . . . well?'

He licked spittle from the corners of his mouth.

'Since you ask,' I grinned, one to me already, 'I can tell you that she's . . . fine. Which happens to be . . . an – '

'Adjective, yes, yes, I know.' He jutted his jaw at me, panting:

'So the article's not yours then?'

'It is so. I've got the cheque to prove it.' Which was a lie but I was expecting it any day.

'You said they're not your words!'

'They are my words. Most of them.' More lies of course, but I didn't want him to think I couldn't do my own job. I'd had enough of this, it was time to get the bastard on his way: 'What would you have written, Reverend? That Jesus never fucked anybody?'

He winced at those words, I give him credit for that.

'For what it's worth,' he said, 'I do like the doctrine . . . *heretical* doctrine,' he hitched his thumbs into his waistband as if that would steady his breathing, 'that if Jesus wanted to redeem us, he'd redeem all aspects of us including our sexuality. And I'm impressed by what you say about Mary of Bethany being the only person who – ' Sarbridge swallowed – 'who loved Jesus heart, mind, body and soul. I never thought of that.'

His eyes slid to watch my reaction. It was Helen's point of course, that one, but I wasn't going to tell him that.

'But you don't think he – ?'

'We've got no evidence,' he cut in, 'that's all. It's perfectly possible he was married, you know, in the Jewish society of the time his parents might well have married him off before he was sixteen, to some local girl – '

'Why?' I said, 'John the Baptist wasn't married.'

'Good point,' he smirked. 'You've played this before.'

'Played what?'

'Theologians call this the hermeneutic of suspicion. Hermeneutic of silence, they call it sometimes too. It means looking between the lines, Patrick, looking at what the gospels left out.'

He seemed to be changing tactic, trying to be one of those chummy, first-name teachers at school. No way.

'Why d'you call it a game?' I asked.

'It's basically guesswork, that's why. Making it up. But it's been keeping theologians off the streets for years and that's no bad thing. Especially the neo-crypto-post-feminists. And it's not often you get *them* interested in silence.' His shoulders shook in private laughter. 'Look at Mary Magdalene's words at the empty tomb,' he went on. 'They've been trying to say for years that meant the Magdalene was married to Jesus. She says "They have taken away my Lord." Do they have the ring of truth for you?'

He genuinely seemed to care what I thought, for about a hundredth of a second before he charged on: 'Fact is the body was probably thrown on a pile for the hyenas to eat. That's what usually happened to crucifixion victims.'

What?

'You mean there was no tomb?' I could imagine my mother in a dead faint from apoplexy. He hunched close to me now. He was so keen for me to understand that our knees nearly touched.

'The stone's a midrashic reference to the Book of Joshua,' he said, 'and Daniel's den of lions. There might have been no stone there at all.'

Suddenly I remembered Helen with her full-length cassock coating the undulations of her body while she explained softly to the school children that Jesus and Joshua are the same name in Hebrew, and a Jew in gospel times would have heard about the stone over Jesus' grave and he'd have thought of other caves and stones in the Book of Joshua and Daniel's den of lions. Had Sarbridge taught this to her?

'Daniel is more significant,' he went on, 'because God was there in the place of suffering alongside Daniel and that's what Jesus does with us.' This was exactly what Helen had told the children.

'Jesus is with us,' she had said, 'in our love and our pain but he's even better than God was with Daniel because he gets past the stone and gets free.'

Sarbridge was still talking, still too close to me. So I cut in and asked him straight: 'Do you believe in the Resurrection or not?'

His voice became vicious: 'You haven't a clue, have you. Just tell me this – did she write the bit about Mary of Bethany polishing the table, did she write that?'

'Did who write it?'

'For God's sake – Helen!'

Every ounce of his body had been dying to say that name. His eyes clenched shut. I said: 'I took it from her book.'

We both stood up. He looked small and old, and I swear I could have shoved him backwards at a run until he fell on his arse out through the window.

'You think it's funny,' he said, 'but there are jobs at stake. Helen Halberd's and mine. And I don't think you've even read your own article!'

'I'm a journalist, not a fucking theologian,' I pointed out more mildly than I felt.

He reached for my hand and shook it.

'Thank you,' he said. I wiped my hand down my leg. 'Will you kindly tell that to my bishop? He thinks you're a reliable reporter. I told him that if you can come up with crap theology like that, you can't be trusted in other things. Like alleging any so-called relationship between Miss Halberd and me.'

He gave a lop-sided smile and made to leave. But I hadn't finished with him yet.

'What do you like best?' I asked. 'The porn or the blasphemy?'

'You'll be asking me my favourite colour next,' he said.

'Very droll,' I said. 'Helen's book, I'm talking about. I couldn't get over the bit about the Song of Songs. Sexiest thing I've ever read without pictures, know what I mean? Did it do it for you too? That bit? Or at your age does your stimulation have to be harder core?'

He scanned me down his nose. Had I got him where it hurt? He tugged his smock down ready to leave.

'Worked for me too,' he said cheerfully, 'worked a treat.'

I smacked my thigh.

'You haven't read it, have you?'

He was trying to open the door.

'You're preaching at me about being a reliable reporter,' I went on, 'and *you* haven't even read her book!'

He turned and locked his eyes on mine.

'Why should I?' he spat. 'Another shitload of feminism? Spare me. That's why I had to get away from your Julia. God Almighty, on and on.'

In two strides I'd squared up to him: 'Don't you dare talk to me about Julia! You stay away from her!'

'No problem, sunshine, she's all yours.' He was so close I could see the fillings in his back teeth and the sinister gleam of his tongue. 'Just tell me this,' he hissed, too close to my face, 'is Helen pleased with it? This article of yours? Does *she* like what you've done to her?'

'No.' I backed away from his rancid breath. 'I don't honestly think I can say that.'

'Why's that?'

'She's taking me to court.'

I watched delight spread from his eyes through his widening mouth to his fingers which he locked together and cracked. 'Ha!' he went and hung his arm over my shoulder as if we might scrum down.

'She won't take you to court,' he whispered deep into my inner ear.

'What makes you so sure? You God or something?'

'No,' he grinned, 'but I could be the answer to your prayers.'

I shrugged away. We were face to face in the middle of the communal hall now.

'Don't be like that,' he simpered, 'I'm going to help you. I'll have a word with Helen for you, sort something out, OK?'

He let himself out of the front door and I watched his shoulders sway like a chorus girl as he sauntered down the path. He paused at the gate.

'Tell you what,' he called, 'I'll drop in on Helen in person. That'll do the trick'.

I had a feeling that somebody's prayers had just been answered, and they weren't necessarily mine.

I cannot think about you any more, I have work to do. I am going to polish this dining table until it shines like a soldier's boot. I've already scrubbed it white as bones. Now I'm going to pound oil into every groove, every ridge of the wood until my shoulders throb with weakness and I never again have to think of the scrape of your chair when you sat here or the way your hands fluttered like doves as you reached past the bowls of olives and chicken and broke bread here with me.

God help me, I need you still. I had lived safely for so long. Then you strode between our linen hangings and oak benches, and you chose me. But the men say . . . they say you met a woman, a Samaritan woman by a well. I anoint this table again, more oil, and watch it roll along the grain of the wood. I wrap my cloth tight around my fist. Did you ask her for a drink? They say you did. Did you ask her for the kiss of life as well? Did you say you were in paradise already sitting beside a beautiful woman like her? The men say she's telling everyone you're the Messiah. That you're the well of everlasting life. She's telling her whole village she could drink you up, every drop.

You have hung weights on my heart, Jesus. My whole body is like a festering wound. Martha says it will pass, all passions pass. She says I must seek God in this, as we all must in everything we do. But where is God in this misery? You said you loved me, Jesus. You said, 'Mary, you are loved.' And I believed you. But you love so many.

I hammer my love into this table until my knuckles bleed. My strap has fallen from my shoulder. I pull it back up and stand straight, with sweat gleaming on my breasts. I close my eyes and before I know what I'm doing, I have bent and kissed the place at this table where your plate used to be.

Dear Julia,

I tried a bit of church here yesterday. Yes, me. I thought it might settle my nerves. Maybe I could imagine Helen in that black cassock or hear her voice wash over me or see her lift the bread to her lips before she broke it at the altar and shared it out. I always loved that moment. I felt sometimes as if there was nobody else in the church but her and me, and it brought me peace.

The service here was in the gym – the chapel's being decorated after somebody's dirty protest – and the chaplain used eight crates of lager as an altar. He whipped the white cloth off at the end and said 'Party'. I might go again.

On the battlefield there are no atheists, he said, but what he noticed was that when men are badly wounded a lot of them want their mothers. Sometimes they want God too, but mostly what they want is their mums.

I want my Mum. A lot. I want her when she was 35, at home, with no jewellery and no holy friends. She hasn't been here of course. When I first got here I sent out loads of Visitor's Orders begging everybody to come but nobody's been but you and Tim's wife Fiona. She came, for thirteen minutes. She's nice, Fiona.

Forget what I said before. To see you again would be wonderful. If you do come, I'll give you what I've written for you so far. Please come.

Love,

P

I didn't send that letter either. I could feel the dreadfulness if you didn't reply again, or even worse if you did. I still haven't got over 'I have the following points', let alone your 'engagement'. I know you're upset, you have every right to be, but isn't getting engaged just a bit of an overreaction?

Number One Guv is leaving me alone, by the way. I p-mailed him that I would throw every game of chess with him until he found me a thoroughly heterosexual bodyguard. There's been no bodyguard. No contact of any kind.

If only I could feel your cool hands on my ribs, Julia. I think they're fractured. They hurt most whenever I'm lying in bed at night and when I try to get up. Both times I tend to be thinking of you anyway so I imagine one of your hands supporting my head and the other gently cradling my ribs as they grind into place. You're good at that. Thank you. I appreciate it.

The minute I'm out of my cell I pretend I'm not hurt though. If I went to the hospital wing, it would just attract attention. I don't fancy another hammering at the moment.

By the Tuesday after Sarbridge's visit he still hadn't been in touch. I kept thinking, how come he was so keen to see me and asked so closely about Helen if she meant nothing to him? On the other hand, if he was the transforming love of her life, how come he didn't know what was in her book?

But most of all, as the days ticked away towards my date with Helen's lawyers, I wanted to know why the bastard hadn't got me off the hook as he'd promised. Maybe that was his thing: all promise and no delivery. Like Jesus and the Second Coming.

So, come the day, I had no choice but to tuck the letter from Helen's lawyers into the breast pocket of my only suit and go to the meeting at *The Truth*. With the Shelly who'd commissioned me and their libel lawyer. I really should have known better, silly of me, but I assumed that *The Truth*'s lawyer would be male.

You know what newspaper offices are like. You explain yourself to the glossy tarts at two reception desks and then wait half an hour in a foyer full of chrome and fountains while people rush past carrying vital information hither and thither about how the world is spinning to its doom. Eventually a pleasant enough geezer in rumpled clothes too big for him leads you via a glass lift to an open-plan warehouse and sits you beside his screen, from which he never removes his eyes while you talk.

The Truth is not like that. It is produced in a two-room shed under a railway arch just north of King's Cross.

I swung along the street stepping between the moaning cardboard boxes and sleeping bags until I reached a sheet metal door that accorded with the address on my letter. I was over twenty minutes early. Damn. This had never happened to me before. Usually I reckon if I'm there before it's over, I'm on time.

To my left an ancient woman in three overcoats stood her full four feet tall and set about gathering up her bits and pieces into a roll.

'Fucking useless tosser,' she growled at me and shuffled up the road on footwear made of frayed newspapers tied together with string.

'How right you are, madam!' I called up the road. 'Mind if I join you chaps?' The pavement company ignored me so I sat down and stretched out my legs, avoiding a sinister stain where the old woman had been lying. Attempts at conversation died in the air so I leaned forward on to my folded arms and did what I do best (not difficult after a night's mental rehearsals of the scene ahead): I fell asleep.

The peep peep of somebody's watch wakened me. My own. Ten o'clock; time to make my presence felt inside. I felt much better for the short sleep and was further perked by what I took to be a good omen glinting between my feet, a pound coin. I put it in my pocket and pressed the buzzer of *The Truth*. A voice crackled through the speaker: 'Give yer nime.'

Nobody greeted me inside or noticed me particularly. I stood there feeling gormless. The small neon-lit room contained five desks laden with plastic cups and sheaves of paper dripping on to the floor. The middle desk was surrounded by women all making that particularly female sound, squealing. One of them said: 'Look at the tits on that poor cow! In't she got old?'

My view of said tits was blocked by their American-scale arses.

'Who?' I had dared to speak. Five faces turned and stared at me. I felt the pound coin in my pocket nervously. Mistake.

'Hands out of the pockets. Don't you dare do that in here. Harass any one of us and you'll be grateful to be left on a meat hook to die after what we'll do to you.'

I had had more gracious welcomes in my time but decided that this was not the time to get sarky. With both hands on my head in the approved manner I approached and asked gently who they were talking about.

'Britney. In the middle there with the sugar on her nipples. In't she got old?' The speaker could easily have given Britney twenty years. I said that I'd always rather fancied older women, there was so much more to loveliness than physiognomy.

'Wha?'

'Talking of which, I'm here to see your editor.'

The oldest one, the editor, was at least twice my age and weight. She'd have been useful in a scrum, except that she had one of those big, loose torsos like a shop display of beach balls, covered in sugar pink velour. She led me to her office at the back and left me alone for several minutes to consider my plight with a dingy cup of coffee until she, Shelly and the lawyer returned.

'Between you and I,' the editor said, ' our sole criteria is, you know, this poor woman's life's ruined, absly heart-rendering, innit, and if she has grounds for slander – '

I hadn't gone out with a lawyer for seven years and picked up nothing at all; I cut in:

'It's in print, isn't it libel if it's in print?'

'Whatever, mate, if she sues, we're all up shit creek without a ladder so show us your proof!'

I produced a transcript of my very first recorded conversation with Helen. While we waited for Shelly to nip across the road to Qikiprint and photocopy it, I wondered if any of them had bothered to read my piece at all before they published it.

A garish travel print on the wall of Blackpool's Big One took me back to Easter Sunday maybe six years ago when we went, you and I, to the fair on Blackheath. I wanted a white-knuckle ride so that you'd have no choice but to squeeze up tight against me and squeal as we swung round and round in some desperately unreliable metal contraption until the flesh almost left our bones. You complained it would be bad for your hair but you went all the same, and I sat with one arm lazed over your shoulders letting the rhythm of the ride and the changing views of church spires and trees and your closeness, your pressure against my ribs absorb me, and I felt that I could die suddenly, cleanly, right then, and be happy.

Shelly hurried back, sweat shining on her dark skin. The editor and the lawyer scrutinised my pages for several minutes.

'Is this all?'

'Well, I did have some other conversations with Helen Halberd but they're not recorded.'

'Why's that?'

'I don't know, I . . . I saw her several times to, you know, get her to confess.'

'And did you? Get her to confess? Yes?'

'No.'

All together now: 'Pity.'

I produced the book, Helen's book full of your jottings and detachable stickers, Julia, and explained our theory that what looked like a church book was actually a description of a passionate relationship between Helen and Sarbridge.

'She wrote up these Bible stories – '

The three women yawned in unison.

'Some of them are, you know, well sexy – '

The lawyer cocked one eyebrow: 'Mr Ronson, I've read the book and personally I'm more aroused by Bob the Builder.'

'Whatever floats your boat,' I said, 'by church standards this book is porn. There's this foot job that's quite horny if you ask me. And a bit further on – '

'Your point being?'

'She takes phrases from one story into the next and the next and there's this build up of a code . . .'

I could feel the words leave my mouth and land cold and indigestible between us.

' – and it finishes up with Mary of Bethany in love with Jesus and he kisses her in a crowd and that's like him walking on water for her, or her walking on the water, I can't remember, and it's because of that she becomes a priest and he took her through the fire which means sex in this other story, so we think they must have done – '

'Done what?' The three voices wanted to know.

'It.'

'Sex?'

'Sex. Look, she even thanks him, here on page seven, it's all nauseating but here in the middle, this one, this acknowledgement it's in the code, to NS.'

'And you think that's Neil Sarbridge?'

'Could be.'

'Or Natalie Spencer.'

'Who's she?' I asked.

The editor sighed: 'The editor of *Country Pursuits*.'

'Or Nina Simpson. President of the Law Society,' added the lawyer.

I should have upended the table, shouted fuck in their faces and marched straight out. Instead, with my voice sounding pathetic even in my own ears, I tumbled further in: 'I don't think she knows them.'

'How do you know?'

'Just a guess.'

Why did I say that? Why?

'Like so much of your work,' the lawyer said. As I watched her slide our copy of Helen's book, our copy full of our notes and memories, in among her crib sheets and pink string, and strain to close her briefcase, I knew it was not looking good. The editor pulled her considerable self to her feet and I knew I'd lost. Among all the scraping of chairs, I seemed to become suddenly invisible except to Shelly who steered me back out into the corridor and through the main office to the door.

'She's loving this, you know,' Shelly confided.

Who, the editor?

'Yeah. It's a bit of a milestone, our first writ. It means somebody's reading the paper, or thinks somebody's reading it, if they're bothered to sue.'

Really. She swivelled her slim hips between the desks.

'Yeah. And there's like loads of readers' letters come in too, so there's less space for us to fill up.'

Nice little hips actually. She pressed the release on the front door and held it open for me: 'Look, Paul, it's been great but we in't going to commission you again. Sorree.'

'Why?'

'Well she says we ain't used to working with incompetents what get us into legals,' she grinned. 'Must go, I got to write up Mrs Halberd's side of it nar, for the Eve's Burden page.'

'Helen's side of it? What's that?'

'Don't know yet.'

'Haven't you asked her?'

'Nah!' She shook her pretty dark curls. 'I'll busk it. I can lift some sexy bits out of her book and stick biog round it. Won't take long. Can I have two quid for the photocopying? You know how it is.'

'Lawyers don't come cheap?'

'Too right,' she simpered.

I dared to feel the milled edging of the pound coin in my pocket.

'One'll do,' she said and held out her hand.

'Can't help you,' I said and swung out of the door into the sour but oddly refreshing air of the street.

Anybody can make a mistake. Even me. But make no mistake about it, Julia, you are in my mind and heart here in this cell, every minute of every day. And night. I lie in bed and miss you. I sit at my desk and write to you. Writing that last bit was especially sad for me actually. What lay in my mind all last night was that cyclone ride in Blackheath, Julia. Years ago when we'd only known each other a term or two. I was rolling around on sea legs desperate for a hot-dog and onions to put me back in order. I had just about survived but was cuddling to myself the certainty that you, my flower, would be grateful that my strong arm had protected you from death. I turned to take your hand, expecting a pale, fearful little face ready to kiss and thank me. You hadn't even been holding on. You smoothed back your hair and strolled off, perfectly straight, unfazed.

My parents were out, and in my room I got to see you tousled and untidy at last, all undone and opened up for me. You have such loveliness, Julia. I know you despise it but it's a treasure, a rare thing, much more wondrous than anything those brassies had to offer at *The Truth*. Your throat, your naked shoulders, your feet always so amazingly small and neat when your boots come off. I know this will disgust you but sometimes here in the mornings I imagine – well, yes, I imagine that, I always do – but I imagine you in the dark before the lights come on and . . . don't laugh. You're feeding a baby or holding a laughing toddler over your head or laying your hand on a child's hot forehead, and I want to nestle with you forever.

I need you deeply, Julia. I forgot that for a while, I admit it and I hope you can forgive me. For the first month or so in here I kept longing to run, didn't matter where, I just wanted to run under a wide sky over miles and miles of grass but now what I want more than anything is to watch you with our baby.

I did forget about loving you for a while, and I'm sorry about that. But it was always there, you know. My love for you. Like the throb of the background music at the fair, sometimes loud, sometimes soft, but always, always there.

Number One Governor's got his own back after all. It was only a matter of time, the creepy old shite. Do you remember when you visited and I told you that all through the first evening I ranted in my cell, pounding the walls and beating my head on the floor, and then in a quiet moment I heard perfectly clearly the guy next door turn the page of his newspaper? The Number One Guv knows that too. He's put an (innocent until proved guilty) crack burglar next door to me and do you know what? He's learning bass guitar.

In the first half hour he learned to play Dom. Waiting for the next Dom was like Chinese water torture. By the time he'd been at it an hour, Dom dom was coming pretty regularly. Dom dom. Dom dom. Always slightly out of time with the throb in my temples. Today he might manage to teach himself another note. What will it be?

Dum.

As soon as I got home from *The Truth*, my bedsit felt cold and hollow and I needed to hear a loving voice. The receiver was hot on my ear after twenty-one rings. Where were you, Julia? Where was your bloody voicemail? At last you answered: 'Oh Julia. I feel absolutely ghastly. I've just been with these newspaper women and the lawyer and – '

'*You* feel awful. I've just had the most appalling experience of my life.'

'Why? What's happened?' Immediately I knew that you must have been attacked in college or smashed the car. You'd answered the landline in your rooms so you weren't in hospital. I was not too fogged to realise that. If I sobered up fast and took it steady on the bike I could be with you by first light. All these thoughts jagged through me. Whatever it was, why hadn't you bothered to contact me? I suppose I'd been out at *The Truth* and then nipped into the pub.

Your voice poured into my senses.

'It was unbelievably dreadful,' you said, 'you wouldn't believe it. I've been to Great St Mary's.'

You in a church? Bit extreme . . . A concert of amateur recorders, you explained: '*Amateur*, Patrick, playing *folk* songs arranged by *Britten. BRITTEN*! On multi-coloured plastic recorders, if you please, originals from the early 60s. Four hours of sitting on god awful tubular chairs from the correct era. My bum hurts. My ears are dead. I want to sleep but still keep hearing parp tiddly parp pee all bloody night. And the minute I do get to sleep, *you* ring up. So you'd better make it good.'

This had to be about Mark. Ha! He'd got on your tits, not literally, I hoped, and at last you'd seen what a useless wanker he was.

So, what was Mark's instrument like? I asked. Chestnut brown? A good ten centimetres longer than anybody else's? Yes, you barked, in fact it was so big he had to have a special chair beside him to hold the slack off the floor.

'Slack? Can't say I'm too impressed by slack, Joo?'

'Don't call me Joo, you know I hate it.'

You were cross but you were being filthy about Mark too, so it was probably safe to bet that he wasn't there in the bed with you. I bet I know exactly what Mark's like in the sack: I've seen him servicing his bicycle. He props it upside-down on its handlebars, yanks off the chain, slaps on plenty of WD40 and says 'I know how to get this going in no time.'

It was time to move you ruthlessly to tears. I described how my career was in tatters, not sparing a shred of my humiliation at *The Truth*.

'What do you mean, career in tatters? You're not a proper journalist till you've been sued at least once.'

'So it's like a badge at the Brownies?'

'Nobody reads *The Truth* anyway. What's your problem?'

Good point.

'But you know, my love,' (I was steadying) 'I keep thinking about Sarbridge. I mean, I think you're right. He must have shagged her. Why would he come and see me if he didn't?'

Why did you laugh?

'When he came to see me,' I went on, 'he didn't seem . . . he didn't deny . . . He just didn't go on as if I'd got it all wrong. He really didn't.'

What was the joke? You were laughing so much you put the phone down and when I phoned back . . . on voicemail. Was somebody there with you? Somebody who wasn't Mark?

I was on the phone again pretty fast the next morning: 'Who were you in bed with last night?'

'Excuse me?'

'Was it Sarbridge?'

'Who?'

'If it was that fucker Sarbridge, I promise you I'll – '

'You'll what exactly?'

And so on. Anything but a straight answer. Am I my girlfriend's keeper, I thought. Too damned right I am. I hadn't put up with your patronising moods for seven years to take that sort of shit. I was going straight up there for the weekend. It was time to put down a few markers.

I stuffed some things in my rucksack, not forgetting a certain small black box and inside it an 18-carat, single-diamond ring. It wasn't the first time I had been in the red but it would only be until my fee arrived from *The Truth*. By then with any luck your financial future and mine would be linked until death tried us to part.

On our way back from The Mitre to the college we were even walking in step together under alternating pink and white cherry trees. A fractious drive up the M11 had been erased by my striding into your lecture room on the dot of twelve, taking your hand and swooping you away to cheers from the top back row and a very pleasant pub lunch. So far this day was close to qualifying as the finest of my life. Then I'd suggested that I'd like to see Sarbridge in action some time, to see why he had such an effect on people, and you'd said he was doing a service that very evening, called Compline, why didn't we check it out. Seemed a good idea then. Less good now that we were walking past your rooms, your bedroom in particular, to go to church.

'What is Compline anyway?' I said, 'Why can't your Dean have normal church on a Sunday like anybody else?'

'Last service of the day. Like evensong. Go on. Say it.'

What! I hadn't had time yet to mention my marriage proposal, I'd been far too busy searching for the outline of your knickers (if any, so far not admitted) under your long skirt, kissing froth from your upper lip and hammering you 15–2 at table footie.

'Aren't you going to make some quip about feeding the oldsters Complan last thing at night or something?'

Some jokes are beneath even me.

'I've got someone coming to see me first,' you said, 'perfectly good student until she found God. This term she's condescended to put in one essay out of four. It was a ten-page diatribe about college hierarchy, why can't everybody have free access to the Master's ceremonial sherry and why do they have to go to lecture rooms instead of just having the notes e-mailed to their rooms.'

'Sounds fair enough.'

'Patrick! She helped herself to post from my pigeon-hole and delivered it to me opened with notes stuck to all the begging letters, you know all the charitable stuff with a free pen, telling me which to reply to first and with how much. When I challenged her about it, she burst into tears and said her therapist doesn't understand her.'

'When's she coming?'

'Half five.'

'Time for a quick one then.'

There was time for quite a long one: the undergrad didn't turn up. I was congratulating myself on having such a wonderful girlfriend who couldn't get enough of me when an inner whisper asked why? I tried to ignore it but the whisper kept saying, why? Why was I getting this unprecedented level of sexual action from you? Which dated, did it not, from your interest in a certain cleric at your college? You claimed to hate him to death and wanted rid. But . . . it just didn't make sense.

I didn't dare ask you straight out. As we walked past the pavilion to the chapel together in horizontal drizzle, I was fingering the corners of the ring-box in the pocket of my leather jacket, choosing my moment to ask you the other ultimate question: would you consider lowering yourself to be my wife?

Close up, the college chapel looked more than ever as if the 1970s concrete god had dropped a deposit at the end of the playing fields and then stepped in it. I had never been inside it before. I'd been at this college three years and not once did it cross my mind. That's not quite true, I used to take deep, sensual, recidivist pleasure in spending my Sunday mornings *not* in church but in the bath on our staircase, blasting my ears and everybody else's with the Sword's

Cock on the Rocks and wanking into lacey knickers stolen from the communal drying rooms and just dropping them anywhere on the floor. But I did remember the chapel watching me, floodlit, the evening I sprinted the length of two football pitches, crawled through the spiky hedge and crossed the road without looking left or right on my way to the Dappled Cow for condoms in the first term. I mentioned this piece of nostalgia to cement our togetherness. You reminded me that we weren't going out until the second term and didn't make love until the March, that time after the Blackheath Fair, when I'd sworn apparently that I was a virgin.

The formal warning came by the swing doors. I was to shut up and behave. If I let you down in the most infinitesimal way there'd be trouble. I warned *you*, justifiably, that if anybody came near me with a kiss of peace, I'd nut them. A few more endearments were exchanged before, I can't remember exactly why, you fucked off in a huff. I could follow you like a spaniel or head into church on my own. Either way, it was fair to say that the moment for a marriage proposal had passed.

Yet, as we settled together in the back row, the old dreads were knotting up. God would perform his one reliable trick, he would command time to stand still so that after about three hours I would look at my watch and only ten minutes would have passed. Everybody else in there would be best friends and they would all turn and stare at me. Even worse, they might 'welcome' me, gripping both my hands through long boasts about their house groups and faith teams. And my greatest fear of all? No, it wasn't standing when I should have been kneeling, lapsing into the wrong version or kissing somebody when I should been crossing myself. No, my worst fear of all, I could feel it hissing and swirling in the pit of my guts, was of doing none of it at all and marking myself out as prey.

I wasn't there to 'worship'. All I wanted was to have a good look at him, this Dean, to survey him on his own patch. I was immune to church. Wasn't I?

About six seats along to the left a girl combed her hand up her neck into her short red hair and held it in a knot on top of her head.

I swung forward with my elbows on my knees and my head low.

I could not think about that, about Helen. Ever since the letter had come from her lawyers, I'd sealed away that tumult of love and rejection and I wasn't going to let it get the better of me now.

'As soon as it's over,' I said, 'we piss off.'

'No way,' you said, 'the best bit's the party afterwards. That is where we draw him fatally out.'

I looked up: 'Can't wait. How about I kick his teeth in? That'll loosen his tongue for him.'

It was meant to be a joke, of sorts, but you gave one of your bored sighs as if you'd be happy if I were anywhere but with you. You explained very slowly that if I used physical violence you'd be happy to fry my gonads with wine and onions for the entertainment of your next Emasculinity Study Group.

I watched Sarbridge sashay into the central space where shafts of orange light converged on the parquet. It wasn't a sashay exactly, he was too small and round for that, so it was more of a sushi. He bobbed on his toes and I was waiting for him to say something like: 'Hi there, let's pray' or 'We want to thank you, Lord Jesus, for this opportunity to just come together in your Majesty.'

But he didn't. Shock or what. The service wasn't like my mother's lot at all. It was Thee and Thou. Sixteen robed choristers twittering like swallows. Instead of a band or synthesiser there were two fantastically beautiful women on violin and cello.

In fact, the place was wall-to-wall with gorgeous women. I was proud to be in your company as always, my love, but I have to say that the competition was pretty sensational. No flowery dresses, no anoraks or mumsy haircuts, these were seriously lovely girls. And apart from the choir (gay to their last chromosome) and Sarbridge and me, there was not a man in sight. As we all stood up to sing, I allowed myself to admire a hand scratching a naturally blonde head just in front of me. Bring me your faith teams, I wanted to shout. Your house groups are my house groups.

As I write this, some bloody distracting, rhythmic Oms are drifting up the wing from the yoga class. About ten of them will be sitting in an education room on patchwork quilts with their big toes stuck up their nostrils in search of peace. It's just one of a thousand perky ways of wasting time in here. The Number One Guv must be due an inspection.

Sarbridge said that Christianity is eternal, unchanging, immutable, perfect. Hasn't changed at all in the past 2000 years. Has it. Except when it decided to include Gentiles. Then they embraced the end of slavery, segregation and apartheid. They allowed women back into ecclesiastical power. Partly. Suicides can be buried by the church now, left-handed people are accepted, mentally-ill people are better understood, even divorced people can have a second crack at happiness with the blessing of our church. Who knows, maybe some day gay and lesbian people will be fully welcome too.

Sarbridge wasn't just standing now, he was prowling, waving his arms, smacking his hands together. He was working that crowd and he was loving every minute: 'They used to say that women have no souls. Change it! The Mass had to be in Latin in case people understood it. Change it! God, all three of him, whatever that means, was all male?'

They all joined in: 'Change it!'

'Only male priests could conjure up the deity, which is ever-present anyway?'

'Change it!' they roared back. Even you, Julia, you were shouting with the best of them.

'And since the eleventh century all those holy men were supposed to be celibate and now (he was whispering) . . . now what? Now the men don't have to be celibate unless they're gay. And women can be priests, and *they* don't have to be celibate even if they *are* gay. Maybe they do, nobody's quite sure. Eternal truths,' he paused, 'or goalposts running around all over the place?'

He looked so different from the middle-aged constipation victim who had dithered around my place as if he'd just dropped a bottle into the wrong recycling hole. He was bursting out of his cassock, ready to see anybody in the car park. Against all my intentions I was warming to him.

When I had first sat down in the back row of wooden chairs and the slicked-back girl next to me had shifted slightly away, I had had an odd moment of . . . of what?

Part of me was revolted by the modernity of the place and I composed a mental hate-list. To Whom It May Concern, Kindly incinerate forthwith all of the following: that dreadful yellow window shaped like a fried egg, the totem pole candle-sticks, all polished-pine individual chairs, every hassock with a high street bank's name or other commercial symbol woven into it, that funny-angled cross with a chocolate monkey crucified on it, all 'praise-books' and 'worship manuals' with candles and doves on the cover. Oh yes, and the words 'inter-faith' and 'chapelette' *and their very concepts.*

But there was something else. It shocked me more than I can say.

I let my eyes follow one of the choristers as he waddled about snuffing candles. After he'd deposited his taper in the appropriate wherever, he strolled down the central aisle, his hands hidden inside his billowing sleeves in a way I recognised. I used to do it at school. He was so familiar with the place, so comfortable that he jumped down the altar stairs with his two feet together like a child. It could have been me up there revelling in that gait, letting the cassock roll take me over.

Part of me longed to giggle and point. But another part, like Mole in The Wind in the Willows, was sniffing for its long lost home. For so many years I had been fighting the church, peeling its tentacles off me, pushing its weight away, but there on my polished-pine individual chair, Julia, I had a bad attack of inner tears.

I took your hand and held your knuckles gently to my stubble. Sarbridge was still talking. The divine territory, he was saying, is still there. Every time we hear music that takes us to the edge of ourselves, every time we smell a rose, every time we are naked . . . we know. The divine dimension is there, waiting for us.

Without daring to look at you, I took the ring-box from my pocket, put it unopened in your palm and closed your fingers around it.

You couldn't get out fast enough. You were holding out the ring box stuttering What's this? What, what's this? and I closed my eyes and leaned back to breathe in that great big beautiful sky arching from the chapel on one side of us to the college on the other and beyond us over the whole silver glittering mass of Cambridge. I wanted to run across those playing fields, to cover distance, take in great lungfuls of fresh air, and take you with me and make you mine. We didn't stop running until we were just short of the pavilion again.

You demanded an explanation and I think I said: 'I've made a decision, Julia, I want to end it all.'

'Patrick don't be so – '

'It's a joke, love,' I took hold of your shoulders, 'I mean I want to get married.'

And you laughed and shook your head and ran your fingers over your hair and opened your lips but no words came out. You started laughing and then I said Just look at that sunset: a slice of blood orange was sliding into mist above the Gothic rooftops of St John's. I took your hand again and sucked the tips of your fingers and held your waist as we walked, in step, through wet grass behind the pavilion. I remember you kissed me with both your hands around my head. It was a soothing, temperate kiss. You said: 'I'm really sorry, Patrick, but – '

I pulled you hard against me – no, don't skip this bit, I want you to read it, feel it with me, Julia, because we might never make love ever again – and as I kissed you back, my hands smoothed over your silk blouse and down your arms. I led your fingers to my belt buckle and moved my own on down and under your skirt.

I'd been speculating since we left your rooms about your underwear. You were bound to have changed. Would it be something sturdy, the Marks & Spencer sort which pouches so voluptuously when they're pulled up tight? Or a thong? You often wore those, terrific as an ocular hors d'oeuvre, back and front, but any attempt to slip in fast round the thong while you were still wearing them and I'd be sliced like salami. Best of all, no doubt about it, would be French knickers. Dirty buggers, the French, to design underwear specifically for off-chance coupling with maximum opportunity for a penumbral stroke and savour of your divine dimensions among silk and lace before the compliant curtain is drawn aside.

My hands were gathering up fold after fold of your long black and white skirt. You freed me from my jeans with a chuckle – why did you always laugh? – and I could have come any second before I even got to touch your legs.

Why, Julia? Why that particular night? When you'd never done it before, ever. Not with me. Why?

I could have taken you to task there and then, or I could have just taken you . . .

No contest. Braced against the wooden boarding of the pavilion wall in a parody of a press-up, I felt your legs trying to cling round my buttocks and your fingers slip between us, flesh on flesh on flesh.

It's a cruel thing about fantasies. So many times I had lain on my bed, one hand on my cock, the other on my balls, and imagined having you fast up against a wall, your arms high above your head and your mouth, everything, open, sighing and mewing. Sometimes you would speak to me in a foreign accent in those dreams, or suddenly, wondrously, you'd flip upside down and fellate me like a mad octopus and then flip back again. And there it was happening, without the flipping of course, and more clumsily than a dream, with shooting pains in my back and legs and pressure on my hands and worrying about my knees buckling and an irritating drip from the guttering down the back of my neck, but everything more dizzying and textured and dirty and scented, with perfumes of sweat and lemons and, oh Jesus Christ, of incense.

But how could I have come, Julia, with you so different? So unlike yourself? You were different from even an hour or two before, for God's sake. Why didn't you complain that the grass was wet or we hadn't a condom or we should go somewhere comfortable or I hadn't shaved?

And why, Julia – in that chapel of all places – why were you not wearing any knickers?

The story of Jesus being anointed with oil fascinates me. It is so unashamedly sexual that it's hardly surprising that it is rarely heard in church.

Anointing was how the ancient Jews welcomed a new king. So, if the story of Jesus is to show us that he was the King of the Jews, there had to be an anointing somewhere. Jesus himself requested that his own anointing, by a woman, should become a sacrament as central as the sharing of bread and wine at the altar. Christianity has chosen not to rise to his challenge.

So where did this crucial act take place? In Matthew and Mark, it was at the house of Simon the leper. Luke puts it in the house of 'a Pharisee' named Simon, without any mention of leprosy. John, most famously, puts it in the house of Mary and Martha in Bethany, and of their brother Lazarus whom Jesus had just raised from the dead.

Who did the anointing? In Matthew and Mark, it is simply 'a woman'. (Is it not extraordinary that the person who performed this defining act is not named?) Luke describes her as a city woman and 'harmartolos', which Greek word is usually translated into English as 'a sinner'. It is better understood as someone who has transgressed the Jewish law in some way, for example by omitting to observe diet laws. It is emphatically not a word for harlot or prostitute.

Only John's Gospel names the woman who anoints Jesus, as Lazarus' sister Mary, the one scolded by her sister Martha for listening to Jesus rather than helping in the kitchen.

Which part of Jesus' body does she anoint? A simple question, and again Matthew and Mark agree: the 'woman' anointed Jesus' head. But in John's Gospel Mary anointed his feet and wiped them with her hair. (For a Jewish woman to have her hair loose with anyone but her husband would have scandalised any Pharisee.) It is only in Luke that we see the traditional picture of the 'sinner' weeping and washing Jesus' feet with her tears. She then wipes with her hair and kisses his feet before anointing them with oil. In this version alone, Jesus forgives her sins, for she loved much.

So, what do we have here? Several versions of one act? Several acts by several women?

From early Christian times the women in the gospels, especially those called Mary, have been viewed as one person. Debate raged for centuries about whether Mary Magdalene was Luke's misinterpreted 'sinner', and wasn't she Mary of Bethany as well? St Augustine decided that it was Mary of Bethany anointing twice, then he wasn't so sure.

Pope Gregory I (from whom we have Gregorian chant) settled the matter in his 33rd homily in 591 CE. He declared that Luke's 'sinner', Mary of Bethany and Mary Magdalene were all the same person and that was Mary Magdalene. Addressing himself to the 'seven devils' cast from her, he declared: 'What did the seven devils denote if not all the vices? The woman had used the oil to perfume her body in illicit acts.'

Could this have been pontifical wishful thinking? It certainly smacks of, how shall I put it, idiosyncratic fantasy. There is no evidence that Mary Magdalene was associated with prostitution, other than her apparent independence of means which (according to Mark) she uses to fund Jesus and his party throughout their mission. Gregory might have taken time to look more closely at the four gospels: the casting out of devils always signifies illness being cured. Nowhere in any gospel has it anything to do with vice. Luke's 'harmartolos' had no sexual taint.

Mary of Bethany performs the mightily erotic act of anointing Jesus' feet but there is no evidence that her life was in any other way disreputable. As far as the gospels can tell us, she lived quietly at home with her sister and brother.

Pope Gregory's conflation of the women close to Jesus has had several harmful effects. Granted, it has given us the image of love and redemption, of the prostitute made good by God's love, which the Christian church has enjoyed for fourteen hundred years. And if Jesus was anointed by a woman, possibly a sexually tainted one, in the house of a leper, which was as far from sacred ground as you could get in those days, and he was anointed not on his head in the traditional way but on his feet, this string of paradoxes joins a host of others in this wonderful Messiah story, ranging from his birth in possibly dubious circumstances to his execution as a criminal.

However, to roll these three characters into one denies the reality of several women being close to Jesus. More importantly, and this is contrary to Jesus' specific request, the church has chosen to dismiss his anointing as the silly act of a besotted woman. Three disciples feature in the Passion story: Judas the betrayer, Peter who denied Christ before running away, and 'a woman' who triggers the whole final chapter because she risked her reputation and an absurd amount of money to anoint him with the finest oil. We hear much about the first two. Almost nothing about the last.

In 1969 the Second Vatican Council withdrew from the Mary Magdalene/ harlot link and admitted that there might have been three women after all. Mary Magdalene's reputation was redeemed at last. What would it cost us to lead Mary of Bethany out from the shadows to take her rightful place in the Passion cycle too?

As usual it was all my fault. It was especially my fault that I'd lost my hard-on without the customary excuse of twelve pints. Your arse twitched beautifully in that black-and-white skirt as you stamped back to the chapel and into the steamy side-room where a party had begun.

The babble was falsetto, giggly and almost entirely female. I took two glasses of wine from the polished table, downed both and took a third, as you do. I felt . . . I didn't know if I felt rejected or jilted or could still muster the will to live. Bread sticks might help, and cheese, and those olives looked good, green and black. I leaned across a bald singer for four pâté sandwiches and asked him if the Dean was always this generous.

'Aye, he is that. He doesn't believe that Jesus meant the church to interpret the last supper as a sip of cordial and a wee white wafer.'

'Sound man, your Dean.'

'In some respects, aye.'

'So you're not with him all the way?'

His reply was a sort of winey spit. 'The man's an atheist. Good on music though. Excuse me.' He wafted away to join the group of choristers by the door. They looked as if they'd die of the vapours if I forced them to hear *Hell Met By Moonlight*, but you can never tell. The Sword's fans are many and various.

I stood alone. Nobody looked remotely interested in approaching me about my spiritual development or inviting me to a house group. I began to feel incomplete without you among all these strangers. You were somewhere in there, probably flirting outrageously with some poor stranger to hurt me if only I could see, but where? Then I heard you giggle. I turned to see you chatting up

Sarbridge so keenly you were practically inside his wine glass.

'But I thought she poured the oil on his head,' you were saying, 'not just his feet. Where do I get that from?'

'Quite right, Doctor.' Sarbridge patted your shoulder, tosser, and went on: 'Luke says she anoints the feet but Mark says that she "takes the box and poured it on his head". I dare say the truth lies somewhere in between.'

Your eruption of filthy laughter made everyone turn and stare.

I said something daft like 'What you all talking about?' and edged between him and a violinist who seemed particularly keen to keep her left breast attached to his upper arm. You condescended to explain: 'We're discussing the contradictions in the gospels. Martha of Bethany . . .'

'Mary,' he interrupted, 'Mary, Martha's sister. You'll remember the Mary who oiled Christ's feet – '

'And wiped them with her long hair,' you said, gathering yours behind your head and slowly letting it drop over your shoulders.

'Terrifically potent image,' he purred, 'profoundly erotic, isn't it.'

I longed to wipe him off my shoe.

'Is this your husband, Doctor Julia?' He hadn't recognised me. Bastard. Maybe he only notices women. You just couldn't reply fast enough, could you?

'No. I'm not married.'

I looked at the circle of female faces around him. He was old and would have rolled right over in the united puff of any international front row but any one of those gorgeous women would have volunteered right there to pour oil the length of his naked body just to see where it flowed.

A girl radiating health by the wine table was having trouble taking off her sweatshirt, the sort of trouble my father would have helped her with. The gap between her navy T-shirt and her low-slung jeans and the tousling of her hair as it became visible again and the slight flush in her cheeks mesmerised me. When I looked back, you and Sarbridge were alone. He might have braced his arm against the wall by your head, or maybe I just remember it that way.

'No, nobody has seriously believed that Jesus thought he was

God, not for well over a hundred years,' he was saying, or similar. You bit your lip like a teenager: 'So are you saying that we can only understand by going to your classes?'

'I'll let you have a copy of my pamphlet Giving Godhead. But what you were saying there, that's most perceptive. In the beginning was Logos, the word, and Logos was with God and Logos was God.'

'Isn't that from Genesis?' you asked.

'John the Divine actually,' he ran his tongue down the cleft in his lower lip, 'but you've caught the allusion to Genesis . . .'

So this was the legendary Sarbridge charisma at work: a combination of intellect, dirty bits of the Bible and sheer physical presence. Why did you fall for it, Julia? He was hardly subtle. Only days ago you wanted me to take him out with an ice pick but now you were simpering and giggling and going 'oh you're so right'. And all of it in *no knickers*! The Julia Bailey I knew and loved would have called him a patronising old fucker. Why didn't you? Why?

Something had to be done.

'Excuse me,' I butted physically between you, 'sorry to interrupt but what *is* that Word? You know, the one at the beginning, In the beginning was The Word?'

Your voice was the sweet, light voice of a teenage nun: 'Oh yes, Neil, is it life force? Or is it – ' as if you could hardly breathe – 'is it love?'

Somebody had to say it, and it had to be me: 'Hey, life force, yeah, doesn't that mean the word's you know . . . Fuck?'

Your eyes stretched in horror. I was aware of pain firing through my left big toe as you stepped on it hard. But I was on a mission; torture was nothing to me.

I looked down. One of his laces (plain, black) was lolling on the floor beside my right trainer. I swivelled my right foot across until that shoelace lay under the ball of my foot and I tamped down with all my weight.

'Any left in that bottle behind you, Dean?' I asked brightly.

I still can hardly believe it, he actually patted your bum first. Then he tried to step back towards the wine table for another bottle.

His face puckered in disbelief as he started to topple. His hands went out in a circular motion like a skater until they connected with the wine table and pushed it and about two dozen open wine bottles to the floor. When his backside hit the floor, he yelped like a girl and collapsed flat out as if somebody had pulled out his plug.

I regretted it briefly when it crossed my mind that I might have killed him. But then five or six young women rushed toward him and he made the heroic decision to be helped into the sitting position. An older one with a short dark bob and a truly exceptional embonpoint pushed through crossly and laid a heavily-ringed left hand on his shoulder. Skulls, goat's heads, she had a fistful of them and in the midst of it all a naked wedding finger: 'Neil, darling, what on earth do you think you're doing?'

I swear I heard him whimper as she dabbed at his brow with a balled tissue and helped him up. As she led him away by the hand, you caught me with a flinty look and I knew I was in trouble deep.

First you bollocked me for being puerile, then for failing to apologise (I still refuse to apologise) and for upsetting your so-called plan to extract his secrets.

But I still don't understand. It doesn't add up. You weren't interested in Helen Halberd that night at all. OK, before I turned up and 'wrecked it all', Sarbridge told you that he and Helen were summoned to see their relevant bishops about my article. Very good. But what was that about a God-shaped hole in all our lives that I was too dim to recognise? I could recognise holes in my life all right. A car-shaped hole for a start. A job-shaped hole. A wife-or-loved-one shaped hole. A telly-of-my-own shaped hole. A home-shaped hole. I may be dim but I think you have to be bloody well off before you can make out among all the other holes the one that's God-shaped.

And it wasn't that you accused me of soulless materialism. Me! The one with no proper job and no pashmina cushions. It was when you started bellowing that I was obsessed with trivia, myself in particular, and that I wouldn't know what a soul was if it stuck its finger up my bum in the middle of the night. Such a nice choice of phrase you have when you're being religious. I only grabbed your wrists to defend myself, I swear. When you started to pray.

So there I was the next morning, lighter by the weight of that engagement ring and any hopes I had for our future, with Pug bawling 'Women Are Just Hassle' through my earphones, half way up the long M11 hill from Duxford. The Honda was striving like a real trooper through the morning sleet. I could hardly see. I wasn't sure whether it was the moisture streaming across my visor or tears knocking at the backs of my eyes.

It's just, I couldn't help remembering the way your hips tilted just a fraction in his direction every time he said your name. Your hips, in the black skirt with the white flowers on it, your hips in no knickers, and that little tilt each time. Julia, he said. And I was thinking about your hips tilting toward him in reply as the fox ran out in front of me and the bike lurched and started sliding up the carriageway.

I fell fast towards the horizontal and somehow I had plenty of time to think, how will Julia know about this? Who would tell you? Some paramedic? An undertaker? And if they found my head some distance from my body, as happens sometimes in bike accidents, would they know to tell you how much I loved you?

My wing mirror was sparking along the ground. Who would tell my mother? Would she look up from her Bible long enough to say Who?

Gravel juddered against my knee. How long would it be before somebody told Seb, my big brother who had long since put from his mind the leisurely blows to my head, the knees in my groin, the lordly thefts of my pocket money? And what about Tim who's always too busy earning enough to pay the school fees and the scuba lessons to say sorry.

My left handlebar dug into the hard shoulder, and brought me to a stop. As I settled with the bike leaning on my left leg and my head at a lousy angle on the ground, I wished I'd said goodbye to my father. I wished I'd told him that I totally understand why he escaped.

The diamond pinpricks of drizzle on my visor were astonishingly beautiful. I tried to get up and couldn't. My arm was hot. The road was burning through my sleeve, the sleeve of the leather jacket you made me buy, Julia, from that market stall where we had our first argument.

I thought, I'm not going to survive this. I'm not sure I want to. I crawled away from the bike and sat there with my elbows on my knees, my head in my hands, and slush from passing lorries on my face. There was only the hard shoulder to cry on and I thought I'd probably never see you or that bloody ring again.

Something had got to you, body and soul, and it wasn't me and it probably wasn't the tosser Mark either. As I tried to light a fag with one wet match after another, and tears fell out of my eyes, I tried to phone you but the voicemail told me you'd taken leave. Of your senses? I left a simple message, no snivelling, just asking you to phone me if and when you could spare a minute.

I closed my phone. That's when it started. One sob out loud, on its own. Then another. In spite of me, they gathered momentum until they were like serpents spewing out of me, cries forcing themselves out of my mouth, loud, raucous, primal. A name was on my lips but I couldn't let it escape. It was a name that came to me every morning just before I woke, as if she tended my soul while I slept. A name of smoke and roses. I had to survive this, get myself up and get home, or I'd never see Helen again.

It took me an hour to stop shaking from shock and by then I was almost solid with cold. I straightened the handlebars and mirrors, lumbered back on to the bike, and eventually, my hands frozen in the grip position and everything hurting and every stitch I wore steeped, I coaxed the bike into action again.

It took everything I had to haul the bike on to its stand when I got back but I did it. The pain of lifting my arm to unlock the door brought bile to my throat and tears back to my eyes. I lay on my bed. Everything ached. Everything was spinning. Closing my eyes made it worse so I decided to run myself a deep bath. I tried to sit up, and passed out.

I'm staring at my hands wrinkling in the water bucket, and I know that if I don't raise my head soon, I'll cry.

'Foxes have holes and birds of the air have nests,' he said, 'but the Son of Man has nowhere to lay his head.' How could he not know how much that wounds me? How much I long to enfold him in my bed with his head close to mine, and caress him until our faces age and furrow like the river-bed in June? He wanders over mountain and hill and forgets his own resting place, here with me.

He came to save the lost. I was lost. I was so lost I didn't know there were maps any more, until he locked his eyes on to mine and held my hands in a storm and said my name. Then the world stopped jolting too fast and too slow and he said, 'Mary, come to me, you are loved.'

When my brother Lazarus walked from his tomb, he said 'Loose him, let him go.' Loose him from his grave clothes. Let him come back among the living. Come back and loose me, Jesus, I beg you. Free me from this living death. My soul is rent and my heart splits like a stone. I long to don sackcloth and ashes and cry in a loud voice, 'Why have you forsaken me?'

Instead I shake my hands and smell them. That aroma of spikenard clings to them still. I will wash again. Stupid of me, I mustn't weep, he promised me nothing, except that I am loved. Passive tense. Passive I sit and wait. Tense. If only, he would come and be alone with me. Privately together, I could ask him at last, do you love me, Jesus? No jokes or stories, no bushels or talents, just tell me honestly: do you love me in the way I long to be loved by you?

But where is he? Gone again. He and the men. Off up some mountain. On the seashore. Off chatting up some woman by a well. Always away. Always with others.

It's Jerusalem tonight. Passover, so they're in a pub somewhere. A private room. Men only. Jesus and the twelve. I wanted to offer to serve them but I didn't dare, and I wasn't asked. So I sit here, half alive, half dead, with my soul aching to gather him in my arms, hold him to my bosom and bring him safely home.

My phone was ringing somewhere, not among the bed covers, not by the pillow, must be on the floor . . . where on the floor . . . where?

As I reached down, pain scorched from my right shoulder up behind my ear. Twisted up like Richard the Third, I heard a light, posh, female voice say, 'I'm, yah, hi, I'm Vanessa at *The Truth*, features editor, you know?'

A features editor!

'Is that, you know, ahm . . . Patrick Pratt-Nicely?'

I dropped my voice an octave: 'Patrick speaking. Actually.'

'Yah, great.' She honked like a goose trying to break into flight, though what amused her wasn't clear to me. She said, wasn't I their expert on all things religious and could I do them a piece on a new outbreak of the Omegists?

I'd been trying to erase that ghastly visit to *The Truth*'s office from my memory on the basis that it qualified as abuse, but . . . She couldn't mean me.

Yah, I was definitely listed as their religious correspondent and a 'this like huge' meeting of Omegists (which she kept mispronouncing as Omigodists) was due on the top floor of some glossy office block in the Isle of Dogs at five o'clock that Sunday, nobody else was free, would I cover it?

Work at last. A real commission, from somebody other than Cyril.

Is the Pope a Catholic? I said.

She wasn't sure.

Here was a chance to put in a classy, professional job, and get it right this time. Besides, if reports in the *Sunday Telegraph* were anything to go by, I just might find myself keeling over into a mêlée of writhing, young female bodies. Could I picture myself flailing about among such beauties and retaining my incisive journalistic objectivity? Just let me try.

The *Telegraph*! If I did go and dig up something new and sexy and suitably arcane, I could offer it to the *Telegraph* as well as *The Truth*! The effective freelance turns copy in as many directions as possible.

Another voice kept whispering in my head. One that blew cigarette smoke suddenly between sentences. I could imagine her combing her hair into a knot on the top of her head as she said: 'He's at St Marty's-Actually. The Omegist church.'

'The one with all the horizontal totty?'

'You should go and see for yourself some time. You might like it. There's also a faint chance, you know' – blow – 'that you might see me.'

I'd been longing to call Helen but I'd no reason to. What I had done was press 141 and her number a few dozen times. Then with my thumb hovering over the call button, I'd bottle out. All I wanted was to hear her voice. Hear her laugh. Sometimes before I was fully awake I'd imagine her phoning me: 'Meet me for a drink, Patrick, please.' Blow. 'I promise I won't' – blow – 'I won't touch you unless you want me to . . .' Then a laugh I could feel all over.

From here on the path is uncharted, Julia. I've kept it from you until now because it's so weird, you would never believe me. But it's true, every word of it. Enter this unholy ground if you dare.

I took far longer than I should have done to get ready. I was trying to carve my stubble into centimetre-wide stripes like Whitehead on the cover of the Believer Fever CD with '*We are all rockers*' tolling in my head, '*of that we are sure.*' Bloody annoying lyric. Pug would never have come up with a line starting 'of that'. Of that bollocks, maybe.

Fuck. My stubble stripes kept refusing to meet under my chin and I wound up clean shaven. With the hangover drooping from my eyes and purple razor rash, I looked like some child-molesting student priest. That wouldn't do at all. I roughed up my hair. Now I looked like a child-molesting student priest who'd just crawled out of bed. On with the black jeans and leather jacket. At least nobody would take me for a Christian looking like that, would they? Or did I look like the token born-again addict? There was always one of those. I put up the collar of my leather jacket Elvis-style and leered in the mirror.

Would they let me in? Time to find out.

As I chained my bike in the couriers' park under the *Mirror* building, I almost crossed myself in respect. The week had been blistering and heat still seeped from the salmon granite footpaths through the soles of my boots. The sky was darkening over Cabot Place's pepper pot turrets. Mirrored clouds rolled across Canary Wharf Tower to blend with the cumulus behind. I was about to enter that monumental mirage to research the wittiest, most sensitive expose of religion the world had ever read. I should even get paid.

Cabot Place was full of families. These were not the usual families you see at the weekend cursing each other in B&Q, all in identical faded denim with their Nan in iron control and everybody smoking, even the baby. This lot looked as if they'd never been outside together before and didn't plan to make a habit of it. Most of the men were those stork-like banker types with tidy haircuts and expensively-ironed chinos. That wasn't a smell under their noses, they just had difficulty breathing outside the office air-conditioning. They clumped together like smokers in the street, probably knocking out a sly business deal or two.

The women were a mess frankly. Badly cut hair clamped in Alice bands or in ugly pins, Oxfam jeans too short for them and saggy, breastfeeding tits. Every one of them was laden with tots and tot-associated paraphernalia. Please God, I prayed, don't let me be seen by anybody I know.

I had to navigate a course through them without being 'saved'. How? Be a journalist, I thought. I whipped out my notebook, lit a fag and I swear to you, they parted like the Red Sea. I went straight to the head of the queue where 'God bless, I'm Emily' asked for my ticket.

'Press,' I shouted back over the rock gig din seeping out from the main hall. She nodded at me as if I was an idiot: 'Praise God, yes,' she was still nodding, 'ticket please.'

'No – Press! Press!'

Over her shoulder I noticed long, badly bleached hair tumbling over a black bomber jacket and leopard-skin jeans. The legs were rock-star skinny. In fact I thought I recognised those buttocks even without a laser light show and fireworks. Could they possibly belong to the holy rock god of Olde Greenwich Town?

'Gavin!' I called. Emily turned in time to watch me sprint past her into the main hall, ready for the interview of my life with Gavvers Whitehead. Who had disappeared.

The big screens, rock kit and laser-eyed security people in the Kingdom Suite were familiar enough – thank you, Mother – but the size of the place was a shock. The hall was about five times the size of my old school gym, all covered wall to wall in lush royal blue carpet. Not that you could see much of the floor. People were still packing in, shoulder to shoulder, being ushered forward by bossy staff.

A small, rat-faced woman next to me already had her palms up in the air and was swaying lightly against my hip. I gave her my recovering addict grin just as a plump man of about forty ran on to the stage in Mafia specs and blue jeans. The place erupted in applause.

'I'm Shane! God bless you, London!' he called into his microphone. Like holy thunder London blessed him back. He closed his eyes, looked heavenward and the place fell silent.

'We just want to thank you, Lord Jesus. For this. Opportunity to come. Together in your Holy Majesty?'

Prayers are always a chance to have a good look around. This lot meant it all right, some of their heads bowed so deep, their chins nearly came out the other side. I couldn't see my favourite living rock star anywhere. Maybe he was backstage. No sign of Helen either.

The preacher looked up. A light show twizzled around him as he knocked on his microphone.

'When opportunity knocks,' he murmured, 'what you gonna do? Opportunity is knocking at your door tonight, people. You gonna complain about the noise?'

Already I was biting my cheek to fight the annoyance building in my chest. I'd heard all this so often in my mother's church. Any minute now he'd say that thing about when life hands you a lemon . . .

'And when life hands you a lemon,' his voice was rising in crescendo, 'what you going to *do*, people?'

You'd think they were kids at a birthday party, the way they all bayed: 'Make lemonade!'

Shane's spotlight shrank to become a dot on the dreaded over-head screen. Where I saw a version of a Sword single. The one that goes:

Being a rocker's fantastic, our rock is so pure.
We are all rockers, of that we are sure.

OK, it's not worthy of Dylan, I grant you – neither Bob nor Thomas – but in the right crowd with ten pints inside you, bloody fantastic, mate. What do you think their Omegist version was like, with a light dot bouncing along the syllables? My sensibilities are still jangling:

Being a Christian is brilliant, our love is so pure.
We are all angels, of that we are sure.
In a crowded tube
Full of heathens, all lost,
I know you're another Christian,
All the others are dust.
We're saved and we're loved and we aren't going to die,
There's a beautiful place for us up in the sky.

Rock atrocity. Gavin rock god Whitehead had better atone. I couldn't wait to tell Helen and share a laugh about it.

The saddest thing was that by the time they were singing 'There's a beautiful place for us up in the sky' for the fourteenth time, swaying in time with palms up in the air, I was – yes, I have to confess this – I was swaying too.

The music clanged to a standstill and Shane simpered into his mike:

'People . . . listen up now, people, we have a special guest here tonight.' Whitehead dared to show his face after that lot?

'I want to introduce somebody who's soon going to join our Faith Team. Put your hands together for – ' he reached toward the wings where a spotlight found her – 'The Reverend. Helen. Halberd!'

I clapped too loudly as she walked on stage with a smile of complete embarrassment. She had dressed the part in trainers, close-fitting jeans and a loose, open-necked pink shirt. She could have fitted in here with us cons actually.

The applause stuttered to a stop. Shane took a minute to place her so that we all still had an excellent view of him. Then he leaned close to share a little of his spotlight, as if any minute they'd be crooning 'True Love'.

'Wasn't the singing lovely, Helen?'

Helen's eyebrows shot up to her hairline.

'I've never been a fan of Westlife actually.'

Shane backed away a fraction.

'That song, you've reminded me, let's just give a great big thank you to our good friend Gavin Whitehead . . .'

His picture came up on the screen: hair tied back, loose kaftan, azure pool behind him, not here with us after all. Bastard. Shane took his microphone and strutted off to the centre of the stage: 'Helen's here to help us, people, you're looking forward to that, aren't you, Helen? Helen's going to help us bring the light of Christ into a dark, dark world.'

Helen chased after him and said something but as Shane and the mike were centre stage, we didn't hear. He stood, arms folded, waiting for her to join him.

'What was that, Helen?'

Helen whipped the mike off him: 'I said, they're nice sunglasses, Shane, did you get them in the Seychelles?'

Shane's hand rose to his Mafia specs. A skinny blonde girl ran on with an extra mike.

'Sure did,' Shane said, 'you know, people, last time I was there, I was just having a quick burger when a woman asked me if Jesus Christ was my personal Saviour. I said I was proud to say that he was!' When the cheering subsided he went on: 'And as we talked and exchanged testimonies, well, you know what I mean, people, when I say the Lord touched her – '

Helen cut in: 'You mean *you* touched her?'

'Couldn't stop the power of the Lord, people! That woman crawled on her hands and *knees* to share Jesus with her family!'

Helen's voice broke through the cheering: 'You had her crawling through the litter on the burger bar floor?'

'And before you could say fries, her family hit the floor too!'

'Why would the Lord,' Helen had to shout, 'Shane! Why would God want them lying on the floor of a burger joint?'

'These people were lucky, Helen. It doesn't always come so quick, some people have to get blessed many times before it's the Lord's will for them to fall. So don't you be afraid, Helen Halberd! We want the Lord to bless you too, don't we, people! With you we are going to *persevere*!'

Helen blinked into the spotlights, considering this remark. Shane strode across her: 'Our badged helpers here, people, they are going to come round and touch each and every one of you with the love of the Lord. And while your hearts open up and obey the Lord in joyous . . . sacred . . . purity, let us sing a new song.'

Some short-haired teens appeared behind him, wearing crosses over their 'FOR CHRIST'S SAKE, ROCK!' T-shirts, and bashed out a few shy chords.

'Another song penned for us, people, by our good friend, Gavin Whitehead!' Shane dangled his hands to his knees like a chimp, then reached high and punched the air.

'*The name is CHRIST!*' he went.

He crouched and punched again: '*The name is CHRIST! The name is CHRIST . . . JESUS!!*'

The chorus took off through the crowds and over all the stamping and applause Shane favoured us with a verse:

He knocked on my door
He said I see you is poor,
I said, Get out, man, you see all my stuff?
Got my iPod, my trainers, my home entertainers?
He said Sure, kid, you got it real tough.
Your cupboard is full but your soul is bare!
You haven't a clue what you're doing or where!
Open your heart to me, man, I'm your dad up in heaven,
Got a place for you, son, open 24/7.

'*The name is CHRIST!*' they all bellowed, '*The name is CHRIST!*

The name is CHRIST . . . JESUS!!'

As the ushers moved among us, people began to drop. Women tended to fold discreetly with their floral skirts tucked around their bottoms. The men tended to be more flamboyant, crashing down like trees. In front of me a man in a pin-striped suit dropped carefully on to his wrists and knees and writhed on the floor giggling. Somewhere behind me I could hear sobbing, gut-wrenching, inconsolable, on and on, why the fuck did nobody comfort that person? I felt that stomach pain you get when you're stuck in the bus near a crying baby and nobody's doing anything about it and it would be rude to say something so you don't, but every note is skewering your guts.

That's when I realised that the more people fell, the more obviously I was standing there resistant. A female wrestler type, fortyish, had been watching me with her meaty arms folded, giving me the evil eye when I didn't sing. Shane put two fingers in his mouth, whistled, and she waddled up onstage, shining her palms at Helen's ribs like a sun lamp. Shane closed on Helen from behind. Helen said later she was praying for the Lord to tell her which one of them she should punch first. A woman beside me gave a shriek, more a beep really like an answerphone, and somebody lolloped down the aisle just in time to help her slump between his sandaled feet.

I looked back up at Helen just in time to see the wrestler put her in an armlock and try to crumple her to the floor. Shane stood by with his eyes closed, whispering to the microphone: 'Don't resist, Helen, let the Lord do his work.'

I was up. I was running. I was on that stage head down, ready to butt him in the chest. I say I was ready: my spirit was willing but years of smoking had left my flesh pathetically weak and by the time I reached the top of the stairs to the stage, my knees were buckling. Helen smiled as soon as she saw me.

'Patrick! What are you doing here?'

She told Shane I was a journalist, he should be warned. Shane bellied me off him no trouble. His voice boomed down the hall: 'Patrick! Welcome! I see you're here to let the Lord into your heart.'

'No, I'm not!'

'The Lord is knocking on your door, Patrick. Come, your Saviour wants you up here to become a Christian, he is begging you right here and right now to know the power of the Lord.'

The stage filled with the ugliest crowd you've ever seen outside a Cabinet meeting, shuffling toward me, some crawling on all fours, all repeating one word, 'Patrick'. They clasped my legs, tugged my clothes. Somebody was breathing damply on my neck. Hands were on my shoulders pushing me down. I was dying to yell my head off in blind, piss-scented terror but Helen was there. I had to be a hero. How?

I caught sight of Shane smirking at me through the crowd.

'Wanker!' I shouted. It made sense at the time.

He tilted his head as if I'd called his name, then pushed through and placed his mouth close to my ear, as big as a sink-plunger.

'What's the difference between a wanker and a journalist?' he hissed, 'Hm? At least a wanker knows what he's doing.'

Before I could think, my right fist rose up through the multitude. It happened to catch the elbow of the person who was interfering with my shoulders, who involuntarily punched the wrestler woman whose head shot forward and nutted Shane who fell backwards on his arse.

Result! I wish I could say that he dropped like a stone, slain, but the Lord must have been busy elsewhere. The crowd was surrounding me, chanting, praying. Somebody was bumping against my backside. Where was Helen? Had she gone down? Was she being trampled to death?

'Helen! Helen?!'

A bizarre noise seeped almost imperceptibly through the insanity, bizarre precisely because it was normal. It was the sound of a sane, non-hysterical, familiar female voice.

'Faint, Patrick.'

I turned. She was beside me.

'Are you fainting, Helen?'

'No, you. Faint and I'll catch you.'

Her smile creased her eyes in the most delicious way. Slowly, so as not to hurt anything, I leaned into her scented cleavage and collapsed. She knelt beside me smoothing my brow. If I'd had the sense to wear a proper shirt she would probably have undone some buttons. I closed my eyes for a moment while she took my pulse. Then she yelled: 'Needs a doctor! Coming through!'

She hauled me up and we pushed together through the crowd and through the swing doors and down the fire escape stairs, a million of them, and ran out through the marble atrium until fresh air smashed us in the face.

'Don't stop!' Helen yelled. She looked back at me, still running: 'Come on! Run!' She put on a turn of speed and I watched the pumping globes of her arse reach the DLR station before me. I can still hear her, smell her leaning against the wall, panting, laughing as I caught up and held her face in my hands. No, I didn't touch her actually, that's just the way I wish it had been. In fact, I was gasping with my hands on my knees, dying to spit.

'I thought I was going to die,' I coughed.

'So did I,' she grinned. 'Oh, Patrick, I'm so glad you were there.

You saved me! I'd never have got out of there without you! How can I ever thank you enough?'

I could think of one or two ways actually. Several, in fact. She named one of them.

'Come on,' she linked her arm through mine, 'let me buy you a drink.'

The light railway took us like a fairground ride through the skyscraper toyland of the Isle of Dogs. Helen stood all the way to Lewisham staring at her shoes. While the train took us under the river, I had a chance to study the reflection of her face in the windows. She was so closed in on herself that I thought maybe I should disappear quietly after I'd seen her safely home.

The doors opened on to Lewisham station and we were up those escalators two steps at a time, out past the taxis and the bus station when I realised she was going to be true to her word. We turned into the first pub we saw.

The door was worn by decades of shouldering by bastards too drunk or idle to use the handle. I held it open and followed her into the familiar, acrid fug of people who had homes to go to but no wish to be anywhere near them. Some of the clientele seemed to have gone to considerable lengths to lose the sight of one eye so they could focus better on the dartboard. Why their teeth had gone missing was harder to guess. Maybe it had something to do with years of sucking down stout that looked like school gravy.

Helen strode up to the skinny East European girl behind the bar and asked if the owner was about. He bustled out from behind the bar and gave Helen a bristly hug.

'The usual?' he bellowed over canned pop music.

'Please,' she mimed back and introduced me.

He leered at me: 'You priests. Get it where you can, that what I say. What you like to drink, young man?'

I gaped. I hadn't a clue. What was happening to me? I was being offered a drink and I still couldn't speak. Had Shane cursed me or something?

'He'll have the same,' Helen yelled and the owner explained to the barmaid that Helen was 'very important lady, she like this kinda Irish whiskey, vairy large, three measures for price two. And for him. OK.'

'Thank you, Luigi, I like it to hurt when I feel like this. With tap water please, no fizz, no ice and – '

' – and no black straw,' he cut in, 'vairy important no straw.'

'Straws are for children and animals, aren't they, Luigi?'

'Children and animals.'

I parked one foot on the brass foot-rail. Why is it easier to drink with one foot higher than the other? Preparation for the honky tonk stagger home?

'Feel like what?' I asked. She had to bend deliciously close to hear me. 'You said you like it to hurt when you feel like this?'

'Oh! It's just. I'll probably get the sack tomorrow,' she laughed. I laughed back, too loud, not sure why. I was watching the way her tongue stopped on her lower teeth sometimes and the way she held the whiskey in her mouth for a second or two before she swallowed. She ordered two more.

'Why will you get the sack?'

'Well,' she bent so close I could see the central join of white bra inside her pink shirt. I suddenly felt immeasurably tired and wanted to lean there.

'I've made two terrible mistakes tonight,' she said hotly in my ear.

'That fucker Shane had it coming,' I shouted back.

'Not just that,' she laughed back. 'I did it in front of you.'

She gave me a look from under her eyebrows as if I were a puppy who'd shat in her slipper. I was desolate.

'Look, this racket is doing my head in,' she said, 'Beer garden?'

Garden was far too grand a word, it was a small back yard crammed with sticky tables covered in tin ashtrays the size of plates.

After the din in the pub, the background hubbub of trains and sirens felt close to silence. We had this Eden to ourselves. Helen's stare made blood rush to my face.

'So what are you going to write, about today?'

I squirmed, shoulders hunched. I longed for a cigarette too. Nicotine might help me think straight. She slid them across the table.

'The truth?' I said.

She rolled her empty glass between her fingers. 'I've got a date with my bishop tomorrow. Do you know how that feels?'

'Like seeing the headmaster?'

'Worse. It's not the first time either.'

'What was the last one about?'

She stretched out every consonant: 'Blasphemy.'

'Because of your book?'

She laughed: 'You know, Jewish scholars were crowding the internet, queuing up to lament my pitiful grasp of haggadic midrash but the Anglicans? I still can't believe they took it so seriously. Anyway, tomorrow at two thirty I will be in the bishop's palace. Again. He doesn't like the Omegists any more than I do but we have to be seen to "embrace" them.'

'And you've fucked up?'

'The very word, Patrick. Though it's not what the bishop'll say. He'll stroke his beard and wipe his specs with his cashmere jumper and he'll explain kindly – because he's a kind man – he'll explain that what I did tonight won't solve anything. And he'll be right. He, we mustn't – ' she stirred the air with her hand, 'what am I trying to say? The trouble is we can't, you know, nobody can be seen to criticise anybody else's beliefs. You won't tell anybody I said this, will you? Please? It's just . . . it depresses me so much.'

'What?'

'I'm trying hard *not* to say that they make me incredibly angry.'

'The Omegists?'

'Yes. There are probably as many ways to believe in God as there are people in the world, aren't there? We're not all the same. So why should we all buy into the Omegists' medieval little world on their terms? But it's their sort of church that's taken to be the right one, the only one. By so many people. By people like you.'

'Me?'

'Journalists. I'm sorry, I shouldn't rant like this.'

I was afraid she would stop. She didn't.

'You know they're using Gavin Whitehead to get at the government?'

'The rock singer?'

'He lends his revoltingly large yachts to cabinet ministers. And his spread in the Maldives.'

'Aren't all politicians corrupt? In the job description?'

'And the Archbishop of Canterbury dines with the Prime Minister, and quite right too. But churches like Shane's are very rich, and they're growing. You've seen what's happening in the States. Soon those churches could hold the voting balance in this country as well.'

'Helen.'

'Yes?'

'You're drunk.'

'Not drunk enough. Your round. No straw please.'

Everything was funny after that and got funnier the more drinks we put away. I told her about my mother getting her stained glass specs from Chanel and she told me about the time she was flying to some conference in her dog collar and the turbulence got terrible and the steward asked her to have a word with God about it and she said 'Sorry, I'm in sales, not management'.

'Old joke,' she smiled, and as we came out of the pub she hooked her arm into mine as if we were best friends. We walked together up towards Blackheath under a wide, indigo sky. What a beautiful word sky was, I thought, and I felt with the motion of her body close to me, that everything in the world was comfortable, balanced, and everything belonged.

'You don't see, do you?' she said quietly as we came up to a clearing bound by seriously wealthy houses. 'Blasphemy's nothing.'

'In your book, you mean?'

'Stop a minute. Look at me, Patrick. D'you know why I've got to see my bishop tomorrow? It's you. It's thanks to you I'm accused of the big one.'

'What's that?'

She looked shy for a moment, almost young. Then one syllable came out of her mouth like an unexploded bomb.

'Sex.' That word. 'You've accused me of an affair with a married man. A married priest. And I'm the Whore of the Anti-Christ, you know' – her crow's feet were crinkling again – 'nobody's safe around me.'

This was the most flirtatious she'd been so far. I was about to step up and surround her with my love right there among the Blackheath gorse bushes when her face shadowed and she folded away into herself again. Disgust soaked her voice.

'You made those allegations.'

'About Sarbridge?'

'Yes. Out loud and in print, and to a bishop, that's what really matters. You've dumped me in it. You really have.'

I thought I'd done a good job with that article for *The Truth* actually, I really did. I'd even accepted most of her suggestions. I'd had my agenda, yes – to prove that she and Sutherland had been at it – but there'd been evidence. Hadn't there? Some?

She breathed. Sighed. It could have been a sob. I realised for the first time how much damage my words had done.

Suddenly she marched past the willow trees and the pond to where the Heath opens out. I chased after her.

'Helen, I'm sorry, what can I do? Can I talk to your bishop? Can I explain? Please, I'll do anything.'

She turned: 'Just be careful. That's all I ask. Think what you write this time. Please. For my sake.' She turned and scanned the Heath. 'I do care about my job, you know.' Then as if it were all the same thought, she went on: 'Just look at this view. Isn't it amazing?'

Herringbone clouds streaked down towards jewelled horizons in every direction.

'You don't get stars much in London,' she said, 'but they're doing their best tonight.'

I pointed at a pin-prick of light over Canary Wharf Tower.

'Look,' I said. 'The Star of the East.'

She laughed as if I'd said something fantastically clever: 'I think you'll find that's north, Patrick. And it's a plane, look.'

We watched it grow, develop red and green wing-lights and bank away left to Heathrow.

'I love a dark night,' she murmured. 'We should have church services at night in the open like this. Maybe I'll suggest it to the bishop tomorrow.' She sucked her teeth. 'After I've resigned.'

'You won't do that.'

'I might have to.'

'You love being a priest.'

'But does being a priest love me?' She sighed.

Everything in my life had been churning and frayed until that evening alone with her. I'd watched her drink and smoke in the pub and felt that this might be a bit like living with her, being able to be with her every day. But those sighs of hers cut into me. I had to help her.

'I was ordained because of a dark night, Patrick,' she was saying, 'Dark night of the soul. After my car accident.' She closed her eyes briefly.

'Were you saved, Helen?'

She snorted: 'I hate the way they've stolen that word. I read somewhere that the Hebrew word for saved just means to be able to breathe freely. No, I don't think it's for us to turn God on and off at the flick of a switch. We're all precious and loved, Patrick. We all matter to God all the time. Us. The real, flawed, marvellous individuals we are. That's what I think. And the church has very little to do with it if you ask me. See that star there, Patrick? Over the church?'

Her church was gleaming in the distance, floodlit and elegant, and above it like a prop in a Nativity play was a white star.

'Is that a star or a plane, what do you think, Patrick?'

'I, I don't – '

'Quick, decide now. You never know, you might be right. Pretend I'm Shane and I'm asking you to be born again, just do it!'

I should have told her I'd been born again before and was quite happy to be dead again, thank you. But Helen wanted to me to do something for her and it gave me nothing but pleasure to be at her side and obey.

'Star,' I said, 'it's a star, we're looking at the most beautiful star.'
She pushed my arm playfully.

'You did it. You decided. You opted in. That's all we can ever do,
I think. Opt in. That's when the work starts.'

'What work?'

'Oh, trying to understand it all. Uh oh, look, your star's just
turned for Gatwick.'

'I need more faith,' I cried. 'Shane! Where are you when I need
you? Shane's star wouldn't have turned into a plane, would it?'

'Faith can't change facts,' she beamed, 'and that's the truth.
So . . .'

Drizzle sparked on me as she looked me square in the face.

'So, what are you going to write about the Omegists, Patrick?'

In my pocket I felt my copy of my Truth article about her and
Sarbridge. It was folded, as manky as a beer mat and frayed with
being carried about so long. I don't know why but I unfolded it and
offered it to her. A drip of rain fell on to my byline.

She took the clipping and stared. Not at the words (my words,
most of them) but at the largish photograph of Sarbridge. He was
rushing out of some back door years ago, grainy, worried, trying to
hide his face in his overcoat. A shiver brushed across what I could
see of her face, no more than a flicker, and she thinned her lips.

It had been such a happy evening of giggles and silly flirting and
Helen ranging from beautiful to breathtakingly gorgeous. There in
the rain, with Blackheath gaping around us and her wet face shining
in the street lamps, she was reminded of Sarbridge. I noticed for the
first time wrinkles like little rivulets along her upper lip. Our
breathing synchronised. A need fell on me, so urgent it squeezed my
breath from me like a punch, a need to comfort her with a kiss.

It was the kiss I was born for, the kiss of my life.

That kiss, that most glancing and most profound of contacts had me walking on sparkles, kind to the world, for three whole days. I couldn't write up the Omegists. I couldn't write anything except poems. To her. (Don't worry, I'll spare you. I couldn't even turn them round and apply them to you, most being endless puns on her name, Helen High-water, Helen Earth, that sort of thing. If she'd been called Helfer, I could have gone a long way with Helfer Leather.)

I tried to deliver one once. I wanted to hand it to her personally and got as far as sitting behind a bush in her front garden watching the vicar's wife put out the rubbish. With rain rolling down the back of my neck, I thought of the shy way Helen had pulled clear of our kiss, that smile as she'd pushed me away and hurried, wiping her mouth under that huge sky, all the way back to the vicarage.

I followed her back, you see, to make sure she was safe. But something in the angle of her shoulders kept me at a distance. Who says I'm not sensitive?

Every second of every day I did nothing but need her, write for her and think of her needs. But she refused to answer my phone calls and emails. In the end I had no alternative, I had to go to her church. It was the only way we could be under the same roof.

People give you funny looks if you're going into church. It's true. As I walked under the trees to Helen's church even the Special Brew Crew dodged my eye in case I came near them.

I tiptoed into the arched porch. That scent of church reached me before I even opened the door: furniture polish and sanctimony.

I pushed the door open, locked eyes with somebody very old and let the door clang shut again. I stood there breathing fast. Why was

I there? To see Helen. Would I see Helen standing out there in the cold? No. I had to go in. I had to.

The somebody inside the door introduced himself as Arnold and offered me a pile of reading material with a nice smile. I sat down at the back, a long way from anybody else. It wasn't difficult to find a spot on my own, there were only about six of us there, and I'd slashed the average age by half.

A sweet voice was reading at the altar: 'Speak the word only, and my soul shall be healed.' Helen's voice. She was still there. She hadn't lost her new Chelsea job as she thought she might. I'd written to her bishop as I promised, and wrote to Sarbridge's too actually, at her suggestion, and a few days later I had nice acknowledgements from the two nice bishops' chaplains and a postcard from Sarbridge. It had that chocolate monkey on it and 'Father, forgive them for they know not what they do.' Her bishop had cunningly extended her notice period in Blackheath and advised them all to pray harder. So I had got Helen off the hook. The trouble was, I'd got that bastard Sarbridge off it as well.

Many times after that, I heard her say those words: 'Speak the word only, and thy soul shall be healed.' She used to say it as if she was thinking of nobody but me but she never once looked at me. Not when I crashed in late and everybody else looked up from their prayers and glared at me. Not when I hung around at the end, the last one of the congregation left in the church, and she was so busy trying to lock up that the church warden had to show me out. Not even while she was giving me communion, placing that little cube of bread on my tongue, bread broken by her fingers, blessed by her voice. I used to hold it in my mouth, my most intimate place, willing it not to dissolve. Closing my eyes tighter and tighter to try and preserve the moment of our contact, the blessing of our love, trying to keep her with me and in me forever. Sometimes as I lie here in my cell I imagine that bread melting on my tongue, given to me by

Kate Winslet, lovely Kate, is holding my head in her hands and breathing 'we'll pray for you' in my ear. One fragrant breast, her left one I think, is damn nearly poking me in my eye and I am becoming aware of other people around us panting, ha ha ha ha. I feel no pain. I should but I don't, I feel nothing but holiness. How I know it's holiness, I can't say but in this dream it's as obvious as knowing, say, that your Mark's a total wanker. Here it comes, Kate says, it's coming, coming now. I swear I feel something struggle and push and fly up out of my head.

'Here it comes.'

'Good boy.'

'Got it? Got the tongs?'

'Yeah, I got it. Wow, it's a big one. That's it, put it down just there. No, to me a bit, there, brilliant.'

As the evil leaves me, all the evil of my life, cheers ring in my brain and I sink away from Kate and ease down to the floor.

'Do there, you reckon?'

'No, shove it a foot more this way, tight into the corner. Don't drop it on your . . .'

'Aow!'

'Shuddup for fuck's sake, you wakened him.'

'Who gives a Donald? Got the keys?'

'What, you lost yours?'

'Just testing. Come on.'

Two screws have just been in my room. Two screws. I can still smell the bacon off them. What were those toe-rags doing in here at 4.55 in the morning? They've left something by the window. Metal, upright, on little wheels.

How kind. They've brought me a spare bed.

HMP GREYMOOR

Julia, my darling, my dearest love,

I need you, Joo. Help me. Please, you've got to get yourself here right now. Here's another Visitor's Order. All you have to do is ring the prison, hold for an hour listening to Celine Dion, tell six different people you want a visit and get cut off each time before you get to mention my name. But you know all that, you came before, thank you, thank you, please come again, I beg you. I mean it. I *need* you, Julia. You've got to drop everything and come. If you don't, I'll die.

Yours until hell freezes, no, don't mention hell. I love you.
Patrick

HMP GREYMOOR

Dearest Julia,

I sent you a rather hysterical letter yesterday. I expect you opened it and decided not to read past the first line. Please accept my apologies but please, I would be very grateful if you could contact me as soon as you can spare a moment. I know you're busy but this is urgent.

All my love,
Patrick

HMP GREYMOOR

Darling Julia,

I've been stabbed *and* I'm in solitary confinement under EC Directive ALLCONSRTOSSRS/2009.

It's all a misunderstanding of course. What worries me most is that if they've put fighting on my tab, I could be stuck here in the block for weeks. You can help me, Julia. Only you. Come and see me again. PLEASE. You don't have to be nice or talk much, just come and plead my case. If you don't, I'll die. Picture me all on my own in this white-tiled cell with its white bedcover and white net curtain at the white-smoked window. Even my face is as pale as death. If I don't go mad, I'll go snow-blind.

I love you. You know I do.
Patrick

HMP GREYMOOR

Julia, my dearest love,

I got up to pee last night and the pain of putting my foot down on the floor made me so faint, I had to lie down for half an hour. Why does it feel as though a thistle has been sewn into my leg? Why did I have to have three agonising injections to 'kill the pain' before I was stitched? Amnesty International should be told. Would you come if I wrote in my own blood?

Now Julia, I'm appealing to your taste for injustice. Show you the motorway protester forced to eat a beef sausage in the nick or a terrorist who needs his mum and there's no stopping you. I do assure you that my being here in solitary is the greatest miscarriage of justice since the crucifixion.

I was sitting in my own room, writing a letter to you actually, when Kitten, the behemoth who got carted off by the police from that pub fight, walked straight in and tried to steal it. Why? Don't ask me. Anyway I fought back and we ended up on the floor wrestling head to toe like a couple of conger eels trying for a casual shag in a whirlpool. You know that slo-mo, all too fast, deep sea feeling when you're in a fight? Probably not. It wasn't funny or brave or perfectly timed like in a film, it was hot and clumsy and extremely nasty. I grabbed his ankles. His Doc Martens kept coming at my face and I hoped my trainers were doing something similarly terrifying to him. I know you don't like this sort of thing but I assure you on this occasion it was necessary. And of course I was screaming my head off like a girl the whole time.

He had a Stanley knife and I didn't, so now I have three stitches in my left calf and it hurts like hell. I want to cry far more than a grown hero really should, but the worst thing of all is being in solitary. I know he's here somewhere too. I can hear him howling. Especially at night. I know it's him because his voice is high-pitched and he keeps wailing for his mum. Nothing to do with me sadly, it all happened too fast for me to hurt him back properly.

My three stitches look like spiders trying to march up the back of my leg. They're very tight. Every time I bend down to do my laces or even put my heel on the floor properly, they hurt and seep. Why not come and see for yourself? I won't charge you for the pleasure of seeing me in pain. Please, darling. If you ever loved me . . .

Your adoring Patrick

HMP GREYMOOR

Dear Dr Julia Bailey,
A screw whispered through the hatch today that I could be out of seg tomorrow. I feel so tired. I never sleep. I just lie around picking at my scabs.

I tried to kill myself last night. I held my breath. It didn't work of course and now I have this awful ringing in my left ear.

Please come. I love you.
Patrick.

HMP GREYMOOR

To Whom It May Concern,
I didn't get out yesterday after all. Maybe today.

My other ear is ringing now too. God, I feel tired. They warned me on the hospital wing that solitary does that. It's the worst thing. I've been in here 12 days and I'm like a wet plastic bag. I can hardly
Who gives a

The trouble with the block – sorry, 'care and segregation' – is there's nothing to do but feel sorry for yourself. That's what Pam says. She's a jaunty female screw with an arse like the Dartford Bridge: great view and available to anybody with a set of wheels. Or so they say. She's been nothing but nice to me.

Kitten and his gang were on the table footie in the lobby as Pam and I came through. There was a lot of jeering about how I'd be all right as long as I had Mummy to look after me. They meant Pam. My real mother is too tied up with her Christian activities to visit her son in prison.

We stopped outside my old cell. She opened the flap, took a look inside and freed up her keys. Back in the same cell? Such continuity, I said, like the kind of high-class hotel that this state of the art prison was designed to emulate. Each neat, clean room was to contain one man alone, like a Holiday Inn. One man alone with his conscience.

I'm sharing. With Magic Marcus, the Number One Governor's most subtle torment so far. He describes himself as an urban sorcerer and purveyor of inscrutable New Age wisdom. Why does New Age afflict so many people in old age? Pam didn't say. She just opened the door, muttered an ugly four letter word – 'Cuts' – and there he was, on *my* bed in the lotus position, dressed in nothing but a Gandhi nappy and an unnatural amount of body hair.

He held out his furry hand as if he expected me to kiss it.

'A little meditation soothes the savage breast,' he said.

I was about to say, it's better than sitting around doing nothing, but fights come out of the air here, so I spoke gently: 'You're on my bed.'

'*My* bed, old man. I've checked them both though. Must be the only clear ones in the place.'

'What do you mean, clear?'

'Listening devices, old man. Bugs.' He dismissed me with closed eyes, 'Now if you don't mind . . .'

Before I knew what I was saying, I was coming on all hard, and me as hard as cream cheese.

'I've just come out of the block,' I said, 'but before I was in *the block* that bed, that one under your arse there, was mine.'

Eyes still closed, he whispered: 'I killed a man once. Twice would be easy.' Then he blessed me like a bishop and offered to read my palm.

Now, for two weeks I hadn't seen a kindly face until Pam took me under her wing. My most intimate contact for six months had been the strip search on arrival, occasional bouts of defensive violence and being stitched over-emphatically in medical wing. I plead all this by way of excuse because Marcus' hands, office-soft around mine, took me straight back to the moment Helen's hand cupped mine on the night she died, while she tried to light my cigarette.

Helen. Still alive then.

No tears. I refused to cry in front of Marcus.

'You could do with a bit of luck,' he said, bolt upright on my bed. News to me, I snapped and whipped my hand away. He sprang off the bed and took it back, careful not to let me get closer to the bed than him.

'You won't die here, you know,' he said – well, that's useful to know – 'but you'll be here a while yet. There's a woman who loves you. But she won't do you any good.'

Hardly unique.

'There's more,' he was rubbing his thumb over the middle of my palm as if he was trying to smooth out the small print, 'but I can't quite . . . there's a man. A dangerous man. Very dangerous indeed.

Letters E and I in his name, I'd watch out for him. Oh and you'll live a long time. Your lifeline's a long one.'

Letters E and I in his name. It was pretty obvious who that was. Kitten.

It's not just the shavings round the sink like nasty little insects out to get me. (How can a man with a beard produce so many shavings?) It's not even the way he shakes his trouser leg every time he farts or goes Slurp slurp aaaah every time he drinks his coffee.

It's the mumbling. He's doing it now, to his Tarot cards. He does his cards thirteen times a day and every time they tell him the same thing: he'll be out of here soon. He tucks them away, tap on the top, tap tap on the bottom of the deck, tap on this side, tap tap on that, before they're folded into their special black silk scarf, mumble mumble, all pleased with himself, then he starts all over again.

He does my Tarot too, by proxy, reading my aura or something. Fucking insolence. But I forgive him.

Kitten came in yesterday, all seventeen stone of him. He growled like a Doberman imitating the lower register of the organ at the Albert Hall, grabbed my feet and upended me, presumably for the fun of seeing whether my eyes or my teeth would fall out first. Marcus looked up from his tarot cards: 'This looks like yours, Kitten. This spread. It says you're a sweet person at heart.'

I could feel bones in my ankles crunching.

'What you're looking for is a creative outlet,' Marcus was saying, 'you're actually a pretty talented guy.'

Kitten let me drop and turned like one of those articulated buses that needs four lanes and all the time in the world, and anybody who thinks they're in a hurry can go fuck.

Kitten walked to Marcus' table, his thighs so over-developed that his feet stood a metre and a half apart, and bent his cauliflower head to receive Marcus' wisdom. Fifteen minutes later he strolled out of the cell purring.

Marcus even had the cheek to charge him ten Rothmans.

And I am still alive.

Ever since then I have been making Marcus' coffee, rolling his fags and doing his ironing. He's just summoned me to pull his trainers off for him.

'How did you get on in solitary?' he asked.

'Survived. Why?'

He folded his arms and breathed at the ceiling: 'The fourth day's the wall, isn't it? First three days you're all alone, going mental, then the fourth comes and on the fourth you begin to like it. By the eighth or ninth, you're flying. Then your problem's not the loneliness, it's re-entry.'

'What's re-entry?'

'Coming back among people. That's why I was careful round you the first week, not to get on your nerves.'

Was he indeed.

'Did you like commune with your gods at all?'

I said I never stopped feeling abandoned by the world and every damned thing in it, living or dead. And my gods or goddesses (if any, not admitted) didn't so much as breathe a word.

'Pity,' he said without a smile, 'mind you I've got an advantage. My dad used to lock me in our cellar. Weeks at a time. Kids these days just haven't got the skills.'

He started to pack away the cards.

'No hanged man?' I interrupted, 'Isn't there always a hanged man?'

'Don't be facetious, boy. And don't be in such a hurry to waste your life.' I pulled my hand away. What life?

'Well, if you're going to do it, do it right. You mess it up and you go on the 20-52s.'

'The what?'

'Dear oh dear. Suicide watch. They peep in at you every twenty minutes, make a little note, sleeping on his right side, sleeping on his left. Drives you up the fucking wall. And if you're on it, so am I. So get it fucking right! And cut out the hunger strike, that just attracts attention. Make a plan, and keep it quiet. That's your best bet. Have you got a plan?'

So I told him. My plan. That I thought I'd hold my breath. Marcus laughed until he coughed: 'You'll sooner wank yourself to death.'

Fuck. I thought I'd perfected the soundless toss-off.

'All right,' I shouted, 'all right, I'll hang myself with my trousers, just you wait!'

Somebody flickered at the peephole in the door. We froze. Can you get put on suicide watch just by talking about it?

No, we were to have the honour of a visit from the prison chaplain. Not the lager guy, he's resigned his job to spend more time with his AA group. They've replaced him with 'Hello boys, are we keeping our peckers up' and just call him Gerry.

Marcus punched him in the stomach and said something about how the church isn't paying him enough, there isn't an ounce on him. Gerry punched back, calling him an old scallywag.

'We were at Chesterfield together,' Gerry explained. 'Still got the old fractures to prove it, haven't we?'

Marcus straightened his left leg with a painful click.

'Yeah, he was the little weed at the front of the class while I was selling weed at the back.'

'Is that what you're in for, Marcus? Or is it the old trouble?'

Marcus flashed him a look like a cruise missile, then: 'Let me do you a reading, Gerry.'

'Ah no, Magic, that's the last thing I need.' Gerry's fingers crossed in the air in front of his frown and he said something about just being here to deliver a message but Marcus raised his hand for silence. Gerry submitted with relatively good grace as Marcus muttered about secrets revealed, a wise man who knows nothing – 'sure isn't that the clergy all over?' – and a feeling of having been passed over by those in charge. At this last one Gerry cleared his throat and stood up: 'It's not actually you I'm here to see, Marcus, it's your friend here. Are you Patrick Price-Johnson?'

I was. Gerry grinned: 'You've got a legal visit. She's in the office on the ones.'

She? A legal 'she' was here to see me? Julia! You were here at last! Were you wearing that navy pencil skirt of yours and the black shoes I hate and your hair all piled up in that tight but loose, sexy way and your briefcase flirtatiously open?

'Go on, quick. She'll be gone if you don't hurry.'

My footsteps squeaked fast along the corridor and down the metal steps. I was in heaven. Julia, my darling, my love, had come at last.

She could have been beautiful, with a soft-fur voice and serenity to calm a devil's soul. But she wasn't. She was a pig in a tan viscose suit and skin like prison-issue cream gloss paint. She leaned across the stained desk, stretching her hand to me – 'Allow me to introduce myself, Mr Price-Johnson' – over the handle of a plastic baby seat.

How could she be so cruel! She was here to see me and she wasn't Julia.

She scraped her hair back behind both ears, a twitch more than a necessity, like the constant shrugging of her shoulders and fiddling with a jacket button. She began to justify her presence:

'I know you didn't ask for a brief,'

'Nothing personal, I've got one already.'

'Says here you haven't.'

'I'm waiting for a friend to come.'

The baby began to grizzle. She scrolled up and down her laptop screen, rolling the baby bucket with one finger of the other hand. I could be ignored anywhere in this prison, I didn't have to take it from her. Besides, my stomach was rumbling. I turned to go.

'Is your friend qualified?' she called. 'You don't have to give details. I just have to know you're in safe hands.'

Safe hands.

'She's a law don at Cambridge.'

'Right. But does she know about court work?'

'I dare say she's better qualified than you. Where did you go to university?'

She tucked the hair behind both ears again: 'I've been at the bar eleven years. My record – '

'You've got a criminal record?'

'My success rate. Is as good as anybody's.'

It's not good briefs that win cases, though the briefs all think it is. It's police mistakes that lose them. You learn that in here. But I couldn't be bothered to argue the toss with her, I just said: 'I thought you'd be her actually. My girlfriend.' I made sure I caught her eye. 'Pretty poor exchange.'

'But I am the one who's here.' Each deadly syllable arrived in its own time, as if it could afford its very own taxi. Which it probably could. How dare she bring her ugly face in here to tell me I've got no hope. My heart's breaking and my world is imploding under the weight of my own uselessness and worst of all you Julia might never come.

I was reaching for the door handle when she hit below the belt.

'You might just tell me before I go why the victim had bruises all along her back, upper body and head?'

I turned and glared at her. She stretched wire spectacles around her face one leg at a time and read to me from a closely typed page:

'Contusions to the parietal and occipital bones. That's the skull. With subdural haematoma in six places, likely cause' – she looked up at me – 'blunt impact.'

Those two words sank to the pit of my guts and lay there.

'What's it to you?' I said.

'Second degree traumatic injury to soft tissues,' she said, 'along the back and upper body.' I closed my eyes and could see an avalanche of books. Too dreadful. I opened them again to see her eyes drilling me from under her bristly eyebrows, 'Ecchymosis, that's discoloration, Patrick, on wrists and inner thighs too. I'm talking about oblong bruises, the size of the pads of a man's fingers and thumbs. Those are later in time, though it's hard to say how much.' She sniffed. 'Perhaps you can tell me.'

I'd been trying to focus on the green panic button beyond her left shoulder, watching it shrink and grow as she spoke. If I concentrated on its centre hard enough, her words might not enter my brain. They might not take me back to the feel of Helen's wrist tendons under my thumb and the weight of the flesh on her thighs.

I made for the door, but the floor seemed to have become sticky and was rising up under me.

'Where are you going, Patrick?'

'Away.'

'Suits me.' She paused to do up the baby's jacket. 'Just tell me why your fingerprints were all over her books too? Why on the day of the murder you phoned your mother from the victim's home? Why you'd been stalking the victim for four months? People are going to testify, Patrick. Good people. Church-going people. In fact they're queuing up. And the best bit, I'm sure you're dying to know, is we've got advance disclosure of DNA evidence. Of some kind. No details yet.'

My DNA? Fuck! I must have left a million clues at her place. But didn't that prove that I was there legitimately, as Helen's friend?

Or could she mean Helen's DNA? Helen's blood? Oh my Helen, my love, your precious blood . . . I spread my hands and stared at them.

'Clean,' I murmured, 'clean.'

'Your DNA, Patrick,' her voice went on, 'your DNA on the dead woman's body. Juries don't tend to like that.' She mopped sick from the corner of the baby's mouth. 'So *now* will you think about having a proper defence?'

There was thunder in my head. I dropped my arms and squeezed my eyes tight shut. I could see it all again. Helen's red hair, her scent, her blood spreading, pouring, pooling.

'I am used to making bricks without straw, Patrick, everyone deserves a defence, but, ssssh baby, we'll go in a moment, darling – '

'*Kneel!*'

One syllable. Helen's voice, out of sight but as real to me as the spit on my lips. I couldn't help it, I kneeled.

'*Kneel. Help me.*' Helen's voice echoed around me: '*Love me please. Kneel.*'

My body folded until my nose flattened on the floor and my forehead came to rest. My outbreath resounded on the vinyl below me and I became all breath, all rhythm, all Helen's sweet voice rising higher, swirling, weeping, crying out until a single high note cut my brain, her cry as she fell, my cry for her and for myself, my cry for all the hopelessness in the world. I did not kill you, Helen, you know I didn't, you know I didn't!

The lawyer shook my shoulders, lightly at first, then as I resisted, more roughly. She was a big girl and before I knew it, I was splayed on my back on the floor. I clamped my arms and knees to my chest: for a second I was back with Seb's old game of cavalry charge where he used to sit on my chest and pump all the air out of me until I went limp. Instead I had a horror-show flash of the darkness up her skirt as she stepped across me to the green panic button. The klaxon roared and I heard staff padding fast up the corridor, eager to be first to get a boot in. The lawyer hooked the baby seat over her arm and the laptop over her shoulder, swung the door open and walked out.

Good. I was free of the cow.

I am more caged than ever.

'What ho, Rotto.' That's Marcus waking up. He's taken to calling me Rotto, short for erotomaniac. A screw told him I'm in for stalking and he keeps going on about how it's outrageous to cut costs by putting loonies in with the normal cons like him.

But am I really an erotomaniac? Am I really mad? Or did I just love her very much? All I ever did was love her. I still love her. Real love has no past tense.

It did cross my mind that I knew next to nothing about Helen. I read somewhere once that that's what being in love means, two people who hardly know each other. But I knew Helen well enough. I'd recorded her life and her thoughts on my machine. I'd read her book. Surely I knew more about her relationship with God than most people. I tried really hard to understand what she said about the midrash thing too and I think I succeeded. Probably more than Sarbridge did . . .

'Marcus? You know a lot, about religion and that?'

'I'm my own priest now, it's safer.'

'Know anything about midrash?'

He started affecting a heavy Fagin accent: 'You mean halakic or haggadic midrashim?'

'Wow! How'd you know that?'

'I used to belong to a Kaballah sect in Westbourne Grove. God's way of telling stars they got too much money. You know Stairlift, don't you?'

Stairlift? His granny's indoor ski lift? What was his drug-addled brain on about now? His aura told me not to tangle with him so I watched quietly as he pulled himself into the lotus position on his bunk with his beard down to his crotch and said: 'Let me midrash Stairlift for you.' He launched into a basso profundo chant: 'The mama who knows . . . sure isn't she the Holy Mother of God who know us all like her very own children?'

One eye opened. He fixed me with it.

'And the stairlift in heaven,' his beard quivered sinisterly at every vowel, 'that's Jacob's ladder connecting heaven and earth. And who goes freely between heaven and earth on that ladder? Angels. So this lady is an angel. That's why she gets what she come for.'

'Fuck me,' I breathed.

'Not very biblical, Patrick. Oo-oo-ooo, ooooo-oooooo,' he sang, or tried to, 'that's to remind us of Jesus in his blessed agony on the cross.'

He leant briefly to scratch his backside: 'Want some more?'

I laughed, which set off his bass chant again: 'There's a sign on the wall – that's the moving finger writing on the wall at Balshazzar's feast, and what did the finger write? That we would be weighed in the balance and found wanting. Which we do not exactly need to be told here in Hell's deepest hole. All right there in that track.'

'Marcus, you're a genius.' So the greatest rock anthem of the Seventies was indeed midrash of one of humanity's most sacred texts. Which explains its enduring greatness.

What would he make of something by the Sword? I sang him their classic anthem Older Than Winter, which he didn't seem to recognise. Maybe he's been inside longer than I thought. By the second verse, he was shaking with the giggles and coughing down the hair on his chest.

Hear the call to be free, where there's spring in the trees
And the mushrooms are dancing for Jesus.

'No, no, stop,' he squeaked, 'mushrooms! Dancing!'

'OK, OK. So what's your midrash on that then?'

Marcus uncoiled his feet: 'That, my dear Patrick, is bollocks. And bollocks is bollocks whatever way you slice it. Now where's my breakfast!'

Marcus is not a happy man when he's hungry. He bellowed through the peephole in the door: 'Where's my breakfast! One more minute and that screw's dead meat!'

Those last words of his sliced me. Dead meat, he said, and dead meat she is. In my mind's eye she's here again. On my camp bed. Helen's body. Dead meat on the bed. She's been breathing, shallow flurries, irregular with long pauses in between, until the one that will be her last.

It gets you like that. You can be about to comment on the shouting outside or put on your shoe or think about reading the paper and you're right back there again. Dead meat.

The men have found the answer. That's what they say. They are all coming here tonight to talk about it and they want Martha and me to feed them again. Peter has given me a list of instructions, look. No need for chicken and olives this time, he says, we are to concentrate on the essentials: bread rolls and plenty of wine. That's Peter for you. He never was a fancy eater.

I'm so hot after all that baking, I'll go for a swim in a minute. Down to the pool shore. Martha won't mind if I go on my own. She trusts me now.

You see, after Jesus died, my sister Martha coped as she always does by keeping busy, until I found her shouting at our mule until her voice wore out and she sank into tears which went on for a week.

I fell silent from the start. I had nothing to say. God forsook me. So I forsook God in return. I went to the pool smiling to myself. My pain would be over soon.

I saw nobody for miles except some small boys chasing and fighting in the distance. The water was khaki and choppy. Criss-cross waves ran over my toes. A high wind whipped my calves. I was aware of an insane excitement as I tucked up my skirt and walked in.

Waves hit my chest. I didn't fight them, I let them pummel me, knock me to the seabed, drag me with their fists and beat me again. My skirt ballooned around me so I took it off. I would not need it any more. Water crashed into my ears like thunder, a sound just for me. I longed for it to bury me.

But there was a man on the shore I had not seen. He yelled and waded straight into the water. He lay me on the beach and, with his little boys all silent around us, he 'saved' me, mistaking my tears for gratitude. Like the Good Samaritan, he took me into his home and charged his wife to care for me as she cared for their sons. So, you could say that in my darkest heartbreak, Jesus was there with me. In a way. Never more than in the half-light of dawn when I most longed to die.

Then came the morning when through my closed eyelids before the dawn, a candle flame sought me, demanding that I wake. The good wife said, 'Come, Mary, it's time to get up now, there's work to be done.'

She dragged me from darkness and as we peeled vegetables together and scrubbed floors, she listened. Sometimes I hummed and sang and spoke to Jesus in my heart and while she listened, she taught me what I had learned. For since the churning of the pool waters, I had learned that my task was to help others out of darkness too. That if I nourish and love them, as Jesus bade me, they might grow to see how God loves us and sustains us whether we know it or not.

'Look at the table,' Jesus had told me, 'the beauty of it, Mary,' and he held my hands. I think of it today, as I always do, as I lay out Peter's bread and wine. But I've not finished. I am going to disobey him for once. Just a little. I don't think the heavens will crack open in horror. I have a bowl of my very best black olives here. I've grown them myself from seed, irrigated them every day throughout the heat and I've picked and washed and pitted them too. I'm going to put them on the table, in the place where Jesus used to eat.

There.

Perfect.

A week after the Omegists' meeting I was still dazed by that kiss of kisses when my phone rang. It wasn't Cyril for once, so I answered it.

'Hallo, hallo, can I speak to Mr Poison please?'

'Poison?'

'Are you Mr Poison, Peter Poison-Smythe?'

I knew who it was then. I said, 'No.'

It rang again.

'Hallo, hallo, is Mr Price-Joyson there please?'

'Price-Johnson. Speaking. Were you on the phone a minute ago?'

'Yeah, sorry, got the name wrong, dinna, it's Vanessa here from *The Truth*.'

'Hello, Venetia. Do I know you?'

'No, I'm new. Shelly says you're like doing us a piece about ah, the Omigodists and I've got to, like stick a few volts up your arse.'

'Ah . . .'

'You know, them religious nutters falling over?'

'Yes, I know, look, I'm sorry, I've been a bit pressed. What I mean is, I can't get these Omegists to sing and dance for me, I just don't see any mileage in it and I was about to call you actually, I wondered if you and the editor might consider looking at it another way. What about a piece on Great Women Priests Of Our Time? I could email you a few ideas tomorrow . . .'

'I'll ask.'

Several minutes of Vivaldi later, 'No, ta. Too boring. But listen, Patrick, you're the religious expert, ever heard of this geezer Neil Sarbridge?'

'I have indeed. Always on the radio and late night telly till you're sick of looking at him.'

'The editor says she's read somewhere he's a bit of a wick-dipper, know what I mean?'

'She may have read that in a piece I wrote for her . . .'

'Oh right. Look, she says it's time somebody done a number on him. Take him apart and spread him over the ropes a bit. No reputation to worry about and no money so you can say what you like. Does that sing and dance for you at all, Patrick? Mmmm?'

The lure of the front page. Of the second page. OK, of any damn page with my name on it. I know, Helen, I know I said I wouldn't do it again but I swear my motives were the best. Something did have to be done about Sarbridge – even you would agree with that surely – and that is why, my love, I wound up going to see Sarbridge's wife.

It was a smelly little terraced house on the other side of the A2, full of cats and washing and I got the distinct feeling that Mrs Sarbridge's relationship with the fat woman in the Bopeep smock was about more than aura compatibility.

That said, Sue Sarbridge was nice. Short hair, thick specs, soft mouth. Years of veganism had taken their toll. I expect you met her, Helen, yes, you must have done.

I was shown into a sitting room that looked like a jumble sale. I sat on the sofa and leapt up again. It wasn't manners, I thought I'd sat on the baby. It turned out to be a doll with a plastic head and a sinisterly floppy cotton body. Mrs S didn't laugh, though I did. She apologised: 'Agnes' was for PODS, her classes for the gynaecologically challenged. Was that tight arses, I asked. Total failure of smiles. No, she and her friend (she gave a simpering smile in the direction of Bopeep) ran 'birthing' classes for people having fertility treatment in the hope that it would advance the successful day.

She spent much of the next half hour telling me more than I could ever have hoped to know about her own five births. Having checked the sofa for cats' turds and other traps, I sat down and turned on my dictating machine. No point in dithering: 'When did you first realise your husband was being unfaithful?'

She straightened her specs with both hands and spoke slowly: 'There's a Browning poem, Mr Price-Johnson, which goes *Be a man and hold me in your arms; Be a god, enfold me with your charms.* I want you to understand that Neil was like a god to me.'

Fuck's sake.

'When did you get married?'

'1972.' No wonder she looked so decrepit. And him.

'We met in 1969, I was working in Boots in Deal and he came in to buy contraceptives. We were both 15.'

Priests eh!

'And the divorce, when was that?'

'Twenty-two months ago.' The gentle voice became fractionally more urgent. 'Until then Neil had been my only sexual partner. And I would like to mention that since he's left me I have discovered how very pleasurable the sexual act can be.' She flicked her eyes at Bopeep.

One of the most disconcerting things about being a journalist is how frank people are sometimes. They really ought to be more careful.

'When did you first know he was being unfaithful?'

'Our wedding reception,' she said lightly.

'Fuck! . . . Sorry, sorry – '

'You look shocked. You're not married, are you?'

'No. No, I'm not. Look, do you mind if I ask you . . .' – it was really eating me, this one – 'can I ask you what you saw in him?'

She clasped her hands in front of her: 'Well, it's very flattering, you know, being singled out by the great high priest. My family were church-goers. The old-fashioned approach, very literal. You had to believe that a dead man ate fish with his friends or you had no faith. You were damned. Do you understand what I mean?'

I did.

'So Neil's theology was terrifically exciting. Liberating. And Neil always was a very passionate person. Too passionate really.'

'Yeah, right, I read somewhere he was the living embodiment of the parable of the seeds, putting it everywhere, stony ground, the lot.'

'But you know, Patrick, it wasn't really sex he was after.'

'You're kidding me.'

'He wasn't all that highly sexed actually, even as a teenager.'

Nobody else in the world could have made me believe that, but there was something about her, an earnest desperation that convinced me.

'It's love Neil needs,' she said quietly. 'He needs to be newly in love to feel close to God. It's not so unusual. For many people spirituality and sex lie in the same chamber of the soul. It might help to imagine two strands wound together to make one rope.'

So that's what he told her.

'Did you get lots of other women sobbing on your doorstep?'

'He specialised in youth work. Sixth-formers about to go off to university.'

'They cry a lot, yeah.'

'No,' she said, 'nobody ever came to the vicarage. Nobody ever mentioned it at all.'

She produced a small pink tissue from her tracksuit pocket and stretched it between her fingertips. Time for me to go in for the kill.

'So how many affairs did he have?'

She looked down at the tissue. Something about the way she pressed her knees together told me she'd been holding in her pain long enough and whatever it cost her, she was ready to tell the truth at last. Her truth.

'Usually the outside world knows nothing about it,' she said, 'until a man like him makes a mistake. Or somebody comes along' – she gave a sigh – 'who actually wants him. Sometimes it's a divorcee. Or a member of the team. Then suddenly the wife is the embarrassment, taking up all that space in the vicarage. There's a clergy wives' help line for when that happens. There are quite a few of us, you know. Do you want the number?'

'Is that what happened to you?'

'No.' A laugh came at last. 'That's the saddest part, isn't it. No, it's not. I'd been waiting for years for the crisis and when it came . . . she didn't even want him. We did try because of the children. Stay together. But it didn't work, we couldn't keep . . .' Sue blinked. Bopeep moved her bulk closer to her.

'Who was she?'

For a second it really looked as though she would give way to tears, right there into Bopeep's bristly cheek. Instead she took a long breath, walked to one of those fold-out desks by the window and jotted something on a page.

'This lady may be able to tell you more, Mr Johnson-Price.

That's all I have to say.'

My mouth fell open at the name on the sheet.

Whitehead. Mrs E. Whitehead. Not the wife of the mighty axeman surely? There was a mobile number too. Maybe there was a God after all.

-

I should have known it would be a God with a warped sense of humour. It was Saturday and Charlton were at home to Leicester (spelt Walkover). There were a million comfortable places I could have been and I was on the bike in streaming rain heading for a church in Deal on the Kent coast. But I was happy. I was about to be in the presence of Gavin Whitehead's missus. Her voice had sounded girly on the phone and a bit naughty.

I found a spot in the car park between an old Sierra and a G-reg Fiesta with a sticker reading THE LORD IS MY PROVIDER. He might provide you with a better set of wheels than that, I thought, and went in. Instead of the usual church atmosphere of inhibiting gloom, inside was a riot. Fat old women were wandering around with armfuls of flowers and vacuum cleaner attachments, all shouting at each other above 'New York, New York' on the radio. I stopped one going past with a tray of chipped mugs of coffee.

'I'm looking for Mrs Whitehead?'

'Sorry?'

After my third bellow she shouted back: 'We've got the Bish tomorrow for confirmation. Hence the attack on the spiders.'

Spiders? I hate spiders. Nobody told me there might be spiders.

'Eileen!' she yelled. Nobody responded. 'She'll be up topsides doing the flowers.' She pointed up at the business end of the church. Tiptoeing in case of spiders, with my wet trainers creaking on the tiles, I approached the quintessential rock wife 'doing the flowers' at a country church altar. Her backside was neat, slim, clad in pale blue denim. The hair was blond and frizzy. The face, when it turned to me, was the oldest orang utang in the zoo. I was in the presence of Gavver's mother.

'He always was a boring little tyke.' Mrs Whitehead shifted an unlit cigar to the other side of her mouth without use of her fingers, which were busy ripping the bottom leaves off a fern stalk: 'He's a teetotal, veggie, non-smoking, prissy little git.'

'You must be very proud,' I ventured.

'He come to church with me for years, sang in his little choirboy ruff and everything, then turned round and said he hated every minute. Not real enough, he said. Normal church wasn't real enough for Mr Squeaky Clean pop star.'

'Rock star. Not pop.'

'You call that rock, son? Where's the guts in it? Where's the bust eardrums? Softer than snot he is since he joined that Omegist lot.'

'You don't like them?'

'Well, it gets him in the news. He's not selling his CDs off a table at the back of the church any more, is he?'

'He did that?'

'Had me taking the money for him! Now he's too busy swanking round Ten Downing Street to phone his mum.'

'Does he ever talk to you about, you know . . . God?'

She massaged the dead cigar with her lips: 'He tried to convert me once, cheeky little bugger. It was as if he was still in the cubs telling me about all his badges. Look, Mam, I've got this one here for speaking in tongues and this one's for falling over and here's the one I got for the time I saw an angel. He's only interested in the big badge now if you ask me.'

'Heaven?'

'A knighthood. Sure he's bought me a Harley and my cottage in Walmer, very nice. But he makes sure you lot know, don't he?'

What a waste. If she'd been my mum, I'd have been a proper rock star with tattoos and a coke habit and getting blowjobs under tables all over the world. And no way would I have joined any Omegists.

As she bent over to gather up her wet stalks from the floor, a rip in the upper thigh of her jeans opened and disclosed a pale tattoo of a heart and a name.

'So Gavin's father's called . . . Snork?' I asked, pen high.

'What you looking at, you little sod? My tats? No, Snork was a very long time ago. Now what you come about? Not what's tattooed on my arse, that's for sure.'

I could feel my neck redden with embarrassment.

'Sorry, yeah, no, I mean Mrs Sarbridge said you knew something about her ex-husband. Something . . . sensitive.'

The old woman's cackle resounded through the ancient rafters, strangely witchy in those acoustics.

'Sue sent you?'

'Sue Sarbridge, yes.'

Her eyes narrowed.

'Poor old Sue. Yeah, I know about Neil Sarbridge all right.' She straightened. 'Couldn't keep his pen in his pocket, know what I mean? Hard on a wife that.'

She glared at the cheap pen in my hand, daring me to blush again. I obliged.

'I found him once.'

'What was he doing?'

'Neil, he'd, you know, stand up there at Christmas and say there was never any three kings and that, but I would just think to myself, I remember that lad in nappies.'

She took out a chrome lighter shaped like a coffin and said: 'Come on.'

I followed her down the aisle and out to the porch where we watched squirrels skittering from one lichened tombstone to another while she lit her cigar stub.

'Sue all right?' she asked.

'Yeah.'

'It was . . . over there. Beyond that tree. Before a concert one night. He liked the musicals ones. Not that they had to be all that musical. They didn't have to be all that, full stop.'

'And?'

She looked around her: 'They were at it.'

'At what?'

'Come on, lad, you wasn't born yesterday? His wife Sue's ever so nice. In't she. We all made sure nobody told the papers. Sad enough for their kiddies without that.'

'Who was at it, Mrs Whitehead?' Her cigar ash dropped. She busied herself with brushing it off her bicycle-tyre sized midriff.

'Who was Sarbridge with, Mrs Whitehead?' I turned and began to push the heavy church door open. 'I'll ask in here, shall I? Tell you what, I might as well shout out loud and see if anybody can help me . . .' Her claw was round my wrist like a handcuff: 'No, lad, no need for that. She wasn't just one of the youth club, you see. That was the problem.'

She took my pad and pen and wrote down a name and a phone number.

Helen's.

I'll never forget seeing Helen's name written on that page. I knew to expect it of course, but I had tried to hope she might have had better taste.

Which was, by coincidence, exactly what I thought yesterday afternoon when I was sitting with a book of Law Reports propped up on my desk and I heard someone shuffling through the door behind me. I turned round to find Sarbridge standing here in my cell.

No hippy-shit fisherman's smock this time, he was in a black suit with shiny shoes and the sort of clerical collar that goes all the way round the back of the neck. How did he get in?

There was a black briefcase in his fist.

'Here to give me the last rites?' I asked, though he was the one who looked in need: eyebags half down his grey face, hunched shoulders. He was breathing oddly too, sucking and holding as if he had to contain something inside himself with a bulldozer. He stood there unfocussed for a moment, before he rejoined the world:

'If you like.'

I started talking much too fast. 'I don't remember sending you a Visitor's Order.'

'You didn't.' He stretched his eyes. 'I've, I'm giving a talk once a week to the chaplaincy staff. I was passing.'

'Well pass off,' I said, 'I'm busy.'

He reached over and tried to pick up my Law Report. 'What you got there?'

I slammed it shut, narrowly missing his fingers.

'I'm getting out of here and this book's going to help me. So's Julia. Remember her? Julia Bailey? At your college, law don, shagged her a few times?'

He looked as though somebody had just found his underwear on the altar and was going What's all this then?

I went on, though it filleted the guts out of me: 'Or was it more than a few times, you tell me?'

He stood there, head bowed, rattling the change in his pocket – a subtle insult that, to a chap in his own cell – before he answered, 'No. No, it was only the twice.'

'What?'

'Couple of times, yeah. Well, she was trying to get me sacked.'

I sucked in air. He'd fucked her, fucked my girlfriend to keep his job, simple as that. I was shocked. Not as shocked as I was about to be.

'Don't worry,' he said, coins jangling, 'it was only in fun.'

There you have it, Joo. In fun. Is that why you've got engaged to the tosser Mark? To show your Dean the real colour of fun? I should feel wounded. I should feel something. What do I feel?

He was still staring at the floor.

'I was at High Table the other night. Friday.'

'Good for you. What did they give you, porridge?'

'Julia, she. . .we had quite a long chat actually. About you.'

I pulled at my lower lip. This was not going to be good.

'One reason she's getting married is so that people won't ask her about you any more.'

'Sweet.'

'That's what she said you were. Sweet. Loving. Annoying too of course.'

'Of course. She always loved me unless I was actually with her. Then I just got on her tits the whole time.'

'She said sometimes you were really . . . young. It wasn't till she met me,' – he was standing too close to me now – 'she realised she was looking for a . . . man . . .'

I calculated that if I stood up very fast, I could crack his chin with my skull and maybe claim it was an accident:

'Out. Now!'

'I – '

Was the fucker deaf?

'Fuck off out of it!' I roared, 'now!!'

'Don't you want to know why I'm here?'

An awful thought dawned on me: 'Is it . . . have you got a message . . . from her?'

Sweat was glistening all over his face and neck as if he was in the vice of a prize-winning hangover. Maybe it was just fear.

'She just . . . she gave me the forceful impression that she never wanted to hear your name ever again.'

His mouth continued in the action of speech but I heard nothing until my mind reran those crucial words in slow motion.

'Never again?'

'What?'

'Julia said never again?'

Far away. 'Yes.'

'And that's the message?'

'It's not a message, she doesn't know I'm here . . .'

Never again. Never again.

Stupid of me. It was obviously all lies.

Suddenly he leaned forward as if he was my best friend. He suggested quietly that confession could be a breakthrough for me. Completely confidential. Nobody would know except God. And him, obviously. I could start where I liked, didn't the papers mention something about 'intimate assault'? How about starting there?

So that was it. My immortal soul could fuck itself, he was here for detail.

And there was Helen again beside me in the red dress, flopped upon my bed barely two yards away. Her eyes were closed as if she was asleep but there was no sign of breath moving between her open lips. He couldn't see her of course. She was only there for me.

'What sort of intimate assault are we talking about?'

'I'm not telling you,' I said, 'I didn't do it.'

He started cracking his knuckles as if he was ready to fight. I should have run away screaming.

'What sort of intimate assault is it you didn't do? You can tell me, Patrick, I won't be shocked.'

His blinks came deeper and faster. Globules of sweat ran into his dog collar. Each of his eyes was like the viscous centre of a jellyfish. And all the time I was thinking to myself, being interviewed is not that difficult. All you have to do is make up your mind

'Don't ask me, mate.'

what you're not going to say

'Don't call me mate.'

and refuse to say it

'Then don't ask me fucking stupid questions.'

right up to the moment he lost his temper:

'Just tell me, you little shit, did you rape her or not?'

Spit was creaming the corners of his mouth. He grabbed my prison sweatshirt in both hands. I was in the full blast of his distillery breath with my head tipped back and my collar cutting my neck like rope. I had to get to the door somehow and yell for help.

'You little shit, you cunt, you fucking stupid little bastard!'

'Nice talk for a clergyman,' I said.

He flung me away from him: 'I came to forgive you. Can you understand that?'

He sat down on the bed again, right on the spot where moments ago Helen had been lying, and sank his head in his hands.

'Every time she, every time she comes into my mind,' he told his shoes, 'God help me, I see you. Your face and hers beside each other in the papers, newspapers' – tears in his voice now – 'the filth of you, the ugliness, always the same and those terrible words "intimate assault"!'

He flung his head up and with his lower jaw out, he sucked air deep into his guts. He wiped his hands hard up and down his red face. He sniffed, and pressed the green release button and in the few seconds before a screw came to release him, Sarbridge finally looked at me. He spoke with a tenderness I had never heard before in his voice.

He said: 'I want to kill you.'

Now please, Julia, anything Neil Sarbridge has told you 'at High Table' about me, ignore it, OK? All of it. Especially about the next time he pitched up. I was lying on my camp bed and Marcus was circling his glass pendulum over my belly button to enhance the balance of my second chakra. That's all. Both of us as innocent as newborn babes, both of us fully dressed, I swear, and who should put his head round the door that very moment but your Dean.

Remember he said before that he was giving a talk once a week to the chaplains? I lose track of time and couldn't tell you whether that was a week ago or a month, but I wasn't expecting to see him again either way. Not least because Marcus had taken against him. That first time after Sarbridge left, Marcus came back into the cell in a dreadful flutter.

'Beware of that man,' he said, 'be very, very wary. The worst ones are the Dark Ones who dress in the light.'

Sarbridge's a Dark One, is he? Does it take one to know one?

'It's in his aura,' he said and started flicking his tarot silk scarf all over the place like a duster.

'You might be right,' I said.

'Course I am,' Marcus gave the bunk beds a good rattle.

'Have you noticed,' I said, stopping a rolling nut under my trainer, 'Sarbridge never catches your eye for more than a second?'

'He daren't,' Marcus said, 'you might see the empty space where the soul should be. He tries to fill the empty soul space with the light from other people's souls. It's a trick with mist and mirrors to make himself look complete. He'll suck you in.'

I shrugged. 'He's not sucking me anywhere, I assure you.'

Marcus wagged a finger and promised that if Sarbridge ever turned up again, he'd help me out. He didn't say it would be by fucking telepathy. One look at the dog collar this morning and Marcus was off down the wing.

If anything, Sarbridge looked worse than before. His facial colour varied from red to ultraviolet, the grey stubble was too long to be deliberate and his rumpled overcoat had pale streaks down the paunch. Alcohol filled out his breath like a ripe fart. He was already inside the cell when he rapped softly on the inside of the door. God knows how long he'd stood there eavesdropping.

'Nobody in,' I quipped, and swung my feet on to the floor. I was on my own with somebody who'd said he wanted to kill me. He must have had some security training because he made sure he kept the release button close. I could have charged past him and away down the corridor, but that would leave him alone with my desk, my stack of writing to you, Julia, and my research about Helen. I couldn't risk that.

He dropped his coat beside me on my bed as if he owned the place and said he understood I was pleading not guilty.

'That's because I'm not. I am not guilty. I did not kill Helen. I didn't.' My voice was fading like a child's, 'My cell mate says he'll, like sort you out if you have a go at me.'

Sarbridge took out a pouch of rolling tobacco. I just knew he'd be one of those smooth bastards who could roll a cigarette with one hand while handing me his black plastic lighter with the other. No filters. He laid the first roll-up on my knee.

I took it, I'm not proud. As the lighter flame caught the fragile paper twist and the smoke shot deep into my lungs, I seemed to catch a background hint of Helen.

'I'm not here to fight you,' he said, 'I want to explain something.'

About time. I had a list of questions for him too: Why did his affair with Helen break up his marriage but they didn't end up together? And why was he with Helen that night she died? He was there with her before I got there, wasn't he?

Before I could get the words out, he said: 'GodSense. I want to talk to you about GodSense.'

GodSense? Oh that.

'It was Helen's idea,' he said.

Helen sat up on my camp bed, naked. She smiled over her shoulder at me and whispered: 'You remember GodSense, Patrick? I wanted to tell everybody about midrash. Same as I did with you. Why should the professionals keep it to themselves? I'm sure nobody meant to keep it secret, it's just somehow' – she smiled as she brought her two fists together – 'nobody had the balls to get it across to people.'

She curled her feet under herself and looked up adoringly at Sarbridge. He didn't even ignore her.

'She thought we should learn from the evangelicals,' he said.

'Yes,' she hooked her hands over her knees, 'write simple books'

'Books,' he said, 'with short paragraphs and lots of headings.'

'Go on television,' she said.

'Hire Wembley.' As he walked the two paces to my bed, she made room for him to sit beside her. He parked one black, highly-polished shoe on his other knee and fiddled with his laces. She rested a hand on his thigh. Stop that, Helen, I thought. The bastard wants to betray you. But I couldn't speak.

'She was,' he spread his hands, 'how can I explain? I'd reached a sort of gridlock at work where the whole thing was just a huge effort.'

She pulled his coat around herself as if they'd been married for years. He went on, the way he does once he's started: 'I knew the maps well enough. The guide books, if you like. Anybody had a problem, I used to say quick as a flash "I know the very book for you." I have a study at home three, four times the size of this cell and every inch of its walls is covered in books. And I have actually read them. But it took Helen to show me what they're about.'

Suddenly he gave one of his deep blinks, 'I'm lost without her.'

In that second she was gone. He was on the bed alone, grey and small with his knees pressed tight together like a girl.

Here comes the bit I wish I'd recorded. I'm writing it quickly, my fingers can't keep pace with my thoughts, but I've got to do it while his voice is still in my head. It's that guttural smoothie one he used so effectively on you, Julia, when we went to his drinks party after evensong in Cambridge: 'I'd had a few affairs, yeah. I don't deny that. You've met my wife.' He flashed me a look as if to say, wouldn't anybody married to that stray or suffocate? I didn't react.

'You think it's easy?' His voice rose: 'Human frailty is a priest's best subject, you know. As my wife kept telling me. You empathise better with a sinner if you've, you know . . .'

He hid his eyes behind his arm for a moment and sniffed. 'Sometimes I wished she wasn't so understanding and she just – '

'Your affairs were your wife's fault?'

He sat up straight with a hand on each of his knees, forcing himself into composure: 'No . . . No, of course not. But . . . she could have stopped me.'

'You could have stopped yourself.'

He blinked twice: 'All that forgiveness . . . it made me loathe myself even more. So I'd go and find another one. But Helen was – ' he made sure I could see how deeply he was suffering – 'I often wonder, you know, would it have been easier if I hadn't been a priest? Just get a divorce, marry Helen, no problem?'

'Why didn't you?'

'She . . . she couldn't understand, you see, she'd never done it, been in that place of . . . loving two people at the same time.'

Cheating, you mean?

He winced. 'I don't have to justify myself to you!'

'Not even in fun?'

He looked bewildered: 'I don't expect you to understand this, Patrick, or maybe you do, there's something in your face, but there really were times when I was with Helen . . . I felt touched by God.'

One more ounce of this shit and he'd be touched none too gently by the toes of my trainers. He wasn't talking to that poor, bullied wife of his now. I stood up.

'I know it's hard for somebody like you to understand, Patrick, but being a priest can be very lonely, and introducing people to God is so . . . so exciting you – '

I finished his sentence for him: 'You just can't help taking your clothes off?'

'Please! What I'm trying to say . . . Helen was so much more than a lover, she was . . . I've . . . I don't know, I've been in the church my whole life and I never knew anybody like her.' He scanned the ceiling, sniffing, shaking his head. Oscar-winning stuff. 'With her,' he went on, 'God help me, there were moments of sheer divinity.'

The word divinity covered me in gooseflesh. My eyes closed and my palms came together prayer-wise. I tried to steady my breathing.

'But d'you know what, Patrick?'

I opened my eyes. He squeezed the last centimetre of his roll-up under his heel: 'You can't make a life out of divine moments, you know. That was a big discovery for me. I had responsibilities. If I'd met Helen at another time of my life . . . But she wouldn't, she . . . wanted to honour my marriage.'

'More than you did.'

'Oh my wife knew.' Suddenly he lifted his eyes to meet mine. 'My wife also knew nothing would have taken me away from my family.' He looked away again, and started rolling us another couple of those mind-spinners.

'But you haven't got family,' I said. 'They left you.'

He blinked deeply and fussed with his Rizlas, needing both hands now to balance his tobacco pouch on his thigh.

'And Helen was single. What stopped you? Why no happy ending?'

His face crumpled. He dropped the tobacco and papers on the floor with his hands flapping, shoulders heaving. Water fell from his eyes on to the fake wood tiles between his feet, five drops, six of them. Shit. Why didn't he just go?

'That's what I . . .' Sob, sob. 'That's why . . .'

'Why what?'

'That night,' he blubbed through fat, wet lips, scrabbling on the floor for his cigarette papers.

'The night she died?'

'I went to see her, yeah. Ask her.' His voice was breaking, 'I wanted to ask her. To live with me.'

I looked across him at the release button. It was easy to reach it with him there on the floor. Two female screws were there in seconds, ready to duff me up. When they found that it was the Dean they had to escort out of the cell, they beamed as if they'd won the lottery. He stumbled down the wing with one of them under each shoulder as if he was on his way to his final meal.

I'd had enough. Enough of him, his piety, his arrogance. Enough of his lying. Because Helen told me exactly why he came to see her that night. And it was nothing to do with living with him.

I'm sitting here at my Law Reports again but can I concentrate? Marcus is holding a meeting here in the cell. An holistic, conscious-ness-raising group, of all things, called CONfidence. For some reason he's talking in a ridiculous West Coast accent: 'Let's relax now and visualise the solar plexus chakra. Breathe in. Chakra means wheel or vortex, so imagine with me a vortex of intense white light manifesting there, behind your navel.'

Your *navel*, isn't your solar plexus up a bit?

'And out. Through our chakras we receive and transmit social, spiritual and sexual energies. People with inner vision can actually see them.'

I look at the group. Everyone's eyes are darting about as if some-body's about to steal their chakras. Anything's possible in here.

'Breathe in,' Marcus says. 'Feel the warmth around your groin. And out. In a moment we'll pick up on our different perspectives but first let's introduce ourselves.'

Darren's squatting in the lotus position on the bog lid: 'I'm Darren, in for murder. I was Nero in a previous life.'

Marcus, squatting under the window, can't wait to say: 'Yes, I could feel a purplish energy in your sixth chakra. You know, if Nero had applied lapis lazuli at the base of his skull, he wouldn't have been so misunderstood. Let's say OM.'

They all say OM.

'OM brings the ego,' Marcus explains, 'into union with the spirit self.'

They all nod solemnly, as if he was recommending the quails' eggs at Waitrose.

There's Warren cross-legged on the top bunk. He's in for raping a twelve-year old girl during her epileptic fit. Arran's on the floor behind me, he's an animal rights man with a grudge against Range Rovers. Ryan's a fraudster who has escaped so often he can't be trusted with bail. And there's Peeler. Peeler's introducing himself: 'Rape and murder, as you know. Being a reincarnated Native American chief, scalping comes easily to me.'

Now it's Marcus' turn.

I don't believe it. I think I'm in shock. I'd been looking forward to the details of his alleged computer fraud. Every time I asked him about it, which wasn't often, he said it would all be far too complex for me to understand. He gave his usual half-smile and tucked himself into the lotus position, hand on his first chakra (inside his pants) for comfort: 'I'm Marcus, as you know.' He closed his eyes. 'Magic Marcus.' Long, slow in-breath. 'Part of a paedophile ring.' Almost endless out-breath, 'but all I did was the camerawork, and heal the little lads afterwards.'

The world has suddenly left me on a freak tide. I need you to hold me, Helen. Julia. Anybody. How can I explain how I feel? I really didn't have a clue. I did not know. I still can't believe that all this time I've been sharing with and, inevitably, being the nice guy I am, letting myself get fond of a nonce.

What's going on anyway? Aren't they supposed to be kept separate in the Vulnerable Prisoners Unit? And where did he get the right to be so up himself about me being a so-called erotomaniac?

Marcus tugged my sleeve. Me next? No way. No way! I am not playing their stupid fucking games, no, no guys . . .

'I'm Patrick, in for alleged rape and murder. Of a woman. I didn't do it actually.'

Eruptions. Everybody's innocent, didn't I fucking know that? This is a remand centre, of course they're all innocent, every damned one of them as innocent as the (Arctic) day is long. I was being called a few things I can't be bothered to repeat when Arran started lecturing me on how you always have to plead innocent whether you did it or not, so then in ten years time some journalist finds a loophole that's not there now. Then as well as getting out, you get on the telly.

Had it worked for him?

Not yet.

What if it doesn't?

'Reload and try full auto,' he said.

Marcus bellowed at them to sit down and shut the fuck up, it was time for role play.

'Calm down, lads, calmly does it. Dum vivimos, vivamos. While we're here, we might as well live, not make things worse for ourselves.'

We were to divide into groups and make up a play. Please, God, I thought, don't let me be first. Or last. Don't let me be picked at all. No chance, Marcus hauled me into his group with Peeler.

The three of us hunkered down between the loo and the sink. Others were whispering near the window. Marcus invited us to 'share' what we thought was the greatest thing about being a child.

Immediately my mind filled with Tim and Seb and bed-wetting and pain, but Marcus and Peeler were well away.

'Remember when the grown-ups pick you up and twirl you around?'

'And you scream your head off and get a big cuddle.'

'Or you're sitting on Father Christmas's knee – '

'And he gets a hard-on.'

'And you get your first cigarette.'

'Look, he's got his bag of sweets, where's mine?'

'And his little trousers off – '

'Do I have to, Father?'

'Sure you do, son, you want to be a grown up, don't you?'

'Never more grown up, than when you're – '

'With a – '

'Kid.'

I hear a howl filling the cell and realise it's me.

'You two have no right to be near anybody's kids!' I shouted. Marcus started bleating that the kids love it, the younger the better, they'll do anything for an iced lolly, anything to please.

'What about when you hurt them, Marcus?' I was shouting, 'Do they smile then, when you're healing them with your chakras and your bit of yoga?'

He stood up and put his hands on my shoulders. I punched them off. Resentment was churning in my chest, resentment that had been building since the day I'd got out of the block and first set eyes on his filthy hairy face.

'Let's say OM,' he murmured right in my face, 'it combines the O of the second chakra' – his brow walloped my forehead – 'with M in the sixth chakra' – and his left fist caught my guts just below the navel, knocking me upright again. I folded and tasted blood.

'Breathe,' he whispered.

'You cunt,' came out on my outbreath.

As I breathed in, I noticed threads of red crowding the whites of his eyes. I wanted no more of this, no more pervs in my cell, and I said so. Marcus sat on the bed, all offended, breathing in gusts: 'It's perfectly natural, you know.' He coughed and thumped his chest. 'I bet there's not a man here hasn't thought about it, getting a child's lovely soft little hand round your prick or parting their peachy little buttocks. Not a man here. Even you.'

That. Was. It.

I was about to punch his brains out, I promise you, when I realised I didn't have to. He had slumped back on the bed and rolled into the foetal position.

Peeler ran out shouting for help. I crouched beside Marcus' face. His mouth slopped open. His cheeks pinched and went grey. His breathing galloped and then stopped, then his breathing galloped again. Fuck. I'd seen this before. Beside him on the bunk Helen lay breathing in exactly the same way. I curled my arm around his head. Tears began to roll down both my cheeks as I bellowed: 'Come on, you pervy fucker, breathe!'

I was in the meat wagon on my way back from another trip to the Crown Court, to establish damn all as usual, when the traffic seized on the A2 close to the gates of Greenwich Park. I was gawping at a bit of normality out of the porthole, sirens bursting my ears, when who should glance up from the wheel of a stationary 4x4 but a face I thought I knew. I stared back for a second or so until he engaged a gear and moved forward, his life totally unaltered by our encounter.

Not so for me. It was Whitehead. Gavin Whitehead, south-east London's tattoo-free axeman, and I realised with juggernaut force that our brief eyelock in a traffic jam was as close to him as I am ever going to get. And you know something? I looked at his rings tapping his plump, leather steering wheel and I thought, he's not fit to lick the late Pug's trainers. Whitehead's got the hair and a voice that can ring the rooks off the tree tops. But he's happy to knock out a rap parody in the name of Christ. Which means he's a wanker and a fraud and I don't care if I never clap ears on him ever again.

On the way back, before I even had the cuffs off, I heard a shout: 'Letter for you, PatPrick.'

I didn't open it then, Julia. I was afraid. The very sight of the envelope had my chakras going apeshit. I called into the hospital wing first, to see if anybody in there had worked out how to diagnose a nosebleed.

The money for clean bed linen had run out. In fact bed linen of any sort had run out, but Marcus was oblivious. As I watched him sleep on the striped mattress on his side with those big fists of his resting under his chin, it occurred to me that prison hospitals might have the only medical staff in the country who let you die in peace. Everywhere else it's against the rules. My plastic chair squeaked under me as I opened my envelope. I closed it again. Marcus always said that that part of the newspaper is the only part you can trust. That and the horoscopes.

No point in waking Marcus to let him in on the news. He was probably sedated anyway. Odd how different his face looked without him inside to animate it. In repose his face looked intelligent, donnish even, and awake or asleep, alive or dead, he was always kind. I forced myself to imagine him taking the hand of someone's child, a boy he'd never met before and saying 'Would you like to come and see what I've got? Mummy won't mind, look, she gave me these sweets to give you.'

I could picture it. I could. And I could picture the child believing him. Going with him. 'Careful, have you grazed your knee? Let me kiss it better, let me kiss you better, see, it doesn't hurt any more. And neither will this . . .'

I thought of praying but couldn't think of a single thing to say.

Marcus is still in the hospital wing. Third day and I'm sitting at my desk not enjoying the solitude.

I can't stop looking at your clipping. It's the *Telegraph* again. Marriage, it says. Marriage. *Your* marriage, Julia! And it's not to me.

Dr M. P. Bothway MA and Professor J. S. Bailey MA, LLM, PhD.

Two names conjoined by fate and newsprint, like murderer and victim. Do you honestly love him, Julia? Your Mark? Or will you just screw him and eat him like a black widow spider? If I had any money, I'd bet you will.

The marriage took place last Saturday at the Chapel of Lancaster College, Cambridge, between Dr Mark Bothway and Professor Julia Bailey. The Rev. Neil Sarbridge, Dean of Lancaster College, officiated.

The most reliable part of a newspaper. It has to be true.

No, you've had it done and sent to me as a late April Fool or something. Please come and tell me it's a joke, Julia. I'll laugh, I promise I will.

Though I speak with brass tinkling in my purse and sports labels all over my clothing, clashing symbols of materialism, I am no fool. I know better than to trust love.

Though I had all the world's faiths in the palm of my hand and could move hearts and minds and governments, I know that faith is nothing but an executioners' trapdoor, a defective parachute, a midnight wail in a hospice to a deaf deity. Your faith healer acts in good faith on your act of faith? Ha! Faith. An empty tin. Like charity.

Of course I'll lend an occasional fiver to a friend and buy *The Big Issue* (and check my change) but I know in my heart that love is as warm as a stream of piss and as comforting as a sting in the eye. Love needs. Love takes. It sucks from us all, our very everything, and laughs as we squirm and the world mocks.

And what does love give in return? A frothy spit.

Believe all things, hope all things, endure all things, it's all the same. It makes no difference. It's there in the newspapers every day. The faces vary, sure, but the message stays the same: never ever rely on love.

When I was a child I loved as a child, with my full heart overflowing with trust. I understood as a child and thought as a child that somewhere in this cold world there would be a warm, loving place for me. But when I became grown, I put away childish thoughts, got a job, got a sex life, and read the papers, I even began to see the point of lawyers, and at last I saw the first and only truth.

We are all on our own.

The toughest part of every day is still when I wake up. For two precious seconds I'm somewhere else. I'm in my bedroom at home with the nurses waiting for me just outside the closed curtains. Or between Julia's wintry satin sheets. Or I'm at home years ago in my Batman pyjamas with the smell of toast drifting up from the kitchen.

Then Marcus shifts or farts, or I do, and I realise.

I'm inside.

I was cleaning my teeth this morning when I looked up and who should be staring back from the mirror – amazing he's got a reflection really – but Sarbridge again, all hail fellow and isn't it a bright, breezy morning.

'Is it?' I wiped my chin on the towel and turned to look at him. We were standing so close we should have synchronised our breathing. He didn't flinch.

'How is Blackheath looking this morning?' I asked him, really wanting to know. 'Tell me. Is it one of those clear spring mornings when you can see every blade of grass and the sky is a heavenly blue dome? Or is it summer now, with kites and football matches and people lolling around half-dressed near the pubs? Or is there a wisp of autumn mist?'

He wiped his hand down his face – I might have been spitting – and said it had been pouring non-stop for weeks, I was as well off in here as anywhere. Well, that was a matter of opinion, I said. He stepped past me a pace and slapped a copy of Helen's book on my desk. As if I'd never seen it before.

Fire Down Below. My palms tingled as I reached for the book and cradled it. A first edition. Pencilled ticks marked the margins here and there until I reached a blank postcard between pages 18 and 19, at the start of the chapter on Temptation. Had Helen touched this copy? The sight of her photograph on the back shook me. Helen. Smooth-faced, keen, her hand to her forehead to establish intellectual credentials, about ten years ago at a guess.

Oh Helen. If I had been different and you had been different and we'd met somewhere else at a different time, might we have had a chance together?

I looked up to see Sarbridge's rheumy eyes studying me. He pulled a white handkerchief from a pocket and blew his nose, examined what he'd produced and put the whole damp package back in his pocket. I backed away toward the window in case he wanted to shake my hand. Thanks a bunch, I thought. Visit a chap in jail and bring him a head cold.

I turned the book over, as I'd once turned Helen's body over, and heard Sarbridge's voice, quiet, almost fearful. What was his exact phrase? If we 'shared our experience of her', we might hope to 'advance our grief'?

I said surely he kept coming because he liked me so much.

I still hope you'll come, Julia, I can't help it. I don't care if you're married. I have no right to care. In fact I wish you and Mark as long, boring and sexually unfulfilled a marriage as the best of them, I really do. But think for a minute, where does that leave me? We did love each other once. We had hope. And for me here now, you are my only hope.

I pulled the sliver of newsprint about your wedding from my bin and flung it at him.

'Was she radiant?'

'Reasonably,' he said, 'It's hard to tell at weddings, people are always so tense. I didn't stay for the piss-up. To be honest, if I heard one more note on a recorder I'd have killed somebody.' He chanced a half smile at me.

I couldn't help it, I laughed. We both laughed. Then I scythed him: 'I'm still pleading not guilty.'

He rocked back a fraction.

'I hear you haven't got a lawyer?'

'So?'

'So how's it going?'

'Great.'

His head twitched sideways as if he was testing ball bearings in his neck. Was I going to get the Adverb Rant again? He leant forward and whispered: 'She was perfectly all right when I left her.'

'Who?' I asked sweetly.

His cough-sweet breath gusted over me:

'You know who I mean.'

'You mean . . . the night she died?' I shrugged away the ugliness of that last word. 'You haven't told the police, have you? That you were there with her that night, before me?'

'If only life was that simple,' he said, pinching his nose. 'Look at it this way, Patrick. Look at what Helen achieved. What she stood for.'

'Such as?'

He sniffed and glanced at the ceiling as if I was trying his patience but he was being saintly about it.

'Helen . . . I . . . For me Helen was everything good about religion. For her everybody was equal, everyone was precious, everyone loved.'

I wanted to go Yeah, even a wanker like you, but I let him go on.

'Hierarchy meant nothing to her. Liturgy the same.'

'Lidgy? What's that?'

He sat on my bed, exactly where Helen had sat the last time he was here.

'Liturgy is the set form of church service,' he said.

'The mumbo jumbo?'

'For some of us it's the endless repetition of those exquisite words that keeps us in touch with God, Patrick. She didn't need that. She was all love anyway. She didn't really need the rituals of church to keep her there.'

Yes. But she made it pretty clear in her book that love equals pain equals more pain, and that organised religion just makes it worse. I didn't mean to but I must have said this out loud because he spoke before I could.

'When people talk about organised religion, it's usually a term of abuse. But the people in it don't call it that. It has its uses, you know. There are thousands of charities and volunteers working away all the time without throwing their religion at you. But it's why they do it, because of their beliefs, and the country would collapse without them.'

The sun freed itself from a cloud and fell on my back through the window. I watched my shadow cover Sarbridge and caught a faint scent of roses as, behind him, Helen – naked again – stretched out on the sunlit sheets.

'I really want you to understand something, Patrick,' he said, his eyes begging, 'How can I put this? If we, you . . . if people got to think that Helen died without hope . . . she would be betrayed. To me that's the most important thing in the world. So many people depend on her,' he said, 'on her memory. Not just you and me. The world mustn't think . . . she ever felt . . . that God abandoned her at the end.'

Helen sat up and rubbed her eyes.

'Jesus' life and death are everybody's life and death,' she said, 'we are all on the cross, Patrick, nobody escapes. But we can come through it if we trust in love.'

Oh I want that, I murmured, I want love so much.

While Sarbridge repeated his nose-blowing ritual, Helen pressed herself close to him and gave me a broad, beautiful smile. 'Maybe we only *deserve* God,' she said, 'if we endure death and the desolation of the cross, and love each other whatever happens.'

Sarbridge was about to put his handkerchief back in his pocket when the blast of sunshine through the window vanished and he shuddered. I sat on the bed and stroked the cold white sheets.

She had gone again, leaving nothing, not a sound or a shimmer. Sarbridge pushed his face into the sleeve of his jacket. My right hand moved as if under water and rested on his shoulder before his gasping gave way to sobs and he threw his arms around me and was crying his heart out.

It was a bit like when you've got carried away at a club and you're having a quick one outside in the dark with some girl, and it smells of pee and over the music you can hear foxes shagging far away and sirens in the distance and your head's bouncing and it's all over nice and quick, it's not until you're tucking it all away again, sticky and small, that you're embarrassed and don't want to look at her or ask her name or meet her eye ever again.

I pulled away first. He cleared his throat, like a gunshot ricocheting around the close walls. We both sat back, each with our arms folded, legs knotted, not looking at each other.

'There is a solution,' he said.

'What?'

'You can plead guilty, no listen please, if you plead guilty, if you say you killed her, then there'll be no trial for months, no more journalists door-stepping me and the wife, no raking everything up. No more of this shit about adultery . . .' His voice was cracking again: 'I – I didn't bloody kill her! Did I?'

His eyes lasered me through his tears. I looked away.

'She was alive when I left her, Patrick. She was.' He smacked his hands on his thighs. 'So there'll be no more nonsense about Helen and despair. Will there? Her memory will be intact. She'll be remembered as a magnificent priest whose parish adored her. A priest whose beliefs are worth something.'

He pulled a page from his jacket pocket and unfolded it. It was a closely typed sheet of A4.

A confession. For me to sign.

'It's what she would have wanted,' he said and handed it to me.

I flattened it on my thigh and looked at it through that haze I always get whenever tiny print comes at me. Especially when the paragraphs are as big as gravestones.

The gist was that I was a nutter, an erotomaniac who stalked Helen. I was in love with her saintly goodness and in her own front room I beat her, raped and killed her.

If I signed the page, Helen would be seen as a martyr.

'You could become a bit of a martyr too,' he purred, all pleased with himself, 'I mean, who wouldn't love Helen?'

'Right.'

'You just took it . . . a bit far.'

He crossed his feet and nodded pertly as if that was settled.

'A bit far,' I repeated. Rage was stirring in my guts, beginning to uncoil. 'You think I raped her.'

'That's what the papers – '

'I'm innocent!' I yelled. 'Until I'm proved guilty, don't you know that?'

'You did rape her,' he growled, 'and I can't stop fucking thinking about it. A slug like you, *scum* like you!'

He was up pacing, his hands over his face. He hit his forehead with the heel of one hand and he was suddenly composed.

'Look. Patrick. We have to sort this. For Helen. For her memory.'

He looked small standing in front of me, his hands gripping his cuffs like a little boy in a goal mouth as he promised he'd be a good character witness for me and so on. Tears bulged in both his eyes and rolled unwiped to his chin. I wasn't to decide immediately, he was very strong on that. I should keep the draft confession.

'Think about it,' he whispered. 'I know you'll see sense. We need to keep Helen's memory safe, we have to. Whatever it takes, Patrick? Eh?'

As he kept saying on the way out, this is Helen we're talking about. Our beloved Helen.

And I might as well keep the book.

As I heard his footsteps fade away down the wing, I kicked the door. Our beloved Helen. Our Helen?

She wasn't 'our' Helen, she was mine. Here with me. I lifted her book reverently to my lips and let it fall open.

Why have you forsaken me, God? Punish David by all means but I did not ask for this woe and I Bathsheba deserve none of it.

It was here, wasn't it. This, this spot here at the water's edge where I stand now sprinkling water on my baby's face. This is where I was washing myself that day when David, your anointed King, walked out upon his rooftop and saw me. He blamed my beauty. I never asked for beauty, it was you that gave me beauty, God. And I had no reason to curse it until David your anointed King sent men to bring me to him. I walked through his courtly hangings of red and gold and longed for the white walls of my own home. I saw your anointed King oiled and handsome, pacing like a tied bull, and cried in my heart for my fine husband at home who loved and needed me.

As soon as David saw me he ran and fell on his knees before me: 'Bathsheba,' he said, 'I cannot breathe without your eyes upon me.' He gripped my skirt. 'I cannot think unless I have the scent of you beside me.'

The might of the kingdom was at stake, he said, if I did not do his bidding. It was not enough for him to take what he wanted; it had to be given. Obediently I gave and obediently I said I was grateful.

Choose me not again, God, for such honour. Choose me not. The baby he put in my belly that day, this little son that I wash here, you made him kick and squirm in me until I loved him in spite of his provenance. And this morning I saw his chest flutter. Then you took his last breath. His eyelids veined like crocus petals, you made them shut.

You wove me too in my mother's womb. As I lay in my mother's

233

arms you taught me hope. But my baby boy is beyond hope, and so am I.

Is your king watching me now, God? Make him watch me. Make him see what he has done.

My breasts ache for this baby. I hold him close to my belly and wash his brow and eyes, his ears, the crease of his neck. I wash the scabbed umbilicus, which will never heal.

A hand is on my shoulder. I hear David's voice.

'Is the child dead, Bathsheba?'

I rush away into the water. I clutch the baby tight.

'Don't torture me, Bathsheba.'

'You talk to me of torture? You have pierced me, hands, feet, heart and soul and belly.'

I stumble deeper into the waves.

'Let me die with my babe,' I cry. 'Let the water cover us both.'

David is kneeling at the shore: 'Then I die too, Bathsheba. I cannot live without you.'

I look down and see my baby covered in water. I panic and raise him up, and kiss his wet face. Cold kisses. Cold kisses. I roar to the deaf heavens and clutch the baby tighter.

'Bathsheba!' David calls, 'give him to me!'

I crash the water with my fist. 'Let me die, I can take no more.'

David wades in, his strides long and strong like that first day when I saw him come to me. He stops an arm's length from me. His face is red with tears.

'My heart suffers too, Bathsheba. Let me hold him just once.'

How could I not?

He takes our child in the crook of his arm. With the fingers of his free hand David strokes the baby's face, and his chest heaves with woe. With his brute fingers he caresses our baby's belly, legs and arms and cradles the feet. He does not look at me until he has touched the little corpse all over.

I am disgusted by this show. How can I watch this murderer, this anointed King indulge for once in ordinary human pain?

I turn for the shore. As I wade away from my dead baby, I hear you, God. I did not hear before, over the tumult of my heart.

I stop.

You say, 'Turn again, Bathsheba. David is flawed but you can love him. He has great work to do and he cannot do it without your love.'

'My baby is dead!' I shout, 'do not ask me to love again!'

For once you hear me, God. But your answers are never easy.

'Your pain will bind you to him tighter than happiness, Bathsheba. You can run to the ends of the earth but you and he are tied by your grief forever. Turn, Bathsheba. Trust me. You will find love.'

Still longing to be one flesh with my baby, I turn. David is bowed over the child, whispering to him. I come softly close to them and David leans into me.

'Stay with me, Bathsheba, and be my comfort,' he whispers.

I reach my arms around him and feel his mighty chest judder. In the silence broken only by our tears and the lapping of God's water around us, I am aware that the tiny cadaver is joining us at the heart.

I'm sitting at my desk. Helen's book is under my left hand. The printed confession Sarbridge concocted for me and a pen are under my right. It's what Helen would have wanted, he said, to keep her memory safe, whatever it takes. I've been filling every letter O with ink and find that if I trace the F in 'confession' down into a nose and up into a pair of goat's horns, I'm looking at a fair enough likeness of Sarbridge himself.

Help me, Helen, what do I do? Pain binds us, you and me, but I can't think straight any more.

Stupid of me, I mustn't cry. You promised me nothing. Except that I am loved. I am loved. Passive tense. Passive I sit here and wait. Tense. Here in my cell, half alive, half dead, with my soul still aching for you after all this time, aching to love you back to life.

Peeler's just appeared at my door, in his bad news face.

'Charlton beaten Chelsea again?' I asked.

He shook his head like a dog out of water.

'Medaillons of boeuf off the lunch menu again?'

Not that either.

He managed to say: 'Marcus.'

'They've told him his chakras are shite?' I said, half jovially as you do. 'His etheric intelligences don't want to play with him any more?'

Peeler's face sagged as if he'd taken his teeth out and lost both glass eyes. I couldn't help it, I stood up and reached for him: 'Steady, steady'. For the second time in one afternoon, I held a sobbing man against my chest. For some reason my own tears stayed where they were, dammed up, swirling in my head.

'He knew he was getting out soon, Patrick,' he blubbed.

'But that's great, that's *good* news.'

'Not like this. He was such a lovely man.'

Ever partial with the truth, our Peeler. But whatever Marcus was or did, the cell is damned empty without him and, by the sound of it, that's how it's going to stay.

I'm not going to that chapel again. It's too dangerous. My right hand is trussed up again like a bunch of jumbo sausages, in cling film this time, for burns.

All in honour of Marcus. He wasn't in the chapel of course, his family incinerated him last week, but somebody must have felt that ten minutes in a south London crematorium didn't do justice even to old Marcus, so there we were, about twenty of us, a heady mix of cons and outsiders, reminiscing about his heart attack and reciting his misdeeds.

At the chapel door an old bird in a white shift handed me a candle and a song sheet. All I could think was . . .Helen. Darling Helen. I missed Helen's funeral, being stuck in here with so much of my DNA gone to forensics I was a shadow of my former self. What am I to do, Helen? Do you want me to do what Sarbridge wants? Do you?

I sat near the back and flopped forward with my head on my knees. I may even have moaned a little. Behind me I heard Number One Guv arrive, Hello hello, isn't it a jolly morning, all fuss and grovel. What was he doing there? Laughing is what he was doing there, laughing with Pam. On his way to his special seat at the front he took a moment to lay his hand on my shoulder, heavy as a slab. His whisper breezed the back of my neck: 'We'll have to get you a new cell mate now, Johnson, know what I mean?'

That man deliberately put a nonce in my cell. A nonce I'd grown fond of but a nonce all the same. What new horror was he brewing? He could move me in with Kitten who would gladly hang me by the neck until capital punishment becomes legal again. White terror filled my eyes.

The old girl in the shift was busy forming everybody in a circle.

I tried to sneak out through the crowd but Pam hooked her arm in mine and held me close to her. The next thing I knew, I was having incense shaken at me. Powerful stuff, incense. I'd forgotten.

'By the ineffable and incomprehensible (something or other, can't be that, it sounds like Fiat Uno) I conjure thee Mark to appear before us here in this circle.'

He might come if she got his name right.

The old girl started spinning on the spot and I had to duck to avoid her left hook. The rest of us stood red-faced, looking at each other slyly the way you do when you're holding hands. She stopped and hung her big arms like doner kebab spits up in the air: 'Mark is here! His spirit is with us! I want you all to turn and look at the person beside you.'

Hello Peeler.

'And I want you to say to that person, "You are a beautiful person." Say it in Mark's name.'

Peeler was scowling and chewing the inside of his cheeks.

I said 'Up yours, cocksucker' and he laughed. The fucker laughed. He was at Marcus' funeral and he was laughing. Pam was laughing. Even the fucking Number One fucking Governor was laughing now, what were they all laughing at? Was it me?

Of course it wasn't Peeler I was cross with, I know that now. It was . . . so many things, how dare Marcus die? And die so fast? How dare Julia fuck that priest? What exactly did Sarbridge do to you, Helen, to make you write like that? And how dare you, precious you, my precious, darling Helen, why are you too so very, very dead?

Peeler put his candle close to mine. The old girl had lit his and our two candles joined and both are lit now, sharing one big flame with one white hot heart. I look at it stretching away from me, going into miniature in the distance as if it's at the wrong end of a telescope, or I am. They're all singing again, mouths opening and shutting all around me, mad caverns of dark tongues, and I hear your voice, Helen, in my head, in my mouth, my most intimate place saying The Body of Christ.

Stay with me, Helen, and be my comfort. Will I regain my soul if

I give my life for you? Can somebody like me seriously do something like that? Is it possible? I hear your voice say from very far away: *The light shineth in the darkness and the darkness comprehendeth it not.*

The candle flames dance in and out of my sight, jumping like my heart, jumping all over the place, my heart, I have to hold it down, get it in my hand, hold it down to keep my heart down or it will break. Out. I rise several feet in the air and watch myself walk over to the Number One Governor. I look at his mouth opening and shutting, singing, and I shout FUCK YOU! The words rattle off the ceiling, up high where I am and I am not. I see the Number One Governor shiver slightly and keep singing. FUCK YOU, I shout again, FUCK YOU ALL. Both of us are shouting this time, me and myself, and I watch me down there scream at me up here in the rafters. My mouth is wide like a lion's yawn. A bubble of sadness pushes from my guts, explodes through my mouth and floats up here, where it touches my heart and showers me in sobs.

I am wet. I fall, float wearily down and find Pam guiding me out through the swing doors to the corridor. She's half hugging, half carrying me – luckily she's a big woman – saying something about me being beside myself.

The hot wax did the damage as much as the flame, they say. Wax all over, all on fire and my hand in the middle of it, gripping hard, holding on for dear life

Helen's dead. Helen's dead. My darling Helen is dead. I could run to the ends of the earth but my darling Helen, my one and only true love, will never be anything but dead.

Sunlight blazes through the stained glass and I turn to look at you. A shaft of pain sears up my neck but oh, the reward. You look so beautiful, Helen, as you come up the aisle to marry me. You leave your father's arm and stand happily beside me, lifting that luminescent veil to show your face more wanting and lovely than I have ever seen you before. Choral music fills my soul as I bend to kiss you and we glide, entwined, slowly to the floor where we meld and move and consummate before we've even wed.

'Holy, holy,' sings the choir and with every sacred syllable my body worships you that little bit more roughly, all glory, laud and honour, I hear you moan and cry as my power overshadows you and we descend, beyond the crypt, the sous-sol, into the earth below. Earth is dusting your cheeks, dust thou art and have but a short time to live, let me lift this veil of dirt from upon you, my love, let me wipe the brown earth from your lips, let me hold you, don't cry, we cry together, my heart suffers too – God, help me, you're not Helen under me but if I press harder, shut my eyes and fuck you deeper, I might just get my Helen back again. No, don't look at me like that, I want Helen, not you, go, get out, I want Helen with me in this grave, not you, not you, not *you*, my *mother*.

I never felt my dick shrink quicker than when I woke up from that one. But I remember learning in school that it's perfectly normal to shag your mother in your dreams. The time you worry is when you enjoy it. But I must be psychic, because who should they tell me is coming to the prison for her very first visit today but

I was asleep when the chaplain dropped a duplicate visitor's order on my face.

'She's waiting for you,' he pressed my shoulder, 'she's in the visitor's centre now.'

I shuffled after him down the wing and out through education to the holding pen where the harnesses are handed out before we're allowed to go in among the humans. They're hi-vis green belts with shoulder straps to give the staff something to get hold of in a punch-up. I told them I wouldn't need one, it was my legal advisor come to see me, my Julia. But if I'd seen the name on that duplicate VO there'd have been a punch-up all right. I'd have thrown myself around till I broke bones and smashed the place down. Anything rather than endure a visit from my mother.

She'd dressed down for the occasion in slacks and a black cashmere sweater. I can still smell her halitosis. At least she came straight to the point: I had broken every damned rule in the Bible and what was I going to do about it? I said I didn't remember lying down with a beast of the field but would work on it if she got me out of here. Meanwhile the sooner we forgot we were ever related and agreed to ignore each other, the better for us both.

'Honour thy father and thy mother,' she started.

I finished it, 'That my days might be long? But I don't want my days to be long, Mummy. The last thing I want is for my days to be long.'

'Behold my son!' she moaned and pulled a bit of newspaper from her handbag. A clipping from the *Mail* about some Yank on Death Row looking forward to his lethal jab because it was just what God wanted.

'It says here,' out came her red-leather bound Bible from her bag, 'Genesis 9, verse 6. "Whoso sheddeth man's blood, by man shall his blood be shed."'

Nice. I knew it wouldn't be long before that Bible appeared. Until I left home, her Bible had belittled, chastised and humiliated me just about every day of my life.

'A life for a life,' she murmured as she laid it on her knee and twitched it open with its ribbon. I stared at the crown of her head, where her grey hairs emerged into the world as stiff and steely as her heart, and I felt an almost overpowering urge to kill her. Instead I found myself asking her something I've always wanted to know, why she believes in God.

'It's like riding a bicycle, darling,' she said, smiling at a female warder who was strolling past pretending not to listen. 'One day I just could and it's never gone away. Simple as that.'

What, I asked, if you haven't got a bike?

She allowed her precious Bible to move into the care of her left claw while she pulled a tissue from up her sleeve: 'I can't see why you find my simple faith so offensive,' she sniffled, 'why do you want me to suffer like this?'

So she was the one who was suffering. I was glad we'd cleared that one up. She was actually looking very old, like a building with the stucco still in place but where everything behind it was cracked and crumbling. Maybe it was finally sinking in that her flesh and blood was within prison walls.

'I never asked you to come.'

I'd never seen her cry before. Not even when my father died. The staff standing along the walls turned and watched but, thank God, they did nothing more. Even in her deepest distress, her Bible was the whole focus of my mother's attention. She cried into it, she cuddled it against her dusty cheeks, she clasped it to her belly. Little wonder the bookmark was so frayed and the leather worn as thin as prosciutto. That Bible got more action than my father ever did.

So different from Julia's pristine confirmation Bible. Julia's Bible. Parked on her naked stomach as she sat back among her pillows . . .

My mother's voice cut through like razor wire.

'Patrick! You're not listening!'

Correct. I had no intention of thinking about my mother when I could wallow in that last glorious weekend in Cambridge with Julia. We spent the whole time delving in and out of Helen's book and each other and I remember so well standing in front of Julia's fridge on the Sunday morning wondering why everything women ate was so tiny. There was a tiny brown loaf, a pretty little half pint of milk, some miniscule yoghurty things, pancakes the size of a baboon's thumbnail, cherry tomatoes, mini-cheeses and a couple of boxes of dinky speckled eggs produced by something about the size of a starling. It crossed my mind that God (if any, so far not admitted) does have an evil sense of humour. He's crippled us males with worry in case our dicks are too small, and all the time the girls would probably rather be wrapping their tongues around something the size of a cocktail sausage. Anyway. Eggs and milk plus bread equals French toast. I set to.

Twenty minutes later Julia was by my side in the cardboard dressing gown going, 'and another thing!'

Now what?

'When you see Halberd, ask her about Bathsheba. I've been looking on the net – Patrick, what do you think you're doing?'

I was soundly bollocked for using up the quails' eggs she'd bought for an MCR meeting as well as scoffing her blinis. (Blinis were the poncey little pancakes I'd eaten to stave off the pangs while I cooked.) Any sign of thanks for cooking her a delicious breakfast? It was the finest French toast I'd ever cooked, and was all the more delicious for being eaten with fingers that still smelled of Julia.

I sniffed my fingers.

'Patrick!' My mother was scowling at me. 'I'm talking to you! You don't know how I suffer, knowing that my child is in a place like this and never even thinks to call his mother?'

The woman I love is dead, a woman I thought I loved is married to someone else, a man I thought I didn't love but did has gone and died, a man I know I hate keeps visiting me to persuade me to take a fall for him, and the woman I loathe above all else and who gave birth to me is patronising me and there is no way I can get fucking rid of her.

'Are we bound together, Mummy? You and I? Like David and – ?'

I stopped. I didn't care what she said. I was more interested in letting my mind mosey back to Julia with the cardboard dressing gown falling off one shoulder every time she raised a sliver of French toast to her lips.

'I've been looking on the net,' Julia told me, 'Bathsheba's baby did die. They thought it was God's punishment.'

'Why?'

'David stole her from her husband, didn't he? He got the husband killed. In the war.'

'What? David? King David? In the Bible?'

'Yep, and after the baby died he and Bathsheba got married.'

'And God made them happy ever after?'

'Not exactly, but their next son was King Solomon. So it's all God's plan or something. What I don't see is why Halberd chose to write about that moment when the first baby died. That's the weird thing. And,' Julia went on, 'why does she put Bathsheba there in her book? Bathsheba's from the Old Testament and in Halberd's book she comes near the end. After *five* New Testament meditations. That makes it arguably the most important chapter in the whole thing. What is Halberd trying to say? Patrick? Patrick, you're not listening, are you? Patrick! I'm talking to you! Patrick, listen to me, I'm telling you about my priest!'

My mother was hacking into my consciousness again: 'He's so good to me, you know, my priest. I'd be lost without him. It's because of him I'm here.' She stroked a thumbnail lazily up her cleavage. 'Your prison chaplain bumped into him at a party and told him you were on hunger strike, so they got me to come. I'm supposed to persuade you to eat.' She twisted her body away from me.

'I eat,' I told the table. I could feel something stroking the back of my head. I'm lost, I told Helen silently, I'm wading through a million mad emotions and my mother is only interested in herself. You're the only person who cares about me, Helen. Deliver me from this hell . . .

You walked from behind me and sat primly on the low table between us. Naked with your red hair loose around your face and smudged make-up. Just like the night you died. You leaned across my mother and whispered: 'You know what I was saying about Bathsheba, Patrick.' Your dark nipples jiggled as you rocked back and laughed: 'It's simple. We suffer, we love, we suffer, we love. Two strands of the same rope.'

It's what Sarbidge's wife had said.

'We have to keep loving, whatever happens. But it's not easy.'

My mother says it's easy, I thought. Seek and ye shall find, all that?

'That may be how it works for her,' Helen smiled.

'It *is* how it works for me,' my mother said. 'Oh yes, he can nit-pick all right,' she snarled, 'he can win any argument and make a bishop look a fool.'

'Who, Mummy? Jesus?'

'Sarbridge. On television last night.'

I hear Helen laugh. Her trucker's laugh.

'It's no laughing matter,' my mother said. 'He knows his scripture but he avoids the God who wrote it.' My mother caressed her Bible again. 'You can't pick and mix, you know. What with divorced priests marrying queers and archbishops writing poetry, what next? What next? It's tearing the church apart. Making us all look silly. And your friend Sarbridge – '

'He's no friend of mine,' I said.

'On that at least we agree.'

I looked at her hand resting on the Bible on the table, her knuckles as baggy as an elephant's knees and the nails all seashell pink. I took her hand and covered it with both of mine.

'Let's just sit here together, Mummy, and not talk. We get on best when we don't talk.'

'Yes,' she sniffled. But there was no stopping her.

'We can pray instead.'

'OK,' I said. 'Have your bit of fun. What'll we pray for, eh?'

She cleared her throat as softly as a puppy: 'An easy death.'

I leaned over and whispered close: 'I could help you there.'

Three of the staff spotted that the distance between us had closed to less than the permitted twenty centimetres and circled, scanning us one-eyed like sharks. My mother tugged her hand free and wiped it on her skirt. Her mouth worked as if she had more to say and was struggling to keep it decent . . .

'And to see that man Sarbridge thrown out and shamed!'

God wouldn't want us to tear the church to shreds, she said. The case would drag through the papers for weeks, putting the church through all sorts. Bad enough having a son in prison (though her church had formed a support group to comfort her, her!) but couldn't I just stop making a fuss and plead guilty? Couldn't I see how much better it would be for everyone if I did?

I watched her play her thumb along the gold-edged pages of her Bible. No point in shoving her bodily against the wall and shouting into her baggy eyes and snaggled, brown teeth that she and her personal saviour should fuck off and torment somebody else. 'Give your heart to the Lord,' she used to say. 'Be saved,' she'd go, on and on, 'be born again.' HOW? I knelt with her so often, squeezing my eyes so hard that the bright pentagrams and rhomboids blended into a searing white light. I prayed, really prayed for God to save me. My mother wanted it and I wanted it and everybody agreed it was a good thing, so time after time I tried. Why didn't it happen? Was I defective? Why did God want everybody else's heart but not mine?

I could feel Helen's palm rest between my shoulders. She knew.

My mother's voice was ringing like a car alarm in the distance. The aubergine lipstick was still in motion in front of me.

'Obey your parent in all things' . . .

Shut up, Mummy! Shut up! *Shut up!*

'Let's open the Bible together, Patrick.' Not that old trick. 'Let's just let the holy book fall open between us and He will show us His will.'

'Don't be stupid!'

My mother swung her whole torso to face me: 'Don't you mock

the Bible, Patrick! It's not just for experts. We don't need to study it at Cambridge to love it any more than we need to know physics to enjoy the sun!'

The Bible fell open. She ran a pink pearly nail to the top of the left-hand page.

'We are born to misery as the sparks fly upward.'

'Not Job again, please!'

She patted my knee. It was a maternal gesture like electronic torture. She shuffled the Bible to another page and handed it to me with a look of pure victory. A shiver ran over me. Isaiah 6, 7.

God help me, I'm skewered. I've been skewered by the Bible: '*And he touched my mouth and said Behold, this has touched your lips, your guilt is taken away and your sins forgiven.*'

Touched my mouth. You touched my mouth, Helen. You laid the holy bread on my tongue, blessing my turbulent love for you, making me want you all the more. Am I to be forgiven? Who can forgive me? Hot, fat tears poured down my cheeks and into my mouth. Helen, my love, my darling, do you forgive me? Where are you, Helen? I can't see you. Helen? Don't go, for God's sake don't go!

My mother pulled her chair close to mine and took it into her head to press me to her musty chest: 'It's all right, darling, I'm here. Tell me all about it, baby, tell me what happened.' She was stroking my back, smoothing my hair, squeezing me tighter and tighter. Don't, I shouted, don't, the way I used to when she started slapping my legs when I was six years old and I couldn't run away. I scrunched my face. Don't breathe. Don't breathe. If I hold it, hold it, I can die here now and it will be her fault. My vision was red turning to orange and white, white, white filling my skull until as I reluctantly gulped in air, my whole body felt suspended again, far from sensuality and hunger, far from pain and my mother, free from all wants and needs.

The staff said later that they could have done with a harness on my mother as they dragged us apart. All I knew was that Helen was with me again, shining. She covered my eyes from behind when I hit the floor, and laughed into my hair. I leaned back into her shoulder and let her fingertip trail down my forehead between my eyebrows, over the centre of my nose to rest on my mouth. Briefly she caressed the little hollow under the septum, rested her finger again on the fat of my lower lip and then pulled away, leaving me with a long, lazy sssssshhhh.

I sit here alone. Silent. Eyes dry, legs crossed, arms folded. It all balances now, question and answer, like the perfect engine, the perfect simultaneous equation, the perfect sentence.

Prison is freedom, you see, prison is peace. Outside is full of dangers, outside is fear. And my biggest fear, God protect me, my greatest fear is that if my mother ever chooses to visit me again, I will be guilty of murder for real.

But I am not alone. As long as Helen is with me, I am safe. Soon I will know what Helen wants of me. I will open her book again and hear her speak to me.

I'd expected to find inspiration in Mary Magdalene. She is a saint for our times. She upped and left her family, a more significant act for a woman than for the male disciples, though it was a big enough step for them. She (with other women from Galilee) supported Jesus and his party financially. When the authorities began to close in, the men ran away like rabbits but Magdalene stayed for the crucifixion and beyond. (Incidentally, only one of the four canonical gospels – John – lists Jesus' mother as being present at the cross.) Mary Magdalene was first to see the resurrected Jesus when she recognised the way he called her name outside the tomb. According to the non-canonical Gospel of Mary, Jesus also came to her in a vision after his death.

I was ready to be inspired by Mary Magdalene but again and again Mary of Bethany pushed herself forward. I'd not thought about her much before. She was the quiet one, always being bossed around by her more forceful sister Martha. It's Martha who takes charge of feeding Jesus and his disciples. It's Martha who summons Jesus when Lazarus is ill. She is first out of the door when Jesus finally turns up and when Jesus sees her, he uses her name twice – 'Martha, Martha' – to calm her before they talk.

Mary is a listener. The way she sits adoringly at Jesus' feet used to irritate me, I must confess. But she's a woman of action too. When she decides to anoint Jesus, she plans it meticulously and carries it through even though others mock her. The moment when Jesus vindicated her action must have been a high point in her life. Is there a hint (Matthew 26, 7) that she knew the significance of her act before he did? Would this be a rare occasion when a disciple or follower understood something of high theological significance before Jesus did?

I believe that before she anointed Jesus, there was another turning point in Jesus' life. I believe that Mary of Bethany led him to his destiny. Without her, it is possible that none of the Passion story would have taken place at all. Her sister Martha is credited with recognising Jesus as the Christ, even though he had just allowed their sick brother Lazarus to die, but it is the sight of Mary prostrate and weeping that stirs Jesus to perform the defining miracle which foreshadows his own death and rising.

He seems unsure of his role, of quite what he must do, until Mary silently persuades him. Mary moved him so greatly that Jesus 'groaned in the spirit and was troubled' (John 11, 33) and in possibly the most famous verse in the entire canon (John 11, 35) 'Jesus wept'.

Mary of Bethany is the only person, it seems to me, who loved Jesus body, mind, heart and soul. Not only did she sit at his feet to hear his words (Luke 10, 39), she anointed his body sacrificially, in an act she performed with her whole heart. (We should not forget that in the Hebrew Bible, mention of feet is often a euphemism for genitalia.) Like Ruth she fell in love with the goodness in her man. Like Esther she was chosen from a crowd for special attention and I think it is fair to deduce a sexual element in Mary's relationship with Jesus, on her part at least. Mary of Bethany (like Jesus' mother) was not one of the itinerant followers; she loved him from her own home where he was a highly favoured guest.

I wish I were the sort of priest who could tell you that God is my constant companion. It would not be true. For me God is a guest whose visits are precious, brief and rare. I find in Mary of Bethany someone who understands that. She loved Jesus unquestioningly, whatever he did. She urged him to recognise the depth of his divinity and to act upon it. We are not told specifically that she was favoured with a visit from the risen Christ. I suspect that after he died, she was left with a heart full of love and was not sure what to do with it.

I wonder if she remembered that God wove her in her mother's womb (Psalm 139) and taught her hope. I wonder if she felt that while the men had their sips and rituals, her place was to keep feeding them – and anyone else who needed it – in the same way that she'd fed Jesus, abundantly, lovingly, patiently. As long as she did that, she knew that some day she might hear a familiar footstep on the path. She might hear God's love push open the door. She might see in the sunburst of his smile that what bound them together would never be sundered. God's love would stride into her open arms, belly and thighs against her, shoulders and flesh and weight all together, and cup her face and say, 'I'm home, Mary. I'm yours.'

I'm holding Sarbridge's copy of Helen's book here in my hand. Below that final section about Mary of Bethany, two words are written in pencil: *I'm yours.*

I didn't write it. Neither did Sarbridge.

A long tail dangles from the y. Helen did.

HMP GREYMOOR

Dear Mummy,

I've been thinking a lot about what you said and want to say that I've changed my mind about pleading not gui

Dear Mummy,

I've given what you said a lot of thought and wish I could say I've changed my mind

Dear Mummy,

I've made a decision. Here's another Visitor's Order. I want you to do me a favour.

I've wiped all my disks, including the one with all this on it, and I want you to smuggle out all my papers and

There's just been an almighty crash on my cell door. Some sort of rumpus in the corridor. Just keep my head down till it passes. Probably another poor bastard having the shit kicked out of him.

'Pardon your French,' I can imagine you saying. Well, some day you'll stick your head up out of that cosy, evangelical rut you've dug for yourself and get a fucking life, if you pardon my French, Mummy. But for now that's not my concern.

There are people running in the corridor now. I hope the place isn't on fire. No alarms. Yet.

So –

Can I trust them to remember me if there *is* a fire? I daren't look out of here in case I get kicked in too. Have you any idea in your holy cocoon how this feels? I could pray but do you know something, it would make fuck-all difference. Just as it made fuck-all difference to all the saints and assorted other goody-goodies who've been needlessly slaughtered in God's name over the centuries.

I bet you're praying for me now. Well, stop it. Fucking cheek. At least Sarbridge never did that.

I'm so sorry. I didn't mean to lay into you when I started writing this letter, I wanted to

The crashes are getting worse, as if everybody's throwing furniture.

I just want you to do this one thing for me: Come and see me once more. That's all I ask. Come and see me and smuggle out my writings. They are a love letter to Julia, which means they're private, OK? Private. You are not to read them. And they must not fall into the wrong hands. You're the only living person I can ask to do this. I have no choice but to trust you, so please don't let me down. I think I've decided about the guilty plea but I'm not sure, it's a lot to think about.

There's just been a lot of shouting, then a long shriek.

So – if you've *ever* loved me, even when I was just born and you held me in your arms and didn't know me yet, come once more and do this for me. Please.

Patrick x

I wanted to tell her everything, Helen. I longed for my mother to hold me and stroke my pain away like Mary, mother of God. I needed that. But from the moment she and that Bible walked into the visitors' centre, as cosy as a hedgehog, telling me that it was her prayer group that hit on the idea of my pleading guilty . . .

What do I do, Helen? Neil and my mother want the same thing. Isn't it weird that the single point at which the two extremes of the Anglican church can agree lies here, in my cell, in me? They want me to plead guilty, stay here and let it all go quiet. Should I do it, Helen? Do *you* want me to do it? I wouldn't do it for them but if you asked me, if you . . .

Darling Patrick,

You are quite correct. We have been praying for you. The Lord bids us in Thess. 5, 17 to pray without ceasing. In fact all our house groups (37 of them now, by the power of the Lord) have had you on their prayer lists ever since, well, you know what.

Your anger – your French, as you put it – is the devil struggling in you. Let it happen, darling. Let the devil out and you will be free. Free in yourself, even though you are still in jail. I hope you understand. I pray that you do.

I will come on Tuesday. Yours in Christ,

Mummy.

PS: As I have not heard to the contrary, I am assuming that you survived the riot unscathed. The report in the *Daily Mail* was terrifying. We're all praying for the families of the dead and injured. God bless, Mummy.

May God bless you too, Mummy.

The rioters trashed D wing to protest about overcrowding, so I'm on A wing now, sharing with two other cons. I don't know their names, I can't be bothered. They've taken both bunks. I get two square metres on the floor to myself, to share with Helen. She's talking to me as I write this, about whether I should sign that confession Sarbridge cooked up and how I should plead. We talk about it all the time actually.

She's with me all the time.

I'm at my desk and if I turn my head, I can see her sitting with her back to the cupboard watching me. My cellmates are off on exercise, so we're alone. Yes, there she is. Naked. She's just got up and is coming to look over my shoulder at what I'm writing. She's whispering, cold, in my ear: 'Why did you do it, Patrick?'

I should feel her breath on my neck but I don't. I watch her neat hand skim over my shoulder and down my shirt and I feel nothing until she reaches my groin. She grips all of me so hard that breath shoots into me and my eyes water. She releases and laughs and, God help me, I'm sitting there with my first real erection in weeks.

I didn't kill you, Helen. You know I didn't.

Her body presses into my back as she straightens. I'm dizzy with the scent of her armpit as she moves away. She sits on the bottom bunk and drapes herself back on the bed. I watch her breasts spread and her belly fall concave. But mostly I'm looking at the auburn hairs over her pubic mound. She stretches her arms up behind her head and eases her neck. Slowly, luxuriously she opens her legs and I'm transfixed by her dark labial crest.

The heels of my hands are over my eyes before I can stop them. Fear pounds me. When I open my eyes again, she's gone.

I remember so well standing in that Deal church looking at Helen's name on the page Whitehead's mother had given me. I knew then that I couldn't write up Sarbridge, for *The Truth* or anybody else. I'd risk hurting Helen again and I couldn't ever do that.

Meanwhile *The Truth*'s apology appeared in very small print on page 15 under a feature about head lice in the workplace. It was the apology that caught the eye of the *Telegraph*. Then the *Spectator* saw fit to review her book. Fairly, I thought. They deplored her feminism of course but complimented her sexually imaginative approach. Sales of Helen's book rose to double figures for the first time in a decade, somebody from the *Spectator* played golf with somebody on the *Sun* and it was only a matter of time until the tabloids smelt a love rat.

I'd never seen a tabloid siege before. Cars parked any old place, pizza boxes and cans everywhere, lazy football matches under the street lamp. For all the world like a scorching bank holiday, except that it was December. I thought I spotted my hero Paul Kibitz in the crowd actually, and was gathering the courage to go and say how much I admired his work when Cyril was on my mobile again: for once in the history of the *South London Chronicle* we had the chance to scoop the nationals. Get in there, he said, talk to her. Listen to her, don't forget to listen, get her to loosen up. Take wine.

Was he going to pay for the wine then? The line went dead.

I wasn't clear in my mind – am I ever? – but I thought maybe I could ask Helen to write something herself. Or I could just see her and write nothing, I'd done that before. One way or the other, it was a legitimate excuse to be in her company.

The crowds were thickest, in every sense, around her vicarage front door so I put my hood up and mooched down next door's path in the dark. With my sleeves over my fists, I pushed through the privet hedge and hid behind some bins to think.

The vicarage side door was only a few yards away. Light from the street lamp slanted across the gravel path, so in theory the press lads could see me if I walked over there. They were concentrating on the front door but if even one of them noticed me trying to breach the precious citadel from the side, they'd be all over me in seconds. Then Helen would hate me for ever and all hope of my scoop would be lost. But I couldn't sit there freezing my tits off by the bins all night.

I grabbed a sizeable pebble from the gravel and bowled it into the street. It landed on the bonnet of a parked Merc with a satisfying clang and while they all turned to look, I ran across the slice of sodium glare to Helen's side door and tried the handle.

Not even locked.

I was hit by combating smells of dog and stew and as my eyes softened to the darkness, I knew I was in one of those big, farmhouse-type kitchens full of tall cupboards.

'You're back.' Helen's voice.

I closed the door softly and felt around until I found a light switch. Photographs curled on every wall of jolly types in yachting colours. Piles of Wellingtons from giant size down to toddler lay around a range with about a hundred socks drying on the rail and four dog bowls beside it. Sticky paper garlands hung everywhere, obviously made by the vicar's adored offspring, and at a long wooden table Helen herself perched on a stool in a red dress with her feet bare. She was alone except for a bottle of champagne, bowls of olives, hummus, crackers, grapes, and two glasses.

I dithered by the door. She was flushed and smiling. Then she saw it was me.

'Well aren't you an answer to prayer,' she said and lurched for the champagne bottle, showing me at least four inches of freckled cleavage. The champagne was lively and climbed out of the glass as she poured. She dipped her index finger in the spillage and sucked it, glowering at me, before she drained her glass and weaved out to the hall.

The effort of switching on the hall light seemed to exhaust her.

'Do you want your shoes?' I called. There was a pair of red high-heeled shoes lying on their sides under her stool.

'No, thank you. Just the bottle.'

I knocked my thigh against the corner of the table, I was in such a hurry to get that champagne bottle, and the two bottles of Turkish Riesling in my coat pockets, into Helen's company as swiftly as possible. I'd managed to be with her, alone and uninvited, and here she was asking me to follow her with champagne?

Possibilities danced like dust in front of me as I stood in the hall. I remembered the Georgian fanlight above the front door from before and worked out in reverse that if I pushed open the stained glass door on my right, I'd be in Helen's flat.

Her mantelpiece was smothered in Christmas cards and although she didn't have a Christmas tree she'd tied lavish red bows everywhere. I remember noticing that she'd emptied the ashtrays. She laughed when I came in, a light sort of what-the-fuck laugh, not her full-bellied trucker one. At first I couldn't quite see her – the room was lit only by a small lamp at the bedside – until she stood up from where she'd hunkered down to look at a Nativity scene in the fireplace with figures three inches high.

'Thank you,' she said as I put the champagne bottle on her desk. 'You can go now.' She waved an arm at the street just outside her drawn curtains, 'And take your friends with you.' She stared at her feet: 'Where are my shoes? Look at those poor feet, what on earth can you think of me?'

'Do you want me to get them?'

'What?'

'Your shoes?'

'Did I say this would be a good time?' Her voice was hyper-polite, 'I'm so sorry, this is a terrible time actually.'

She gave a washed-out smile and dropped her head full on to her chest. There was something so desperate about her that I couldn't leave her even if I'd wanted to. So I did the next best thing I could think of. I refilled her glass and knocked it back myself. One thing I've learned about a drinking party: there is absolutely no point in being the only sober person in the room. I refilled the glass and drained it again. But the more I drank, the more deathly sober I felt. I'd been longing to see her so much. I'd lain awake with excitement all night, my soul seething with imagined scenarios. Now I was with her, I felt nothing but fear. I yanked out the first Turkish Riesling and unscrewed it.

'Of all people to be here now,' she said topping up the same glass and sucking it dry. 'Are you proud of yourself, Patrick? Are you? I need to sit down.'

She grabbed for my hand to steady herself.

'You're a bastard, God!' she called to the ceiling, 'You send this boy to me now? Of all times!' She poked me in the ribs, 'Why did I ever speak to you in the first place? Why did I ever think I could treat you as a friend!'

We made it together to her oatmeal chair by the window where she sat heavily and tucked her feet under her skirt.

'My mistake,' she said, pointing at the air, 'I let somebody find my vocation for me. Funny, you know, I didn't even know I'd lost it. He brought it out into the light and said Look, Helen. This is it. This is Good. And you know what? He didn't even take off his over-coat.'

Who didn't take off his overcoat? Sarbridge?

She opened her packet of cigarettes on the little table beside her and dropped it. I jumped forward dying to help and we grappled on the floor, heads together. I let her win. She knelt back and offered me one. With her palm supporting my knuckles, and her shoulder under that red dress touching mine, she cupped my hand and lit it for me. It was the last gentle touch of my life.

'Chaotic in here,' she said, kicking at some books on the floor, '*I'm* chaos. It's not in the Bible, chaos, but it damn well should be. I don't mean evil, evil can be terribly orderly, what, is there wine down my chin? Is that better? What I love about Jesus, that talent for chaos, stirring people up, going No, not like that!' – she was wagging her cigarette at me – 'not like that just because it's the usual, try this. Instead. Not all chaos is good though. Ho no. It does damage too. It has done, for me.' She swallowed, and winced. 'Done for me.'

She slopped more wine into our communal glass. Her aim wasn't great but she didn't care.

'That's why I couldn't do it to you,' she said.

Do what to me? As far as I was concerned, she could do anything to me, especially sitting there with that full silky skirt around her and one strap falling.

But you know what women are like when they're drinking, next thing I knew, she started sobbing, awful, ugly sobs, and in between she was laughing too, saying she could see that I loved her but how could she take my love? Even though she wanted love, by God she needed love from somebody . . . but no, she couldn't, wouldn't if she couldn't return it. Did I realise, she giggled, her face all blotchy, did I realise how hard it was for her, a priest, to try and put me off coming to church?

It took me a while to realise what she was saying. That she had actually wanted to enjoy my love.

'Oh Helen,' I said and dared to sit on the floor at her feet.

She rolled away from me a little, as if she would like to get up but had to shelve the idea until she'd revived herself with a smoke. A long tube of ash fell on to her red dress.

'I did my best to be a good priest, you know. I loved it, I really did. But you . . . no, let me speak, Patrick, what you did was important. Are you listening?' I nodded. 'When I decided to become a priest, it was because I was in love, and I thought it was with God. But it wasn't. You made me look back into my heart.'

She rubbed her face with her free hand.

'The thing, saddest thing, he never knew . . .'

'Who?'

'I wrote in, you know, his copy of my book. And he never saw it. Isn't that the funniest joke of all? I wrote the whole thing for him, to tell him how much I love him.'

'Like Mary of Bethany?'

'And he never even read it!'

So you were right, Julia. Her book was a love letter.

'Were you raped, like the Virgin Mary?'

'No,' she breathed. 'I told you I wasn't and I meant it. I never had a baby either, dead or alive. That was part of the midrash, things I put in that didn't happen literally but meant something. We had these plans, you see. But they died.' She rested her hand on my knee. 'We could have saved the world. We could have set up a new church, brought world peace, anything! Midrash was a way to say that.'

'Why didn't you just tell him straight?'

She was patting her face and head as if everything might spring apart at any moment: 'Somebody told me once that unrequited love is the only love that lasts. But it hurts so much. Doesn't it. You understand, Patrick. You say nothing, but I know you do. Say nothing. That's best.'

Her cigarette fell on the floor. I lifted it gently away. She bent forward and whispered that she'd like to lie down now. I helped her over to the bed and watched her drape herself back, eyes closed.

'Kneel,' she moaned.

I knelt at the bedside like a child at prayer. She raised herself on her elbows to look, an action which flopped her hand over mine. It was cold. I turned my hand to enfold it.

'Were you lovers for long?'

She stopped as if I'd said something shocking. Then she laughed, and rested her thumb on her lower lip the way Sarbridge does. I'm sure she wasn't trying to be girlish in that big frock with her thumb at her mouth and her feet crossed beside her, that was not her way, but she looked enchanting. She smiled. When the words came, they were almost inaudible: 'We were never lovers.'

My heart blossomed. Did I hear correctly?

'You were never?' My darling Helen. My love.

'Lovers? No. We weren't. Didn't you know that?' She shook her head and laughed silently: 'He never cleared his life for me. Simple as that. I think fidelity . . . terrified him. I was not allowed to cling to him. I had to let . . .'

With her eyes half-closed she reached for the bottle from the floor and sucked it dry.

'I thought you were him, you know. What a joke. Him coming back.'

I wanted to hold her sweet face in my hands and say it's all right, Helen, you are loved. I love you. I'm here and I'll love you till the end of time.

Instead I tried to kiss her.

She bit my tongue.

She apologised immediately, and so did I. It didn't hurt all that much to begin with, but so much blood. It wouldn't stop falling all over my shirt so she wiped my mouth with her skirt, and made me promise by nodding that I would not call anybody. I would not call for help.

Whatever she wanted.

'Don't call anybody, Patrick,' she said thickly, wiping her hand down her breast. 'It ends here.'

What ends?

She shook her head and brushed a lock of red hair from her eyes. 'God, I'm tired, I have to . . .'

She sighed. She pulled away. I could feel her fingers hovering in the tender creases of my palm, then drawing down the length of my fingers until, tip to tip, our hands parted. She curled away from me on the bed, tucked her bare feet close to her bottom and wept.

Sarbridge. She'd known he was coming. But he didn't eat her sacrificial food or drink her wine. He did not ask her to live with him. He didn't even take off his coat. He must have left through the side door before I turned up. The very thing the journos outside were after and they missed it.

His visit ended her life. He knows that. That's why he keeps coming to see me. He could have wrapped her in his arms and told her that he'd always loved her and that his heart was as broken as mine is, though I think that his is smaller and not so heavy. But he ducked it. Don't ask me why, maybe he took fright at the crowds outside or she came on too strong. Instead he begged her not to speak to the press. Best all round if she said nothing to anyone. Best just to be discreet.

They were back pain tablets she'd been prescribed after her accident. Co-proxamol. She'd been saving them for months.

'How many?' I yelled, when I found the packet by the bed.

'Enough,' she said.

In bright terror I made for her phone, her landline, if we got the ambulance quick and got her pumped she just might –

She lurched off the bed, dragged herself across the floor and drawing every remaining brain cell she had to attention, ripped the receiver from my hand and dropped it rocking on the floor. She retched with the effort and swallowed. Pale. Curled up foetal on the floor.

I helped her back to the bed.

Helen dying. Wanting to die. My brain would not accept this. It could not be true.

He did not stay. I knew that was true.

I would stay. As long as I breathed, Helen would not be alone.

She was shivering. I lay on the outside of her bedclothes while she lay beside me under them and I tried to warm her. Can you picture me lying on her pillow drinking in the scent of her hair, feeling her weight beside me, pulling the covers higher for her, stroking her hair and cheek? Imagining what it would be like to be married to her? I turned off her bedside lamp, it seemed to be bothering her, and lit a thick, red candle on the bedside table. She caught me staring at the crackling flame.

'Sparks,' she said. 'As sparks fly upward we are born to woe . . . or is it sorrow, no, not woe, pain, it must be pain? It's Job, isn't it?' The warmth of my body beside her must have brought on a burst of energy because she lumbered over to her bookshelves to check the quote.

She was laughing when she fell. Like a tall building going down in slow motion. She rolled against the shelves, one hand out, and the whole lot toppled over her. God's truth. Two huge hardbacks started it all, a matching pair about the end of civilisation or something. They thudded on to her head and chest and the rest followed and in seconds she was buried.

I propped the shelves back up, shoved the books off her and knelt beside her pleading Get up, don't die. I straddled her legs, leaning over her, pushing her hair off her face. Her breathing was weird, hardly there so I started kissing her mouth, her most intimate place, to warm her, wake her up. I was panicking of course, but I . . . I . . .

Don't ask me why, I just knew that if I caressed her, loved her, somehow I could persuade her to breathe again. That red dress was all askew so I sat her up and undid the zip, God she was heavy, I wanted to free her lungs, her breasts, oh God her breasts, so I smoothed my hands over her, no bra, just soft jelly breasts, the nipples as hard as stones. I kissed one and heard her moan, a sound just for me. I sucked the other and held its weight, its underside, and felt her hands flap against my chest pushing.

But you want me, Helen, I know you do. You said so.

Her hip bones were cold under my palms as I pushed the dress up to her waist. She stretched her arms up behind her head and mewed as my little finger teased along her inner thigh. I'd imagined that first daring swirl of my tongue around her navel so often and now I dared to do it, with my fingers deep in her pubic hair, hair so unfashionably long that I dared tell myself that nobody else had ever seen that russet forbidden forest . . .

Gently I unwound her legs from her white pants. I unzipped myself, ready for worship. She said it again: 'Kneel.'

I did, and moved in between her thighs. I smoothed both my hands over the pale belly skin still crinkled by the elastic of her pants and heaved her lower body up to me. I'll never forget that first sweet genital encounter, first with my fingers, two, then three, and her shudder as I entered her.

'Kneel,' she said, 'Kneel! Love me, kneel, help me, love me, please, kneel!'

The bruises, the fat lip, God help me, she reminded me of you, Julia. You remember that time when you put on the make-up to look as if I'd thumped you to make me find the dirt on Sarbridge? I'm not saying it was your fault, what I did, of course I'm not, but can you please try to understand this?

I know she would have wanted to spend the last minutes of her life being loved. Being cherished. That's how I know she's alive now. Somehow all of time, all eternity is here with me, all at once and forever, past, present and future. And so is Helen. I know she is dead. I also know she is with me. In me. Her wisdom and her warmth are here, and her love. She led me through the fire of our love and now in the silence of my cell, I know at last what she wants me to do.

I am to say nothing. As she did. That's best. That way she can be mine and will abide with me for ever.

You're not going to get this, are you? There is no way you are going to underst

In a sense he never leaves me. Every evening when I wash the day's work off my feet I remember my fingers sliding between his oily toes like seaweed. That laugh of his as I lifted his heels to caress them. His groan as he held my head. I treasure these memories like a miser. But my greatest treasure of all, I have told no one. Until now.

My brother Lazarus was taken suddenly by fever and could not see the sun without pain. A rash patrolled his body and on the day he did not recognise us any more, my sister Martha wrote to summon Jesus.

'Sign this,' she said, 'put your mark and he'll come.'

'When has he ever come because of me?' I said and wept, for my heart broke daily for need of him. Martha thought I was weeping for our brother but I did not yet have a true sense of Lazarus' danger. He was young and strong and should pull through.

Martha pulled my writing hand away from my eyes and forced me to make my mark. My tears fell on the letter. Martha wiped her wrist across the ink for greater effect.

'He's not far,' she said, 'if he comes by sundown tomorrow Lazarus could be saved.'

But Lazarus was in his grave four days before the village boys shouted, 'Jesus is here, he's coming, he's coming,' and Martha stormed straight out to meet him.

I stayed put. I knew why he had not come to us sooner. In every silent minute when he must have known the urgency of our need, I knew there was only one reason why he would stay away. Only one thing could have occupied him so.

Half an hour later Martha was back, slamming the chairs hard against the table.

'Lazarus will rise on the Last Day,' she blurted out.

'*Like the rest of us?*' *I said. She folded her arms tight under her breasts.*

'*And he wants to see you.*'

'*Me?*'

'*You know how he is about you, Mary.*' *A smile broke her tears.* '*If anyone can get him to heal our brother, it's you.*'

A crowd followed me all the way from the village. Some were my friends but most of them were just tagging along for the show, knowing that Jesus was not a man to disappoint them.

I will never forget the sight of him that day. He straddled the path like a mountain in sunlight.

'*Mary,*' *he said with that lop-sided smile of his,* '*you know me so well.*'

I stood mute, away from his touch. He was bathed and oiled and his beard was trim. I was right: he had not been spending his time only with the men. He came closer and caressed my cheek.

'*Come on, Mary,*' *he whispered,* '*you know you're the only one. Forgive me.*'

The command in those two last words caused such turmoil in me. He had doubly broken my heart. He had let my brother die while he . . . while he . . . My mind whipped between exhaustion and fear. What if Jesus did not raise Lazarus? What if he turned and went away again?

But to forgive him was the one order I could not obey. For one simple reason. His bed was not my bed, it never had been, so it was not for me to forgive. Yet he sought my forgiveness. Could it mean that he wanted me to be the woman who commanded his bed?

The crowd pressed closer. My brother's name was buzzing in their mouths. They did not care about my grief or about the night Martha and I had sat watching our brother's last breaths or the day we laid him out. They were there for a miracle and they wanted the best. They wanted Jesus to produce a punch in the face to the Romans right there in front of them. They wanted him to bring our Lazarus back to life.

My stomach knotted. I longed to yell at them all to leave us alone. But if they went away, Jesus . . . Jesus . . . Jesus was still filling my ears with his urgent whispers, 'Don't treat me like this, Mary, I beg you.'

My legs buckled first, as if God Himself were pressing my shoulders down into the earth. My hands went out too late to save me and my knees crashed on to the rocky ground. I fell full length among the grit and droppings and let tide upon tide of tears overwhelm me.

Jesus sat down beside me in the road with his legs straight out. He pulled me on to his lap and surrounded me and we groaned and sobbed together. He was pleading still: 'I cannot breathe without your eyes upon me, Mary, forgive me please.' I let my breathing blend with his and held him close.

The crowd darkened over us. A chant rose up: 'Lazarus! Lazar-US!'

Later, as we watched Lazarus loosen his grave clothes and walk scowling from his tomb, Jesus said that no command could have moved him as much as my silence. My grief spilled into his soul, he said, and spoke to him of his destiny. He knew that I wanted his destiny to be our life together. If only that were all that God asked of him, he said, kissing my palms, how happy he would be.

I didn't know what he meant then. I knew only that as he lifted me from where I lay upon the road, held my hand and led me to the crowd, I felt bridal.

HMP GREYMOOR

Dear Mummy,

Yes, please come on Tuesday. Tuesday is not one of my busy days.

You must not read anything except this letter. When you come I think it's best if we don't speak. If we speak, we'll just argue, won't we. Also I don't want the bugs to bite. I think you know what I mean.

It's a funny thing, I found a postcard in Sarbridge's copy of Helen's book. It's a blank copy of the one he sent me, with the chocolate monkey on a cross. I'm looking at it now. Odd how religion gets itself organised to bring the best out in people and ends up crucifying them instead. Look at me. All I wanted was to love. Oh well. The light shineth in the darkness and the darkness comprehendeth it not. Or something like that. You won't understand, Mummy, but I don't want you to worry. I don't understand you either but I know you've tried to do your best as you see it. I appreciate that. I really do.

I've changed my mind about my writings. They were for Julia but there's no point in bothering her. She won't read them and even if she did, she wouldn't understand. They can't stay here. Since the riot, the staff keep spinning our cells every day looking for weapons, drugs, signs of life. If they find these papers my life won't be worth living. Which would be sad because for the first time in my life I have a feeling that it is. Worth living. So I just want you to shred the lot. Would you mind just doing that small thing for me? I won't bother you with anything else, I promise. Thank you.

Your loving son,
Patrick.

Dear Bishop,

RE: MURDER OF REV. HELEN HALBERD

Remember me? I wrote to you last Thursday and have your chaplain's acknowledgements of my eleven letters last month, so I know you will get this one. I hope you don't mind if I trouble you once more?

My son Patrick was convicted of the murder of the Reverend Helen Halberd at Bellfen Crown Court last month. You've probably read about it in the papers. As far as I can gather (which is quite a lot, being his mother) he has fallen completely silent since I last saw him. Our meeting was not a happy one. Almost as soon as I arrived he said I was stupid, which I pointed out was no way to observe the Lord's commandment (Exodus 20, 12) to honour his mother. In retrospect I wonder if he had already planned to 'go Trappist' and was indulging in a final flourish.

He has been sentenced to stay in Broadmoor prison for the insane for a very long time. The prison chaplain there tells me that Patrick spends most of his time in silence, often inside a *Roman Catholic* confessional box where he sits for hours on end, just breathing through his mouth. He makes no complaints or demands of any kind, except for one. He doesn't want to see me. I quite understand that. He must know how hurtful it is for me to see my own son in such circumstances. But the Lord giveth and the Lord taketh away (Job 1, 21). And although no murderer has eternal life abiding in him (St John's epistle 3, 15), my priest has helped me to see that Patrick could be leading a prayerful, austere life of which any saint would be proud.

We will probably never know what really happened to Helen

Halberd that night. While Patrick was on remand, he wrote up his version of events and gave me his scribbles to destroy. Respecting his wishes, I did not show them to the police or the court. There was no shortage of other evidence against him:

(1) He always was a violent child. The signs of a struggle at the murder scene were no surprise to me. His two elder brothers can testify to the truth of this although they could not bear to attend the trial. While Patrick was on remand, his violent nature came out in a knife fight and he had to be segregated from other prisoners.

(2) His ex-girlfriend Dr Julia Bothway gave evidence that she left him because of his increasingly aggressive behaviour, particularly in their sexual relations. The Rev. Neil Sarbridge also made a statement that Patrick attacked him for no reason in his prison cell.

(3) Several people, church-goers, confirmed that Patrick had been stalking poor Rev. Halberd for months. The wife of her vicar said he used to lurk in their front garden behind a bush.

(4) There was Patrick's blasphemous display in the prison chapel at a memorial service. In fact, his prison records show a history of rudeness to the Prison Governor who, poor man, perished in the recent riot.

(5) I testified in court myself that when Patrick phoned me on the evening of the murder, he was rambling and incoherent. Imagine how I felt when it turned out that this was just after he had killed her.

(6) There was of course Patrick's written confession to stalking Ms Halberd and murdering her, though his defence team did their best to try and prove that he did not have the mental capacity to mean it.

(7) Most crucially, there was the DNA evidence found on poor Rev. Halberd's body, including saliva and semen. The *Daily Mail* said, correctly if you ask me, that this alone would have moved any jury to a guilty verdict.

I think you will agree that challenging Patrick's conviction would do the church no good at all. The publicity has been bad enough already. That is why I have not bothered you (or anyone else) until now with the enclosed. However, after much prayer, I have decided that you ought to know what my son had to say about Neil Sarbridge.

We all suspected for a long time that Rev. Sarbridge's view of his wedding vows was as liberal as his interpretation of Scripture, but there was no proof. Before Patrick fell silent, he told me that Sarbridge visited him, not only before the murder but three times in his cell. Each time Sarbridge tried to apply physical as well as emotional pressure to suppress what Patrick had discovered about his many infidelities.

So I have not in fact destroyed Patrick's collection of writings as he asked. Knowing that the Lord will guide you wisely, I enclose them with this letter. I also enclose a cutting from last month's *Daily Telegraph* written by Paul Kibitz, a journalist my son admired. It is an excellent summary of the case.

There is no need to acknowledge receipt.

Yours in faith,

Pauline Price-Johnson.